RIVER IN LIGHT

RIVER'S END SERIES, BOOK TWELVE

LEANNE DAVIS

Raw, Real, Emotional
Romance

Print ISBN: 978-1-941522-78-3

River's End Series, Book Twelve

Edited by Teri at The Editing Fairy (editingfairy@yahoo.com)

Copyediting: Joan Nichols (www.jrtediting.com)

Cover Designer: Steven Novak (novakillustrations@gmail.com)

For JMS
Now and always.

CHAPTER 1

*R*OSE RYDELL STOPPED DEAD and let out a small but quiet groan as she stared at what lay ahead of her. *No. Not him.* Not Mateo Alvarez. Crap! Shit! Damn! She all but kicked her foot into a large rock along the river trail of the Rydell family's private beach. Despite it being a private beach, there were always people on it. From her aunts and uncles to countless cousins, second cousins, or cousins once removed, they often arrived to enjoy the family beach.

But of all the people that frequented there… How many? Maybe three dozen that had permission and full access at the beach this particular afternoon… Why freaking Mateo?

Mateo worked for her dad, Shane, in his mechanic shop, Rydell Rides. Shane personally built custom motorcycles for clients, and the other divisions of his business fixed and repaired ordinary cars as well as motorcycles. Mateo was one of the car mechanics, along with Rose's sister, Iris.

But Mateo looked more like a gang member. Rose didn't know what exactly why. She just knew he was something different. Something very scary. She avoided him at all costs.

He showed up two or three years ago, and she failed to pay him much attention at the time. He came there to work for her dad after he finished serving his sentence. As in jail. Actually, prison. Rose had little interest in any one-on-one time with Mateo.

Later, Iris became best friends with her new co-worker, but thankfully, the time they spent together was either at the shop or River's End Tavern. They never hung out at the apartment. The shop and tavern were places Rose rarely, if ever, visited, and she thus managed to avoid Mateo for months at a time. Giving him wide berth, she never allowed him to approach her or she him. She saw his truck and him, but always from a distance, of course. It was a small ranch and town and she lived right across the river. She often gazed back at the ranch where she was raised. The beach usually served as the perfect place to avoid seeing Mateo.

Why?

Simply stated, he scared the living piss out of her.

Not like a creepy guy at the bar coming on to her... No! More like he could murder her in her sleep and steal her wallet. She wondered if he was still a gang member. He had all the tattoos and a prison record to document it. His demeanor totally convinced her of the danger he presented. And she didn't trust him one bit. She wondered when he would hurt her... or them. She expected him to rob the shop or the family members in the house. There was serious money made on the ranch so the opportunity definitely existed.

But her naïve dad decided to give him a job.

And now? He dared to swim in her favorite spot on the damn river. Rose stopped dead and she took a step back, then another. She was instantly determined to sneak away. But... damn it. He stopped his long, powerful strokes and his legs touched the river bottom as he flipped his head up out of the water, lifting his face and wiping his eyes before looking right at her. As if he were boring a hole through the center of her chest, he kept staring at her with dark, black, bottomless eyes. She was always flummoxed when she made eye contact with him. Was he soulless? How could he stare so deeply at her without blinking? Was he secretly planning something? Her ragged nerves expected it would involve violence. No matter how much Iris raved about him, and her dad touted his skills and whatever else he could do, the only thing Rose saw in Mateo was the chance he might be plotting her murder. So she harbored an honest fear of him.

Although she went to great pains to avoid any and all contact, the chance of being thrust into one hundred percent contact by being alone together, like this, never entered her wildest nightmares. And despite all of her careful arrangements never to be caught alone with him... here they were.

Mateo finger-combed his black-as-a-moonless-night hair, squeezing it between his fingers until the droplets formed tiny streams that ran down his sculpted, inked chest, shoulders and back. She realized her gaze had nearly eaten him up before she quickly turned away. "Trying to run away from me, Rosie?"

She gritted her teeth. He was the only one on the planet who dared to call her that. Her given name was Rosemary and she'd spent her entire childhood as Rosie; but when she'd entered adulthood, she'd insisted on being called Rose. Everyone except damn Mateo called her Rose.

"N-N-N..." she stammered, hating her stupid nerves when she almost bit her tongue. "No. I forgot to bring sunscreen lotion. I'll burn and turn as red as a lobster... can't risk it..." Perfect excuse. She turned to leave and his voice followed her.

"I got you covered, Rosie; it's right there on my towel. Don't wanna get skin cancer now, do we?"

Her eyebrows popped upwards. Damn it. She stole a glimpse that way and sure enough, she spotted the damn sunscreen lotion. Stepping forward, her heart hammering and sweat popping out all over her forehead, she wished she could vanish from his watchful gaze, he made her that nervous.

"Feels as hot as bacon sizzlin' on the devil's ass out here, huh?"

"Umm… yes. It does." *Bacon? On the devil's ass? What?* His graphic depiction of the high nineties' temperature remained etched on her brain.

She dropped her bag, which contained everything she needed: sunscreen, towel, phone, water, beer and chips. She intended to indulge herself for several hours here. It was only two o'clock. And so hot. And still summer. Maybe her last summer here where she wasn't working full time.

Having earned her bachelor's degree in secondary education and a master's in education, she planned to pursue a course of extended training in Orton Gillingham. A name few knew anything about, even those in the education community, and that was the career she intended to practice. Despite her broad background in education, she had no intention of joining the community as a teacher. No. Instead, she would become part of the small, but growing dyslexia advocacy society.

Her mother worked as a tutor for twenty years and Rose planned to join her mom's business and become an activist for the cause. Tutoring remotely, as they lived in the middle of nowhere, today's modern technology allowed their students to come from all over the Pacific Northwest. And due to the shocking lack of effective remediation and providers for students with dyslexia, her mom's client load was always at maximum capacity. Rose would have to juggle a full case load from the start, even though she would be teaching the basic levels of the tutoring program her mom once taught. The upper levels, which were more difficult, would remain in her mom's expertise.

Rose had planned to do this kind of work for… hell, for as long as she could remember. She admired what her mom did. And decided, it was a good cause that she could support unconditionally. There was also a personal connection: Erin. Rose's aunt, Erin, was twenty-six years old when she was pronounced completely illiterate. Her dyslexia was never diagnosed and consequently, never addressed, treated, or remediated. Erin failed to grasp the traditional public school reading programs. And the usual special education services merely doubled down on these teaching strategies, which made any dyslexic student less likely to learn, resulting in more failure and defeat.

For Erin, the damage was already done. Erroneously believing she was stupid, Erin became hopeless and unwilling to try anything new. She feared she could never learn to read. She believed she was severely mentally challenged and incapable of learning. End of story until Rose's mother, Allison, offered Erin the remedy that opened up her mind, heart and brain. She first had to convince Erin that she wasn't stupid or a hopeless failure; she was simply never exposed to the correct therapy. Reading allowed Erin to glimpse an entirely new world, the written world. Fiction, non-fiction, newspapers, magazines, and the internet were once things Erin never could access or understand. Allison redefined Erin's world.

And that miracle impressed Rose. She listened to the story, which was usually recounted by her dad with pride shining from his eyes. He had to push her mom, who was then working as a public school teacher, to help Erin learn to read. First, she had to define Erin's learning disability, or as her mother and Rose agreed to call it, her learning *differ-*

ence. Anyway, her dad was the motivation and her mom found the fix. Her mom pursued an entirely new career from that experience. She saw her niche and began tutoring dyslexic students from then on. That was her mom's career while raising Rose and her sisters. Her clients came from all walks of life: young kids falling behind in class, and middle and high school kids that were on the brink of dropping out from pure frustration. There were also adults, like Erin. Allison managed to change people's lives. It was slow progress and nothing happened overnight. Her program was two to four years, depending on the student, and the level of dyslexia. There are mild, moderate, severe or profound forms of dyslexia; and some of the older students and adults were forced into traditional reading curriculums that had adverse results on their confidence and abilities. Half of Allison's job was repairing the damage before they could start an effective learning plan.

For as long as Rose could remember, she wanted to work with her mother. She also wanted to change lives by tutoring… one hour at a time. Rose was so passionate about the subject, she could not wait to dive in and do something about it.

For the past few months, she was on a sabbatical to work online and complete her Orton Gillingham training. It was the icing on top of her two college degrees.

And why, on Wednesday at two, she could spare to be at the river. With Mateo.

"Why aren't you at work?" Rose asked as she exaggerated her placement of things beside the beach chair.

"So damn hot. Iris and I started early to finish up before the heat of the day hit. We do that a lot in the summertime."

Right. So that meant he could swim at their beach with her. And she didn't notice Iris coming home wearily. Frowning, she glanced at him. He was standing in the water, staring right at her. "Iris didn't come home early today."

"Iris is a workaholic; she's still there working on one of her side-gigs."

Iris was always fixing something. Mechanically inclined, she was incessantly following their dad around. A *tinkerer* was what Shane often called his profession.

Rose wore a white, lacy coverup over her swimsuit. Despite any sort of attraction toward this man, she felt oddly strange dropping the coverup. Her comfortable, loose, and rather ugly but very functional one-piece swimsuit was one she'd had for years. Eight years. She only ever wore it here at the family beach where she could be alone to relax and enjoy herself. Trolling up and down the river and rapids was a pastime she enjoyed very much. She found meaningful purpose in the gilded colors of summer and their reflections in the warm, silky water. This, for Rose, was the essence of summer, capturing its vitality and mood. Hot afternoons and cool evenings beside the river.

How many days and nights did she spend there in her youth? So many she could never count. The huge family: cousins, siblings, aunts, uncles and their offspring, always coming and going as they headed to and from the beach. Mostly they stayed right around the main swimhole, floating up and down along it.

But life moved on. Rose graduated high school and moved far away to college. It was something she'd always wanted to do and she felt proud of herself when she'd accomplished it. She'd always excelled in her grades and often joined clubs and extracurricular activities that fully engaged her in campus life. She began living in the dorms and eventually shared an apartment with friends she hoped to sustain for life. She'd replicated that experience in grad school, becoming well-known, well-liked, and well-adjusted.

Living away from home and her parents was not much of a challenge to Rose and her homesickness was easily tolerated.

There was only one thing she'd sorely missed and that was summertime in River's End. Those long, sunny, summer days of unrelenting heat before melting into the river.

She always spent ridiculous amounts of time here. Not so much now, not with Mateo here to witness it.

Tugging on the hem of her coverup, she flung it off and threw it on one of the large rocks that peppered their sandy beach. It served as a natural table for their personal things. She didn't glance back to see if he looked at her pale, white, freckled body. She had to slather on the sunscreen, reapplying it hourly in the hot sun or risk getting burned until she was uncomfortably pink and miserable.

She grabbed an inner tube and floated further away from where Mateo was. He seemed to undulate with the current. The water was only waist-deep, but he let his legs float behind him as he held onto the rocky bottom with one long arm, anchoring him. The pleasantly cool, sun-warmed water engulfed him. Natural air conditioning. Rose often did the same thing.

She kept her gaze averted from him as she floated away. Kicking her legs, she let her body adjust to the temperature. Rose let the current carry her downriver, past the rock and moving out of sight from Mateo where she stayed for hours. Swimming and sunning herself on heated rocks, she relished the radiant rays of the sun as her skin absorbed them eagerly. Finally, when the sun dipped to the horizon, she crossed the river and walked along the edge. She was far above the beach when she saw her uncle Jack and aunt Erin swimming below.

No Mateo. A sense of relief engulfed her.

She'd waited long enough to flush him out of there. Pleased, she crossed the river and swam into it again. Jack and Erin greeted her, unsurprised when she seemed to show up out of nowhere. She always did that. Going half a mile upriver and floating in hours later to encounter an entirely new group of beach-goers.

They exchanged the usual pleasantries. The couple had obviously planned to enjoy some quiet, alone time. Jack sat in the inner tube, his legs poking out and his arms folded behind his head. Erin swam all around him, popping up now and then. Both smiling, they laughed and spoke softly to each other. Erin held onto Jack and they exchanged quiet looks. Rose very discreetly got out, dried off and left them to their privacy. Their undying affection for each other was undeniably evident. It made her heart glad but Rose could only wonder what that would be like?

Her relationships weren't like that. They never looked anything like that. Soft looks, secret smiles, something warm and glimmering in each other's eyes as they gazed cow-eyed at each other… Hers were much more sterile. Rose grew up with parents who adored each other and yet, she remained unable to find anyone who would look at her the way that they did at each other. She didn't know why, but something always went wrong whenever she tried to get romantic. Or sex got involved. She was the problem. Rose didn't know how to act although she didn't really know why that was so.

She was already home, parking her sedan within four minutes of leaving the beach. She hung her towel over the railing to sun-dry and ducked into her room to strip off her wet swimsuit. She glanced into Iris's room, but it was empty, before wandering into her kitchen and preparing a quick dinner.

Grabbing her laptop, she began finishing the certification work that was required for her dyslexia tutoring work. She worked as the sun set, the twilight lingering for what seemed like forever in the June nine o'clock sky until she finally went to bed. She knew tomorrow she'd be doing exactly the same thing. She only hoped Mateo wouldn't be anywhere near the beach then.

MATEO TILTED THE BEER BACK, letting the ice-cold liquid slide down his throat. Emitting an exaggerated "Ahh" after the last swallow, he set the glass bottle down on the table with a slam. "I really needed that after dealing with such a bastard all afternoon."

Iris Rydell, his co-worker, best friend and coincidentally, the boss's daughter, laughed and emptied her beer as well but without as much relish as he displayed. Beads of condensation slid down the two bottles. The ice-cold beer and the ambiance of the River's End Tavern were well worth it. A red-necked place to chill, the old timers lounged on the bar stools and half the small crowd were clad in flannel shirts, jeans, cowboy boots and cowboy hats too. Not Mateo's favorite look, even if it appeared to be the established uniform of the small ranching and farming community of River's End.

Mateo stayed there to fix all their damn cars, tractors and machinery. The good stuff. His outfits and tats didn't match the area. "You didn't deal with him. I did. You grunted and scowled and did that creepy thing with your face that scares people until they are too afraid to talk to you. So I had to placate his whiny, complaining ass."

Mateo grinned. "True. I did. This can come in handy around this place," he said, swiping a hand over his neck tattoo. It was a firefly and there were more signs and script all over his hands and arms. He had plenty of others, but those were just the visible ones. Combined with his neutral, cool look, he managed to scare off more than one person. He toned it down sometimes with nicer, more polite people, the ones he preferred to deal with. But if his desire were lacking, his sheer demeanor could effectively shut anyone up and he rarely had to say the words out loud. "Half these farmers almost piss their pants when I give them my steely-eyed prison look."

Bless Iris, she merely rolled her eyes in reply. "If they only knew what a true wimp you were. And please stop with the 'prison look.' All it does is give me more picky people to deal with. You hide under the hoods of their cars and leave me to listen to all their bitching and whining. Not appreciated."

He drank a gulp of a fresh bottle. "So works for me. I love hiding under the hood. I'd love my job even more if I never had to talk to people."

She rolled her eyes. "At least a quarter of our job revolves around customer service, jerkoff, and I don't appreciate getting stuck with yours."

"But Iris, I'm so damn scary…" He gave her a cool, hard look, one that could intimidate grown men who were bigger and physically far more fit than Mateo. But Iris never spent a single moment feeling intimidated by him.

"I'm not Rose, doofus. You just look constipated to me."

Mateo couldn't restrain the laugh that nearly forced his mouthful of beer to spew from his mouth and nose. He rubbed his nose and covered his mouth. "Rose is afraid of me. Any idea why? Did you say something about me to her?"

Iris yawned, over-exaggerating it. "Why the fuck would I talk about you when I'm away from you? I'm too busy trying to forget about you." She fluttered her eyes sweetly.

"Well…" He leaned forward. "We both know that you're only covering up your secret desire for me… but seriously, why is Rose so afraid of me?"

She snorted. "Mateo, I would no more fantasize about you than I would a billy goat. But as for my sister? You act really stupid when she's around. You glare at her and barely utter any words, and she's too polite and genteel to call you on it, so of course, you scare her."

"She *is* polite." That was one of the things that first drew his attention to Rose. "But she acts like I'm about to assault her or maybe she's worried about the shop getting robbed."

"Well… why don't you ask her? She just walked in. What the hell? She never comes in here," Iris muttered as she rose to her feet and waved her hand to capture Rose's attention. Mateo glanced back, straightening at Iris's words. Damn. The fastidious, prim Rose was standing in the doorway. She remained tucked back as if she were too timid to even take a look around. She might have been a native of this town, but she looked like more of a transplant than Mateo.

He focused his gaze forward, taking his beer in his hand and trying to appear casual. Stay steady. He would not show anything towards the woman he may have purposely sought out at the river. Her river. Her beach. He knew she spent all her spare time there. She always did every single summer. Iris had granted him permission to go there anytime he chose from the start. But Mateo was unable to swim and afraid of the water, so he avoided it like the plague for three years. This past June was the first time he actually forced himself to face the river that flowed behind where he lived. It took days before he dared to venture beyond his knees. The swishing current of the water as it flowed downriver scared him most. He worried that he would be swept away.

But he also knew the exact location where Rose preferred to hang out. And he was… what? Planning to hang out with her? After all these years? Maybe. Yeah. Exactly that.

Her unsubstantiated fear of him was already getting old and he was freaking tired of it. Iris, her sister, was his best friend, yet Rose shunned him as if he were a serial killer. As always happened when Rose was near him, all of his senses went on high alert. The freaking hair on his arms seemed to stand straight up and turn towards her. She symbolized everything that wasn't his type; and yet, she totally captured his attention and interest. Way too intensely. He rarely cared how others perceived him, neither from his appearance nor his personal history. Why should he? He refused to defend himself to assholes who could never understand who he was or where he came from. They would judge him no matter what he did so he never sought their approval. Rose's reaction to him was not unusual. Iris and her dad, Shane, had the atypical response. They simply accepted him and offered him a real chance to start his life over. No judgmental remarks or snobby looks about his appearance or his past.

Still, Rose's reaction bugged the shit out of him. He couldn't accept it. His customary *I don't give a damn* attitude seemed inadequate. He felt strangely compelled to convince her to move past her own biases towards him. That was why he learned to fucking swim. Him. Swimming in a moving body of fresh water. Terrified of any body of water, large or small, never mind the idea of swimming against the river's currents, Mateo convinced himself to do it anyway. It was a great excuse to spend more time around her.

To what end? So Rose could see him in a different light? Why? To possibly arouse her interest in him? He almost snorted out loud. Even if she managed to get past his outer appearance and give him a fair and equal chance, she would never truly find him sexually attractive or even someone she'd choose to be friends with. He was stupid to be so interested in pursuing her.

Yet he couldn't deny or end it no matter how hard he willed it to stop or tried to ignore it.

Her hand was on the chair beside him, gripping the back of it. A spray of freckles was splattered on the back of her hand. She wore a silver ring on her middle finger and a chain bracelet hung on her wrist. He snuck a fleeting glimpse of the curve of her torso, pausing over the soft mound of her left boob and slim shoulder. The ends of her thick, red hair were loose and free, ending near her elbow. Then he looked at her face. Her soft, heart-shaped face had such deep blue, beautiful eyes, like the depths of a vast lake.

He hated knowing how much her presence affected him. And yet, she didn't even spare a glance at him but remained simply focused on Iris. "I locked myself out and the keys are inside my room. Can I use yours?"

Iris nodded as she dug into her jeans pocket and pulled out a ring of three keys. She tossed them over the table and Rose leaned forward to grab them mid-air. "That's so unlike you."

"I was in a terrible hurry. Mom wanted me to sit in with her and a new student. He's a middle schooler who is just starting tutoring with Mom. He can't read at all. Not even a few sight words. Imagine the anger and embarrassment he feels. And the sense of failure. He won't even try. His attitude is bad and he's lost all hope, so she wanted to show me how to approach such difficult students."

Iris nodded towards her. "How'd you know I was here?"

"Friday night… you two are always here."

Iris tilted her head. "Are we?"

Mateo kept his gaze fastened on the table so he wouldn't look up at her with puppy-dog-eyes or reveal his true interest. He shuddered. He wasn't trying to appear mean, but he had to hide his biggest insecurity around her. *What was it about Rose?* He snorted. "You never realized that?"

"Never really thought about it. Sit, Rose. Have a beer. Now that you're here."

She wrinkled her nose. "Not really my scene."

"Relax, sis. I'll protect you from all the scary cowboys." She smirked at her prissy sister. Rose gave her the stink-eye before she glanced down at Mateo. He felt her eyes, but didn't have to look up to confirm his perception. He assumed she had a frown of disdain.

She let out an exaggerated sigh. "I'm not afraid." She gripped the chair, pulling it out and slipping onto it. "I just don't appreciate the darkness of this place. Or the overbearing stench of stale beer and hay."

Iris raised her glass bottle in a mock cheer. "Exactly."

Rose laughed with unmasked affection towards her sister. "How could you and I come from the same parents?"

Mateo let out a noise and they both glanced his way. He shrugged. "That's a good question. I've often wondered the same thing."

"Because she's so lame and I'm so awesome?" Iris leaned back in her chair, crossing her arms over her chest.

"I didn't say anything close to that." His mouth twitched. Iris was so full of shit. That was why he loved her.

The table was small and round and the three chairs were crowded around it. They were so close, he could feel Rose's body heat when her arm touched his. He kept his eyes on the label of his bottle of beer but stole glimpses of his bare arm being so close to where Rose rested hers on the table. She had slim, white arms. His dark brown ones were covered in endless designs and continuous ink. Yin and yang. Left and right. Night and day. Easy to see who filled the metaphor of night and who was day. He was the darkness and Rose was the light.

"Well, we know what you meant." Iris smiled as the server walked up. She worked at River's End Tavern for as long as Mateo had been there. Decades if her looks were any indicator.

"What can I get you, Rose?"

Mateo glanced up sharply. The server knew Rose? Surprising. Her head was turned towards the waitress so Mateo greedily ate up her profile. He was mesmerized by the way her throat vibrated when she swallowed and the small smile that politely lifted the corners of her mouth.

"Hey. How about… oh… I'll have the same as Iris."

She drank beer? Surprising again. She smiled and nodded when the server left. Iris dropped her arms and leaned forward. "So, did you see how to handle the little shit's attitude?"

She tilted her head. Mateo was glad he could stare at her now without seeming strange. "Not a little shit. A kid so frustrated he has to act out. And another reason why you should never work with kids. Lord, Iris. Certainly not the way you might handle things."

She gave a cocky grin. "Exactly why you're the saint and I'm not. I'll stick to sculpting hunks of metal instead of malleable minds."

"I'm not a saint." Rose glanced at Mateo, rolling her eyes and then looking back at Iris.

"You are, sis. I live with you. I know you are."

Mateo gripped his bottle to keep from fidgeting. He leaned back and drank a swallow. Setting it back on the table, he smirked. "Somehow, I think Iris is right."

Her delicate, gold-tipped eyebrows descended and she side-eyed him with a glare. "You wouldn't know."

"I would know from one glance, Rosie."

Iris laughed, leaning back on her chair legs. She was at ease. Enjoying herself. He knew Iris's demeanor. She could be quiet and sedate sometimes and hard to read. Except with him. She was all sassy attitude and full of jokes and sarcasm. Even with Rose. Mateo, on the other hand, was all nerves and overly self-conscious. He lived his life with no concern of what others thought or felt around him. Never. Except for Rose. Now his left leg was jiggling with uncontrolled nerves and he second-guessed everything before he replied to her.

Rose raised her hands up in a sign of surrender. "Okay,

you two, tell me what it is about me that makes me appear like the lamest one in a room?"

"Not the lamest one, Rosie. The best one in the room." That was just a fact. Rose was always the beacon of right. Of integrity. Of discipline and obedience.

"Best is boring," she mumbled as she glanced up and smiled when the server set down her beer. She gratefully took a sip.

"Well…" Iris said with a widening grin and the affection she felt for her sister sparked from her eyes. "We need you, Rose, if only to keep the rest of us honest."

"Great. I get to babysit you two delinquents." She winced and licked her lips, glancing at him.

Iris picked up on it and burst out laughing. "You are. But there's only one actual delinquent, huh, Mateo?" She pretended to flutter her eyelids at him.

He almost kicked her shin under the table, but instead, just glowered at her. "Delinquent implies youth, which I am not. And an ex-con, little Iris, is not the same thing. I need far more than a babysitter."

Rose seemed unsure how to reply to that. As always. Even when he was kidding or teasing, based on his history, she never failed to squirm. Rose half feared he might turn towards her with a gun in his hand and commit a crime right then and there. And Iris? Iris merely razzed him about his criminal past and the time he served.

"Then, you're too much for Rose's sainthood."

Didn't he know it? She had no idea how correct she was. He was too screwed up and rough. He would only taint the perfection of Rose Rydell.

Rose gripped her drink harder. "Again, not a saint. Maybe you two should alter your behavior so acting normal wouldn't make me seem so saint-like."

Iris shook her head. "Shoot me if I decide that." She tilted her beer bottle towards Mateo's and obviously wanted him to toast her in agreement.

He leveled a look at her. "Iris, you can't claim any street cred. You're as saint-like in your daily life and behavior as Rose. So nice try. The only difference is you talk dirtier."

Iris glared at him and Rose, for once, laughed. She finally laughed out loud at something he said. "Meaning you're full of shit, sis."

Rose glanced at Mateo and a small smile formed on her face. Damn, his heart fluttered in response. Iris gave Rose the middle finger. "I am more badass than you."

"But not me, little Iris," Mateo interjected. "And you think that's something to be proud of? Bet you wouldn't say so after the first day into your prison term."

Her smile slipped. His tone was lower and the mood changed. "Fuck. You always make me feel bad for what happened to you. Fine. You win, badass."

He stared down at his fingertips. Just below his knuckles were some intricately small designs. "Not a contest anyone wants to win."

Rose's gaze remained on his profile. He swore her eyes were boring a hole into his skull.

But Iris had no qualms or barriers towards him. She reached over and took his hand and squeezed it. "I'm an asshole and I'm just kidding. You're not a badass. That was my point. You're anything but that. In fact, what you had to endure was crap."

"It was not crap. It was actually a pretty light sentence for the crime."

Iris kicked his shin softly. "Ugh. Don't be a martyr. Then I'll have to feel bad for you and admire you and that's just plain uncomfortable."

He squeezed her hand before removing his. "You feel all

those things but you're too out of touch with yourself to admit it." He smirked.

Rose followed their banter: from teasing to serious to bullshitting again. They often spoke in only undertones. As they did now. Iris admired Mateo. She cared about him. She was on his side no matter what he ever did or planned to do. He felt the same way toward her.

Her lips pressed into a small, smug line. "Maybe."

Rose let out a groan. "You two are literally impossible to understand."

"Nope. We just speak the same language."

"Non-language," Rose mumbled as she looked away and wiggled her butt in the chair.

"Come on and tell us how the saintly Rose handled the disgruntled middle schooler."

"Fine. But first you have to quit making fun of me for it," she muttered.

Iris nodded and became more serious as they listened closely and fell into conversation. Mateo didn't add very much. He loved listening to Rose speak, expressing her intelligent thoughts in a calm, soothing tone of voice. It might have been the first time he was attracted to a woman simply for how she spoke and what she said, rather than her looks.

He finished his beer and ordered another mainly for something to do with his hands. He had to keep his rattled nerves around this woman under control.

"Well, I'm starving. I'm going home to eat. You coming soon?" How Mateo wished that Rose was addressing him. But of course, she was speaking to her sister.

Iris lay back, her eyes glassy with alcohol. She ordered a plate of nachos and was evidently settling in for a few hours of unbridled relaxation. Here. With him. Mateo often did the same, which was why they both loved spending their Friday nights together.

He wished rather often that it would lead to something more between them. If only to squash his interest in the wrong damn woman.

"Nah. Go on. Me and my boy wanna discuss how to rebuild this ancient tractor I found buried in ol' man Garvy's barn."

"Tractor?" He raised an eyebrow, pretending to care about what Iris was saying. But honestly? He was watching Rose grabbing a few bills from her clutch to set on the table. He noticed the way her shorts stretched over her small bubble butt. So damn cute. Always. "Since when do we fix tractors?"

"Since this one is awesome and there's a huge market for that kinda thing around here. I see a windfall at the end…" She kept talking as Rose waved and Iris waved back, without lifting her gaze. Mateo tried not to stare up at Rose or reveal the longing he felt in his heart.

Wishing… For what? Everything was so wrong.

He and Iris worked together on several side-projects at any given time from older cars and motorcycles to newer ones and now, apparently, tractors. They restored, fixed, and sometimes pimped out and resold them. Always for huge profits. It also expanded and developed their skills. Plus, it kept them stupid busy. Neither of them sought a personal life. They had friends here and there. But mostly, they spent all their spare time together, fixing stuff. Or talking about how to fix stuff. Mateo got laid from time to time, but he didn't hang out with anyone for very long. There weren't too many guys like him around River's End… just Iris. Thank God, for Iris.

But still, she wasn't the one he wanted something more with. Mateo wanted the last person who would ever want him back: Rose.

CHAPTER 2

*M*ATEO FIRMLY PLANTED HIS eyes downwards to avoid watching Rose Rydell retreat from the tavern. Her figure was one he lusted after in a way no other woman's form called to him. He vaguely noticed hot women, and acknowledged the ones he'd like to tap, but he never longed for any women. Their outfits, and the way they wore their hair from day to day were always irrelevant to him before. But with Rose? He noticed it all.

From the very damn start.

He should have fallen for Iris. He showed up in River's End to work for Shane Rydell after Shane hired him solely because of a letter from his mother. She asked Shane to give him a job after insisting that Mateo was a decent mechanic who could hold his own. She wasn't totally clear about his experience, which actually came from a chop shop, but Mateo assumed that Shane, so world-wise and weary, totally understood that. He had no other references after an extremely recent stint in the pen. Shane knew his dad, years ago, before his dad got stabbed and killed in a bar fight while

Mateo was in prison. The only reason his mom asked Shane for help was out of respect for his history with Mateo's dad.

So Mateo went to River's End. To nowhere. He never set foot in Washington State before, let alone, the small farming and ranching community that was so rural they counted the population in their towns by the *hundreds* of citizens. Perhaps a few thousand lived in the Rydell River Valley, but the small town of River's End only contained a few hundred citizens. It was the polar opposite of Mateo's entire life. The concrete world in which he grew up and barely survived. He could navigate his way around the city and even excelled at it, but coming here? He was the newbie. The fresh transplant. The fish out of water. For real.

He met Shane and was sure the older man would swiftly dismiss him with a sniff of disdain once he saw his friend Juan's son, fresh out of prison with a neck tattoo. Tattoos were becoming fine and acceptable; even full sleeves and body coverings were appropriate nowadays. Billionaires hid them under their three-piece suits. Doctors displayed them on their forearms, and all of that was becoming pretty standard to regular society. But the neck tattoo? That's almost as bad as having one on the face. Like a stamp of disrespect and a true sign of being a punk. At least that was Mateo's experience. But Shane didn't blink an eye. Shane shook his hand, asked about his mom and brother, and listened with genuine interest to what he said. Shane asked about his history, questioning the details of any gaps and asking for the real story. He said, "You learn all that from your dad's chop shop?"

How should he answer? Yes? And let Shane think he's a thief and a crook? Or lie and provide no history to explain his expertise. No schooling. No legitimate work. And only a record of doing time in prison. Yeah, few opportunities lay ahead of him.

Shane added, "I knew your dad. He ran a first-class chop shop."

Mateo smiled unintentionally as he nodded. "Yeah, my old man taught me everything; I used to help him."

Shane smiled. "Well, then I know you're good. He only employed the best. But my place is fully legit so you better keep it above board, and that goes for anything you do on my land, under my business umbrella and under my name. Got it?"

Shocked, Mateo was almost appalled that Shane would... What? Allow him to do legal rebuilds and fixes on his own hours? He was offering him the time and space? Incredible. The fact that Shane so readily trusted him without trying to *fix* Mateo, was new for him. His loyalty towards Shane and the Rydell name, land, business and family was established that day. He trusted Shane unconditionally. Trust was a very rare commodity in Mateo's life.

Especially with men. Older men. Men his father's age and the associates thereof.

Anyway, he met Iris too that day. The mechanic chick turned out to be the daughter of the employer. Mateo assumed, with total chauvinism and a bastard mentality, that she sucked at the work involved. He erroneously assumed she was employed for her quirkiness and whims at Daddy's Say-So. Iris was unappreciated, disbelieved and utterly disrespected by Mateo until they embarked on an all-out battle to prove who the better mechanic was.

Iris was also skeptical about Mateo's position, knowledge, expertise, and validity in the position he sought. She saw him as a pity hire by her dad, and slighted him as much as he looked down on her. They sabotaged each other. They pranked and ruined and hindered all kinds of projects. They gave as good as they got and Iris never once told her dad. She never once backed down either. And damn if Mateo didn't say uncle eventually. Iris soon became the coolest woman he ever met and it wasn't long before she was simply his damn best friend. That was a new experience too. But she was.

Soon after he started working and Iris and he were barely friends, Rose showed up from college. She planned to spend her summer at the house.

Rose. Her name said what she was. Beautiful. Red. Delicate. Fragile. Rare.

He had no words for her looks because they went far beyond hot and sexy and whatever else he could think of. She was exquisite. Special. Stunning. And he became tongue-tied around her. Words failed him. He could only stare at her.

But Mateo still scared the shit out of Rose. He was a criminal to her. Always. Never gonna change that impression. And damn if he could... not as he was. But she didn't understand he really wasn't and he never wanted to be, or that he wished he could change it forever. He wished he could undo it. Bury it as a thing of the past.

But she saw only that. And the tattoo on his neck. Her gaze never left his neck although she was repulsed by it.

Knowing all of that, this hopelessly strange reaction, was truly no more than unbridled attraction. White-hot, sexual attraction. He didn't want it. Not towards prissy, prim, privileged Rose Rydell who was everything he believed Iris was not.

The main problem was he didn't want to just fuck her. That, he understood. His desire would have been abandoned as soon as he saw her reaction to him, if it were only about sex. But this was so much more and so much deeper, like a strange new part of him was calling out to her. He didn't know what the hell to do with it. Since it never was a problem for him before, he had no idea how to solve it now.

Rose attended college, majored in education and graduated early with a bachelor's degree before earning a master's in education. Mateo assumed she wanted to teach or pursue a career in academics. He could not begin to fathom all the things she must have learned. The tower of a person she was compared to him. The multitude of things that crossed her mind compared to everything he still didn't know about. What she wanted to be was always clashing with what he could never be.

Rose Rydell wasn't like her dad or her sister. She didn't give Mateo an unbiased chance. She didn't trust him or like him. Worst of all, she felt truly threatened by him, believing he planned to pull a gun out and rob her or perhaps do worse. She couldn't see past his history or the dangerous figure he posed. It was annoying as shit, but he had the record and criminal history and looks that projected that stereotype to people like Rose Rydell. She was preppy and conservative. Born and raised in this small town, she had a somewhat jaded dad, but lacked any real experience herself with the world. That was what seemed so glaring about her. Even after college, the bubble she lived in became the main source of her beliefs and thoughts, which continued to confine her.

At least she didn't hide any of it. Her expressions were often troubled, startled, shocked and simply judgmental as she watched Mateo.

Mateo sighed as he turned back to Iris's tractor plans. They hung out for a few more hours, remaining sober, before he ducked into his small truck. It was more than twenty years old and barely started, but it usually got him from point A to point B. He went directly home. Calling it home might have been a stretch to most, but it was the closest Mateo ever came to having a home in his life. He drove down the rutted, rocky, dirt road that led from the orchards, down an embankment to the flat spot where decades-old migrant worker housing stood. They were all lined up, ten units per side, with a larger building that housed the kitchen and bathrooms. Back in the day, these sheds were supplied to the transient workers that came to the valley to help harvest the crops. Many still came for that purpose. Apples and cherries are always popular crops grown up and down the river.

The eighties saw the workers living in the sad, crowded, tool-shed hovels. However, the orchard owner refitted all the units and updated them with modern appliances. They were also painted red with white trim to match the theme of The Red Barn Orchard. Included in the remodels were tiny, single user kitchens and bathrooms. A bed occupied the space across from the kitchen, a small table for eating, and a single recliner for seating. That was all there was room for. A single dresser held his personal things.

That was Mateo's home. But it was all his. Affordable and private. Things he valued most of all. After living in prison, his privacy became a rare but significant luxury. Aloneness. His personal space also became a priority. He preferred not to live with anyone ever again if given the choice. And why should he? He could stay here indefinitely. Others came and went, briefly occupying the small rentals, and many transient workers were still working at the various orchards.

Hungry as always, he heated up a frozen meal in his small microwave and leaned back on his counter, imagining Rose being here. That made his lips tweak up. The disdain she'd no doubt feel, and confusion most likely too. She'd ask him outright: *People really live here? Like this?*

Ha. As if they could share anything more than a few disgruntled, uncomfortable words. Rose wasn't a bit like her sister. Iris would always champion the underdog and give people like Mateo a second chance, whereas Rose? Not so much. But he never felt about Iris the way he did about Rose. Stupid hormones. The tragic downfall of so many people.

But not him. He clearly understood how the world worked. He refused to fall victim to stupid fantasies that could never happen. Life was too short and he knew that better than anyone.

He had dozens of encounters with Rose over the three years since he'd arrived in River's End and began working for her dad. He thought she would have trusted her dad's judgment, but no. Rose still feared him. She invariably strained to duck out of his view and avoid eye contact, going so far as to step back to lessen their proximity to each other. He was used to it, but also, each time, he wondered why? Why was she so afraid of him? Didn't the past three years convince her of anything? Nothing happened in all that time. Not one single thing that made him look guilty or convinced her of any nefarious plans. So why did she worry so damn much?

That's why he had to conquer his never-ending fascination with a woman who firmly believed he would commit a crime eventually and hurt her. Yeah, not exactly the makings for a bright anything.

DAYS LATER, after entering the shop, Mateo started working on a local farmer's work truck. It needed an old-fashioned tune-up. Nothing specifically wrong with it, and nothing in general that was hard to do. The brainless job helped him easily pass his day. He glanced up when the door banged shut and Rose walked inside. His heart slammed and he frowned at himself. Why did he physically respond to seeing Rose? Always?

She glanced around, looking for her dad or Iris, of course.

Iris saw her too and rose up from the hood she was under. "Hey, Rose, you here for Dad?"

"Yes. He was supposed to take a look at my car. It's been a making an odd noise."

"I can do it."

"Yes. I know. But he promised me."

Mateo came out from under the hood where he'd been half hiding and half spying. "Shane ran out to meet a guy about some paint samples. He should be back in half an hour or so."

"Of course." Rose rolled her eyes.

Iris wiped her hands on a shop rag. "Rose, I'm free and I can take a listen right now. No need to wait."

Rose gritted her teeth in response. Wow, Rose was so sensitive toward her dad and Iris's relationship.

"My little Iris, she wants Daddy to do it," Mateo snickered. He always called Iris *little*. She was small and tough, which drove Iris nuts. Mateo sensed her shortness was a source of insecurity so he deliberately called her little, oh, hell yeah; and for years she'd railed at him for it. Now? She was resigned to her height and his penchant for commenting on it. He took every opportunity to tease her because he obviously enjoyed it.

Rose glared his way. "Dad will take a look when he gets back. Besides, we were grabbing some dinner too."

Iris threw the rag down and nodded. "Okay, I'll leave you to it. Knock off early then." Early? It was an hour past closing, but neither Mateo nor Iris ever seemed to leave on time. Iris grabbed her bag and keys before she tidied up and waved at him and Rose. "See you later."

"See ya, little Iris," Mateo said, barely glancing at her as he buried his head under the hood of the car again.

"Why do you still call her that stupid name?"

He was startled when Rose spoke right to him. He glanced around, looking almost confused and surprised. When did Rose ever speak to him? Not directly. Not on purpose. He straightened as he looked at Rose. She was standing against Iris's work bench with one leg crossed over the other, and her arms over her middle. Her hair swung around her shoulders, thick, wavy and glorious. The red strands caught the fluorescent lights on the shop ceiling. Her hair bouncing with highlights and competing textures, her blue eyes were suspiciously on him and then they bobbed away.

"What?"

"Why do you call her *your little Iris*? It sounds like she's your daughter or girlfriend or something."

He leaned down to avoid his undeniable desire to stare at her beautiful hair and liquid blue eyes. Her figure prompted him to imagine all the dark, nasty things he could do with her. So yeah, avoiding her gaze was a good idea.

"It bugs her."

"That's it?"

"Yep. Do I need a more profound reason?"

"No. It just seemed like a nickname of endearment. I wondered…"

"Oh? I'm hella endearing to her. Just ask her. But mostly I give her shit and she gives it back. We get each other. You wouldn't understand or like it."

She straightened her spine, her eyebrows puckering downward in obvious disapproval of his observation. "Why would you say that?"

"Because you don't like to give or take shit. I don't know if you even have a sense of humor, but you sure as shit wouldn't have one with me."

Her mouth dropped open, her arms tightening around her middle. "I do too have a sense of humor. I just…"

"You just what?"

"I just don't know you very well. But I have a broad sense of humor."

Mateo rose and quit pretending he was doing something to avoid staring with longing and lust at the rich, privileged woman who could never spare a fleeting glance at her dad's inked-up employee with a bad past. A criminal record. Prison. Yeah, not exactly the ideal man for Rose Rydell.

"You sure about that?" he asked softly, his gaze caressing her face. It was a weak answer. Iris would have blasted him with so much shit at his insult. He liked that about Iris. But Rose took everything as it was, seriously, and without much humor.

"Of course, I do." She made a face. "You can't be Shane Rydell's daughter and not have one. Why do you assume I don't?"

Okay, maybe after that point he could believe it. But whenever she was around him her sense of humor seemed to be hog-tied and muzzled.

"You're kind of uptight. Makes sense."

She glared hard at him and rolled her eyes. "I am not uptight."

He straightened up fully, leaning one hip on the car behind him, trying to appear as insolent as she believed him to be. His gaze roamed from her forehead down to her sandal-clad feet with painted red toes. "Rosie, you're strung so tight you could snap in half. And you're jealous of your sister's relationship with your dad."

"I am not!" she snapped, her voice rising.

He merely smirked in response. "Uh, huh. See? Strung tight." He gave her an eyebrow wag. "I'll tell your dad he missed you."

"Fine." Her lips compressed into a tight line. Then she added because he knew she couldn't resist her own polite manners. "Thank you."

Puzzled by his long look, she scowled and turned around to leave. She was totally unsettled by him. He chuckled and turned back to fix the car. Damn, but he'd like to hit that. But she was so uptight and scared of him... she could be terrible in bed... or she might be a wild hell-cat. He didn't know and perhaps that was the whole draw. Had to be. What else could keep him so tied up in knots over an uptight, red-haired, college graduate and worst of all, his boss's daughter? She was definitely off limits for all the things Mateo imagined doing with her.

Definitely.

But reality didn't have to stop his fantasies. Mateo had a well-developed, vivid imagination. He smiled at his thoughts and started whistling as he dove back into the vehicle.

ROSE WONDERED why she felt so odd at being around Mateo. Even sitting at a small table with him, she was aware of every movement and every twitch he made. She felt on edge, as if she could bolt upright out of her chair if he merely leaned her way. It was awkward and hard to follow her sister's easy-going, comfortable banter and conversation. How could Iris not see how uncomfortable she was? And how could a casual meeting at River's End Tavern unsettle her so damn much.

She escaped as quickly as she could, hoping it would be several weeks before she saw him again, but no! She ran into him while looking for her dad.

Walking towards her beach, she hoped Mateo was out of her sphere finally. No way. It had to be done.

But he was there again. Mateo. Swimming the same as before. She gritted her teeth as she went through the routine of dropping her stuff, lathering herself with sunscreen lotion and finally plopping into the water. Again, Mateo was holding onto the river bottom, his legs floating out behind him as he stared at her.

"How come I never saw you here before?" she finally questioned. She couldn't keep ignoring him, right?

"I used to frequent the resort beach. Iris found out and she stomped her foot at me and said to get my ass here and quit being so stupid. So... that's how."

Iris. Always. Always about Iris. With her dad. Now with Mateo. Iris was funny, sweet, quiet and tough. She was unusual in her choice of career, her interests and styles. And impossible to resist.

For Iris to offer to share this place with Mateo meant she liked him a lot. Why? Rose stared at the stretched-taut, golden-hued skin that covered his throat and displayed the harsh line of his tattoo. He must be very trustworthy. But she struggled with that.

"Oh." Her usual profound answer.

She stayed floating for a moment, and when it wasn't blatantly rude, she let the current sweep her downriver before disappearing into the next set of rapids. There was a small pool to the left side where she could hide and no one could see her. Even the people who were floating down the rapids rarely noticed the spot. Caught behind large boulders that enclosed it and shrubs that grew on top of the boulders, it was well-hidden. The fresh water flowed through it continually, keeping the water crystal clear.

For an entire week that happened. Mateo showed up there every day, seeming to melt into the water. At the same spot even; he never swam around but stayed anchored to the river bottom and half submerged. Rarely did he swim at all. He kept showing up and watching her without any comments, which made all his staring that much more unnerving and weird. She eagerly ducked into the water, glad to be submerged. That was the only time she knew his eyes weren't fastened on her.

Except he didn't show up that weekend. No biggie, she didn't care.

But he appeared again Monday afternoon. And maybe, just maybe that interested her.

And then she immediately dampened that thought. No. No way.

◆

"WHERE ARE YOU GOING? Where do you always go?" His eyebrows dropped down with displeasure as he frowned and his gaze rubberbanded from looking at her holding an inner tube to staring upriver.

"I'm going up the river. Like I've done for… well hell, at least two decades."

"Why are you crossing the river?"

"I prefer the opposite side. It's deeper between the rocks so I can float and push myself up instead of merely walking through the ankle-deep water or the land on this side. Why? Do you want to come across?"

What? She almost slapped her hand over her mouth. Why? Oh, why did that pop out? Out of her habit to be polite, that seemed like the right thing to say. But she didn't mean it. No. Never.

Now, she couldn't unsay it and he was staring up the river and then back at her. Intensely. God, the guy had such dark eyes.

"Uh, okay."

She inhaled sharply. Damn it! He agreed to come.

He grabbed a black, inflated inner tube. They were made of light plastic and had ropes around them to hold onto. A good, sharp branch could easily poke a hole in them, but they usually managed to last for the small float Rose liked to do. She shrugged and turned to walk across the river. Compared to the swimhole, the river quickly became shallow and the bottom rocky and hard to walk on. River shoes were needed if there any hopes of getting across, and even then there was lots of slipping and sliding to get across. Rose kept her tube around her waist; in case she fell, she could land on it.

There was no way to cross the river gracefully. Even for her. She'd been running across, going up and down this river at will, often by the hour, ever since she was twelve years old. That was when her parents allowed her to go there on her own. She swam like a fish. The riverfront bordering the ranch was more familiar to her than her own hand. She knew every rock, every swish and ripple, every current and the layout of the bottom. Every year it changed its course slightly, but she quickly saw it and knew what to expect.

It was hard to restrain her smirk and giggle after she swiftly reached the opposite side of the river and turned to watch Mateo trying to cross it.

He put on a good show at least, wobbling this way and that. His lack of balance kept him teetering and hindered his progress. He fell flat on his butt in the water, cursing. Rose called out, "Put the tube around your middle so you can fall on it next time."

He cast a gaze up at her. He was glaring. The next three falls landed him safely with a soft bounce. He cursed, of course, each and every time. His growling and scowl could have made Rose nervous if she weren't sure he was not hiding a weapon on him. He couldn't have been simply because he wore only a pair of cut-off jeans and old tennis shoes.

He eventually made it to where she stood waiting. She was trying so hard to hide her amusement. Her face must have been glowing as she pressed her lips together to restrain a guffaw, which he would not appreciate. He scowled and asked, "Now what?"

She flopped down on her stomach over the inner tube in the water. The depth varied between her knees and her waist. Lots of huge rocks outlined the river shoreline on this side. She loved to watch the dark green, swishing water as it flowed behind her before dipping into free fall around all the boulders. Some looked like little islands, while others lay submerged like unseen reefs, disturbing the waterflow.

"Now we meander upriver."

She smiled. He scowled. He followed behind her however, asking, "You do this for fun?"

She glanced back at him as she lay on the tube and began kicking her legs out behind her. "Yes. I always do my best thinking like this. The hot sun all around me, warm air, and cool, silky water enveloping me… I like to daydream and make plans for my life. I've made so many plans, most of which I'll never do, but… yeah." She frowned and almost planted her feet to stop the upward struggle against the downriver current. Why the hell would she tell Mateo all of that? Of all the damn people, why would she start gushing to him about daydreaming? Telling him her favorite pastime as a kid? Her youth? She wondered what his youth was like? Getting initiated into a gang and shooting people? She couldn't imagine, but it was definitely not what she was doing when she was young.

"You really like this, huh?" His gaze… (what was that look?) …almost softened.

She pushed her feet down to gain some distance and move upwards. "Yes."

"Tell me what you daydream about." The words followed her. She didn't turn around because she was heating up with embarrassment. What a statement from freaking Mateo. She assumed he was keeping up but she had no intention of waiting around to see.

"I… I don't know. Where to go to college, who my first

boyfriend would be… my first kiss… you know, that kind of stuff."

"Nope. Never wondered about any of that. Always knew I was really into chicks. Never questioned it."

She didn't mean to release a snort as she glanced at him. He was now beside her. He seemed to be pushing hard. He had longer legs and more defined muscles. Here they could relax, without maintaining the balance they required while crossing the current.

"Haha." She rolled her eyes. "Anyway," she said, giving him a strange look, "I just wondered who my friends would be and I'd pretend things were different… you know, I just enjoyed it. I always had a vivid imagination."

"Yeah? I don't remember daydreaming much. I liked to pretend. I think I would have liked to have acted out some of the characters I used to read about." His voice was deep and husky, with a rasp that always scared her… It also made her skin overly sensitive, like a soft, cool breeze that raised goose bumps. His voice was sexy; fine, she'd give him that. But his words stopped her.

She stared at him as the cool water rippled around them. He stopped too.

"Pretended? As in… acting?"

He rolled his eyes. "Crap. Maybe. I was like ten years old. Stupid, huh? I'd just… yeah… I'd think about what it would be like to pretend I was Spiderman or… Romeo or…"

"Romeo. Shakespeare's Romeo?"

"Sure."

Sure? She tilted her head. Wow, that wasn't what she expected. She smiled while trying to imagine a miniature, child-like version of him but it was nearly impossible. All she could manage was to reduce Mateo's height a foot or so shorter. She could not picture him as a youth. Or a child. He lacked innocence. She also tried to imagine his inked skin untatted. She could barely picture him as he was now, only smaller. But as Romeo? Or a reader of Shakespeare?

"Did you take acting in school? You know as part of a play or musical?"

He snorted. "No. Never. No way. I just wanted to be an action hero when I was young and pretended all alone. You know?"

She did and she hated herself. She never believed he could have been a young kid with dreams of his own. She was such an asshole. "It sounds like you wanted to be an actor."

"Yeah… maybe. I don't know. Crap, it was so uncool that I'd have gotten my ass kicked…." His words drifted off and his face remained impassive. His glance darted everywhere but toward her.

Something jolted through her. *That's his tell.* She realized so much in that moment. He always looked cool. Neutral. Okay, and completely scary to her. He never smiled. His face never cracked with any expression or emotion. He appeared incapable of any feelings and always remained indifferent. Cold. But his eyes? They darted around. They showed his true feelings. Unsureness. Discomfort. Insecurity. "It's stupid. Forget it."

Forget it? She wondered if he ever told anyone that before. "Have you told Iris that?"

"Fuck. Iris? She'd laugh her ass off and never let me live it down. Of course not. You… you're not going to tell her, are you?"

He was worried about what her sister thought? He confessed something fanciful, a part of his youth. Something so cute and sweet that it made him more human and adorable. The monster Rose created in her mind vanished. She flushed with embarrassment over all of her preconceived ideas about him. She was terrible. Not him. "No. Of course not…"

She wanted to ask more. She longed to hear more about why Mateo wanted to perform in a Shakespearean play. Wow. But she also felt an overwhelming urge to share her own admission. Something intimate and private and embarrassing. Tit for a tat? Maybe. But also… she'd judged him wrongly. Harshly. She felt obligated to offer him a personal detail about herself if only to ameliorate her shame and total disgrace over her prior prejudice. "I often pretend to be characters from the book I'm reading." She blurted it out so honestly. Her eyes grew large as she smacked a hand over her mouth.

"As in now? Not just as a kid?"

She shook her head. Too late now. "No one knows I do that. Duh. Or the books I read."

"Not even Iris? Or your dad? Mom?"

"No one. You can't tell anyone."

"What stories do you like to read that you pretend to be the protagonist of?"

She blushed instantly… like a sunburn on her skin. "If I tell you, you must take my answer to the grave and promise me you won't tell anyone?"

He squinted. "Wow, you take this shit seriously. Okay. Blood oath. To the grave, Rosie Rydell." He grinned and a weird flutter in her chest caught Rose's attention. Her heart seemed to be flapping like butterfly wings inside her chest. It felt new and odd and weird. What was the source of this reaction?

"Well, um… romance. Historical romances. Scottish highlander romances."

He smiled. "That's not what I expected."

"I like to read them for fun and escape… and they give me

something intriguing to think about at times like this... when I want to escape my real life... you know?"

"How long have you been doing this?"

"Always."

"You just... pretend?"

"It's entirely for fun. Remember? We were just sharing... I don't even know why I do it. Come on. No more about me."

He didn't immediately follow but seemed to be taking in her words. She wondered what he thought. Maybe he didn't want to end the conversation yet. He followed her eventually.

They stayed quiet, treading water against the mild current. Going around the corner, he suddenly stopped dead. "Wait. Where do you intend to go?"

"There. At the top of the rapids."

The rapids were churning foams of white water. Rocks poked out and waves dipped up and down with little time or distance between them. Gurgling river water roared and splashed and soon her words were drowned out by the sheer noise of the splashing water. He followed her, but remained deadly quiet. She smiled. So the big ex-con hesitates at the sight of a little water?

Finally reaching the top, she had to step out of the water onto shore and walk up the worst of the churning. He followed, both of them carrying their inner tubes.

Then, he was running and cursing. "Fuck! Shit! Damn. What is that? Why is it doing that?"

She glanced around. Alarmed. Surprised. He was up the shoreline and standing away from the water. "What?"

"That!" He waved towards the water. She scanned the surface and finally found the source of his dismay... a little snake? He was scared of a tiny, skinny, little snake? As thin as a shoelace and maybe half as long as her arm?

"What? The snake?"

"Why the fuck is it in the water?"

"Because it's a water snake." She bit her lip and her tone was calm and reasonable. He was all but dancing as he alternated standing on one foot and the other.

"No. Damn no. Those things don't swim. Never. Not like that."

"All snakes can swim, but not all hang out in the water, no… Why are you so scared of it?"

He frowned as he finally came closer to her. Cautiously. His eyes stayed glued to the water. The little snake wriggled away further. "No. I just hate how they pop up out of nowhere. All twisty and slithery and undulating… that slimy skin…" He shuddered. Rose wished she could bottle how oddly adorable she found him at that moment. Over this.

"That snake can't hurt you. Just the rattlers and sometimes bullsnakes, but they aren't poisonous. Most will do all they can to avoid you."

"I don't like any of them. Too gross and what? You don't mind them?"

"No, I don't. Not after growing up here. Keep an eye and an ear out for the rattlers but other than that?" She shrugged, then grinned. "Hold on." Stepping into the water, she grabbed the snake firmly behind its head.

Mateo all but turned to flee. "What the fuck are you doing? No! Nah, don't touch it. Just get rid of it."

She bit her lip to hide her smirk as she slowly walked downriver to release it further away from Mateo. She walked back to him and found him all but shuddering… still. "How could you do that? Touching it with your bare hands? Wash your hands… oh, my God!" He nearly convulsed with repulsion and Rose relished the role reversal, seeing that Mateo was anything but tough out here.

She nearly bent over, struggling to contain her laugh. "It's not going to contaminate you. You didn't have any snakes where you come from?"

"No. I grew up on solid concrete, thank God."

"Oh, thank God is right; it worked out well for you. Seems encountering a few snakes here and there is better than the violence you grew up…" Her voice drifted off. She nearly smacked her mouth and head as she realized what she was saying and to whom. The man served time in prison. She was teasing him and frolicking like he was just some guy she attended high school with and knew forever. It was decidedly easy and fast after her previous unfounded fear and reserve with him. But she took it a bit too far. She flushed. "I'm sorry. That was shitty of me to forget…."

"Well, my childhood didn't include all kinds of wildlife popping up out of nowhere. I'd take a gun pointed in my face any day over a snake."

"A gun over a snake? I hope you're—"

"Kidding?" His mouth tilted up a fraction of an inch on one side. "Yeah. Rosie, I'm totally kidding."

She had a nervous grin at his statement. She rushed towards the water and crossed far enough to reach the whirling, whooshing waves of the rapids. "Come on!" she called when he hesitated. He didn't follow her very fast. His gaze darted between the white water and the side of the river where the small snake had been. She almost snickered at that. She wondered which worried him the most? Then she curled up, placing her butt inside the hole of the tube, while her feet and arms were splayed out so she could paddle and hold the rope. "Like this!" she called out behind her.

He stared at her for a long time and down at the water swirling around him. Hard. As if he were willing the water to do something. She allowed herself to quickly be carried into the main flow of the river and up and down she went, churning, gliding, flying and swooshing. She screamed and laughed with unbridled glee and freedom. She obviously loved this!

"GO! Come on Mateo! Don't be a chicken!" she called out with a laugh. Good-natured fun was the only thing behind her pushing and joking. Somehow the joy she experienced made her more brazen and brave toward him where she'd never been before. This adventure revealed a new side to him. He was funny and sweet and totally not all badass. Considering the little snake and him falling all over the river, she began to feel differently about him.

When she hit the bottom half of the rapids, which was a crazy ride, she saw Mateo jump into his tube and finally follow her. She was laughing with glee through the worst of it. She let the current land her on the shore as she set her legs down and turned to watch Mateo's ride but her smile quickly faded. Her gaze filled with concern.

Mateo didn't look right. His face was screwed up. His mouth was twisted. His eyes were wild and definitely off. Shit. He was terrified. Not just nervous or unsure as Rose often experienced with people who were new to the rapids, some of the biggest on the river. But he was like... oh, crap. She pushed him way too far, past what he was ready for. She quickly pushed off the beach to meet him. She grabbed the rope on his inner tube and didn't say anything. The loud roar of water dragged them downriver and back towards their beach. She kept quiet, pulling him along until they landed on the beach. Contrite, she felt guilty and ashamed until she finally glanced at him.

"Why did you do it? I had no idea you were that scared until I saw you." He didn't look at her. His expression was still off. "Mateo?"

"I wasn't scared." His tone was so low, it came out as almost a croak. His denial was weak, and she had to press her lips to keep from smiling.

"I'm sorry. I never considered that. Everyone who grew up here swims."

"Well… I taught myself to swim here on the river but never in that kind of water."

She shut her eyes. *He taught himself to swim here? On their river?* She had no business taking him down the white water rapids. And without a lifejacket. The snake. The rapids. She all but gave him a heart attack from sheer fright. He was also nothing like what she assumed he would be. She was horrified at herself.

"Why would you go down the rapids then?"

"You were daring me, right?" He raised an eyebrow and she flushed with embarrassment to have taunted him so ruthlessly. She was used to the guys in the valley, and the ones that Iris hung out with at the ranch. They were born rough and tough and those who grew up along the river swam, floated and river-rafted with the same ease that she did.

So teasing and ribbing each other was simply part of it. How many summer afternoons did she spend floating for miles down the river with a group of kids from school or around the valley? For years they'd all done it. They dragged her little sisters, Violet and Daisy, as well as several of their cousins with them. It never occurred to Rose to ask if someone could swim or might be scared of the swift current that was actually her playground.

She snorted. "So what if I was. Why would you let me goad you? You don't care what I think of you. I'm not one of the guys at work. I'm not even Iris."

He stared long and hard at her and she fidgeted under his gaze. He always did that to her. It made her anxious and she began shuffling around. Ragged nerves danced up and down her spine. His stare and unrelenting silence made her twitch and she felt obligated to say something, anything to break the deafening absence of language between them. Rose rarely felt like that with other people. She usually enjoyed the quiet and peace, but not with Mateo because she always felt unsure. She wondered what he thought although it did not matter, but for some reason she cared.

"Why would you say I don't care what you think of me?"

Now he totally perplexed her. Her eyebrows shot up and down. Was he serious? How about because he rarely reacted to her presence? Sure, he scowled at or teased her, but never in jest, throwing shade and having fun like he did with every guy at the shop, including Iris. Always kidding around with Iris, but not her. She shrugged and turned away. "Well, I'm not Iris. And I guess what I think doesn't matter to you. Certainly not enough to endure something that terrifies you. I would never have spurred you on if I'd known."

"I wasn't terrified." He bristled, straightening his back and shoulders. She had to restrain herself from doing the full eye roll.

"Yes, you were. I saw the terror in your eyes as you faced down the last few rapids. The waves churning…"

His face crumpled to a frown. Oh, yeah, her words made him relive it. He wasn't at all fine with that. Rose all but tapped her toe to hide her annoyance.

"You won't tell Iris, will you?"

"That's your first concern? I won't tell Iris? Why is that so important? Are you… Have you two…" Her tone lost steam. For some reason, she didn't want to know the answer. Dread filled her. What if he and Iris were… what? Lovers? Bed buddies? What did one call them? But the thing that horrified her most was that if they were, she didn't know it. Iris wouldn't tell her. As hard as Rose tried to be close to her sister, Iris was tight-lipped about her private life that went far beyond what was reasonable. She could have easily taken Mateo as a lover without telling Rose. Even though Rose

asked often enough. If something changed in her relationship with Mateo, Iris wasn't duty-bound to tell Rose.

Mateo's head cocked to the side as he observed her. She
looked across the river as if she never saw it before and had
to study it. She could not diminish the burning blush that
flushed her neck and cheeks, however. Why all the embarrassment? Because the subject of Mateo and sex as a talking
point felt totally off and strange. "Are we what?"

Oh, he knew what she started to ask him, but failed to do
so. He would so enjoy dragging out her embarrassment.
"Just... you know... whatever. I just wondered why you care
so much about what my sister thinks."

"Well, it's not because we're fucking. If that's what you're
asking." He shuddered, shaking his head and shoulders
dramatically. "Yuck. Never. She's more like a bro. My dude.
I'd say sister but that wouldn't be right either. I don't see Iris
as having any gender. And why don't you know? Aren't you
two close? You live together for God's sake."

"We... yes, we're close and we get along pretty well but
she doesn't always confide her personal stuff to anyone. So if
she and you were... whatever, I might not know. Yet you
worry I'll tell her about this?"

"Yeah. She won't let it go. She'll give me so much shit
over it."

"So do you care what she thinks? More than me?"

"I rode down the stupid rapids, didn't I? So obviously, I
care. But Iris can be mean. She'd never let me live this down."

Maybe Rose found that almost more disconcerting.
"She's... I mean, you value her opinion of you very much,
don't you?"

He shrugged, dragging his inner tube up towards the
beach and setting it down. "Yeah. She's great. One of the best
friends I've ever had. Not that I run around telling her that...
but I don't have to, she knows it. I know it. That's enough."

How could this guy, who intimidated her so easily, get along with her sister? And why couldn't she get over her own baseless insecurity about him?

He flopped down on the sand and leaned back, spreading his arms wide, tilting his face up towards the sky. "Ahh, blessed land."

She stared at his figure, now lying almost spread eagle, as he dramatically tried to kiss the land. She couldn't restrain a laugh. "It wasn't exactly a biblical miracle or lifetime accomplishment. It was merely a set of river rapids."

He popped an eye open and moved to a seated position, hooking his arms around his knees and squeezing them to his chest. "It *was* actually. I've been dreading this river ever since I first saw it. When I imagine that current taking me downriver, it never fails to make me shudder. Took me several long days to finally find the guts to get past my knees even when the temperatures were soaring in the high nineties. I couldn't tell anyone why, and I only hoped no one would notice."

"Because you had to hide your fear of the water?"

"Yeah. Duh." His smile hooked up on one side. She tilted her head.

"What kind of friend is Iris if you can't admit your fears to her? They aren't weaknesses, just phobias. Or an inability to swim."

"She'd razz me forever and give me so much shit. I know because if the roles were reversed, I would do that to her."

"I don't get the friendship you two claim to share."

He shrugged, letting his gaze fall forwards, away from her. "The ride-or-die kind."

She tilted her head, looking more confused. "What the hell does that mean?"

He cleared his throat and threw her a glance before his eyes skittered away. He seemed to wish he could avoid her.

"It means, she's the kind of friend that would stay by my side no matter what happened. No matter what I did. She's loyal and true. I'm the same way with her. So we might flip each other shit, troll each other while joking and having fun, and maybe even go too far sometimes with it, but there isn't anything in this world or the next that I wouldn't do for her."

"That sounds an awful lot like more than just friends."

He shook his head and answered, simply, "No. It isn't. If you don't believe that, and you don't have any friendships like that, then maybe you should find a new friend."

She glanced away, staring into the blinding afternoon sunlight that sizzled over the water surface. He seemed to chastise her for not understanding the friendship he shared with her sister.

"I don't need a new friend." She had friends. But she wondered if she and Iris were the ride-or-die type of friends, which apparently was the thing to seek. She didn't think she was like that. Nor did she know anyone else like that.

It sounded kind of nice to be such things with another person. But where would she find a ride-or-die friend? Someone who would even get that? Much less, get her?

She didn't know; she didn't always get herself.

"So, again, you're keeping everything you learned here on the quiet, right?"

Her previous thoughts vanished as she became aware of him once more. She sat down beside him, surprised when his head pivoted around to pin her. Those black eyes that seemed so bottomless used to make her think he had no soul. What if they provided merely a glimpse of his soul and all of the feelings she somehow missed? Stunned, she had to consider how wrong she might have been. And what? Iris was right? Unnerved, she swallowed and stared away. "I will if you will."

He set his hand out. "Done."

She stared at his hand and then looked up at him. "Done." She echoed as their hands met. Their palms touched and sparks nearly sprayed off their skin where they shared contact. Their fingertips slid along each other's and shivers began at her palm, running the length of her arm and ending deep in her gut. She had the oddest tug of awareness. Sensual. But something much more. Was it trust? Like a blood-vow they made to each other. Ride-or-die, they wouldn't betray the other.

She didn't do things like that. Or connect with anyone like that. She was always casual. Polite. Formal. Kind. But she never gave someone shit and later chose that person as the one she most trusted with her life. She didn't know what to think of that. The sparks were real. But it was erratic, off and on, strange and very Mateo. Scary, tatted, ex-con Mateo... What could they possibly share in common?

CHAPTER 3

*T*HERE SHE WAS. AGAIN.

Rose was the only reason why Mateo came there. To the river. In the afternoon. Just like he did all last week. Hoping she'd… what? Come here again? Pretend not to see him? Barely speak to him? Ultimately wander away when she thought she had enough face-time with him and wouldn't be completely rude and off-putting? Despite being afraid, unsure and totally half-repulsed by him, Rose Rydell clung to her middle-class values. She was raised with the need to save face, always be polite and never draw attention to anything unpleasant she might think or feel.

And he… what? Hoped for this? Counted on it? Looked forward to her showing up again? Even after crowing like the fool he was yesterday about the things he feared like snakes and water, which were nothing really, but nightmares all the same to him.

"I… I brought you this," Rose said as she set down the bag in her hand, tossing it as if it were garbage. But it wasn't and she was embarrassed to hand it to him. "If you want to use it, that is. Whatever. No big deal."

She hastily turned and started to do her little ritual. Slipping off the pretty coverup, showing off skin so pale that it should never be subjected to the sun's rays the way Rose exposed it. But when she started rubbing the sunscreen lotion on, he quickly darted his glance away lest she see the lust sparking from his eyes. All the fantasies her actions created... well, hell, when he was alone at night, he could allow his fantasies to run the gamut. But not now.

He rose from the water and moved towards her. The bag was a large, canvas tote she set haphazardly in the sand with little care or regard. He had no idea what it contained. Or why she brought it.

She turned when she sensed his movement. Her gaze ran over his body and she quickly looked away. Did she still harbor fear toward him? He never knew what she thought of his physical looks.

Lots of girls told him he was hot. Fuckable. Above average height, long limbs and dark, bronzed skin that was smooth and clear but for the ink he marked it up with. He had shiny dark hair that fell to his chin and "bedroom eyes" according to some girls. Soulful. Hard to look away from. Whatever eyes he had, Rose could scarcely make eye contact with him. So who the fuck could know what the prissy, pristine Rose thought?

He opened the bag and pulled out a freaking, adult-sized life jacket and then, a box with a brand new rubber raft in it.

He held up both items, frowning at them. She bought these for him? He didn't react at first, he was so stunned. No one ever bought him anything. Never. Not even his own damn mother. What in the hell? He didn't know how to react. His heart slammed into his ribs with shock and a new feeling? Was it pleasure? Fuck. It felt pretty nice.

She witnessed his abject fear of the rushing water and knew how foolish he felt, but she also saw a need... for what?

And she filled it? Did she think she could conquer his fear by giving him a safety device?

She turned and noticed him simply holding the items as he stared hard at them. "You don't have to use them, of course. Maybe you don't want to leave the swimming hole. I just thought if you did, those would... well, they could help." Her words faltered as he lifted his gaze and pinned her with it. She gulped as she repeated,"You don't have to use them," she repeated. "I just thought you could wear the life jacket and I could... well, I could pull the raft by a rope and you could sit in the boat and be safe and all that..."

He released a long breath through his teeth.

She flinched, misunderstanding his relieved sigh. "You don't have to use it. I didn't mean to insult you or anything if... if you're too embarrassed to wear the jacket or you think it's dumb... I just saw it at the hardware store and... I thought..."

"Of me?" He finally found the words. Softly and quietly, he interrupted her nervous rambling.

Her eyes widened and she swallowed again, obviously reluctant to remain under his scrutiny.

"Well... yes. But not like it was dumb to be scared... I mean, you taught yourself to swim and that's so... I don't know... cool. Knowing you'd do that and conquer your own fear and then you even went with me and..."

"Did you purposely go out to get me these things?"

She stared at him. Her flush made her entire face and neck pink. She finally croaked out. "Yes."

"I thought you disliked me."

She pretended to busy herself with the bottle of the ever-present sunscreen lotion. Cocking an eyebrow up at him, she replied, "N-N-Nooo. That's what you thought?"

"That's what I know. That and your basic fear of me."

She let out a long breath that blew the bangs off her forehead. "Right. Yes. I didn't hide that?"

"Not for a second in the three years I've been here."

"I just didn't know… anyone like you."

"And yet you bought me stuff?"

"I'm sorry…"

"No one has ever done something like that for me."

Her gaze slammed into his as he interrupted her. The statement was quiet. Solid.

She shook her head. "It was nothing. Mateo… it's…"

"More than a few bucks. I know life jackets aren't cheap. That's why I didn't already have one."

She sucked on her lip. "Umm… I didn't mean to insult you. I just thought…. We kind of had fun yesterday."

He stared at her. He was still unable to get his brain around the fact she did that. And her undying fear of him. Yet she still went to the trouble of doing that.

"We did. Yes." He cleared his throat. "And now it'll just be better."

He flipped the life jacket over and tugged the tags off. Slipping it over his chest, he pulled the snaps and tightened them. Turning right and left, he asked, "How do I look?"

Her eyebrows puckered down before a slow smile, one of the few she purposely reserved for him, blossomed on her face. "Not so scary."

"No? The life jacket doesn't say pimped-out gangster, huh?"

"Well…" She bit her lip. To keep from laughing? Or from saying no? He still looked like a pimped-out, terrifying gangster. "Maybe not as much."

"So even I can make a lame-ass thing like this seem cool?"

"You looked like you might drown if you hit the wrong type of wave. So yeah, not looking terrified of the water you're swimming in will make you look tougher. Almost terrifying even."

"Well, thank you. No one's ever done something so nice for me."

He let a smile loosen his mouth. She stared at him for a long moment, blinking as a small smile lifted her mouth. Her forehead wrinkled and he assumed she was trying to puzzle out what he said for some reason. He wasn't sure what it was. He was a throwaway kid all through his youth and even as a young adult. No one gave a shit about his safety, let alone, his damn comfort. Nobody coddled him over such things as his fears and phobias. Rose turned and dug out more paraphernalia from her bag. She dumped the contents on the beach at their feet. A towel, water, chips, sunscreen lotion and a handheld air pump.

She opened the box and spread out the one-man raft. Finding the valve, she opened it and started filling it with air via the pump. Without a word, she methodically kept pumping until the plastic floatation device started to take the shape of a little boat.

"You think this is safe?"

"I think it'll make you feel safer. You'll be on top of the water instead of half-submerged through an inner tube. The life jacket will keep you safe."

"You don't wear one even when going through the rough rapids."

She flipped her hair over her slim, white shoulder. God, he loved the russet tones grabbed by the sun before the reflection ended. Silky strands slid carelessly around her exposed shoulders and upper arms, as slim and smooth as her hair strands. He blinked to regain his thoughts and his attention before losing himself in her hair. It was oddly stupid to feel sentimental about her *hair*. He wasn't a guy who mooned after women's hair. Hair. Or her shoulders or her arms, or her smile, or her bright, energetic blue eyes whenever she got excited about something... Anything and everything that pertained to Rose was noticed, obsessed over and eagerly indulged by him.

"Many adults tried for years to get me to wear a life jacket. I just disappeared and slipped away from their supervision, going up and down the river before anyone realized I was even gone. And no one could keep up with me."

"I would never have pegged that of you."

"Well... I never saw you here before."

"Again, I never came near it until this year. I was so fearful of the water."

She unhooked the air pump hose and leaned down to close the valve. "How did you get over that?"

"I didn't. I got tired of being hot all the time and forced myself to walk through it as long as I could touch the bottom. The river in front of where I live is a lot swifter and shallower. It was a good thing I did it alone. I stared for hours at that river, talking it down. We had a contest of wills the first time. After two full hours, I could step past my ankles, going out to where the current moves the water. Sweat streamed all over me and I was..."

"Panicking? I don't know how you made yourself do it."

"Well... I don't have air conditioning and it was a hundred degrees for several days in a row and I wanted to cool off. I had to figure it out or sweat to death for the rest of my time here. I can walk in it now and go to bed still wet."

Her gaze whipped around. "You really do that?"

"On days like this? Shit yeah. I get nice and wet before entering my sweat box. That's the only way I can stand it and get some damn sleep."

"You conquered your fear out of necessity."

She again bit her lip. No doubt she wasn't used to living

without air conditioning. Or doing things purely out of need. Or desperation.

"Yeah."

She rose up from her knees and he stared at her trim, round ass and the crease of her leg and her butt as she moved. He fought the urge to run his hand over it, cup it, pull it and her tight against him, which was nearly overwhelming. He flexed his fists to keep still and turned his ogling gaze from her. What was it about this woman?

"I'm sorry that you had to face such a primal fear like that. If I'd known, I could have eased it. I used to teach swimming in Pattinson at the youth center in high school. There were always kids who were afraid and we found several techniques that made it much easier and not half as traumatic or intimidating."

"I'm not a kid." Mateo purposely puffed out his slim chest. Although he was thin, he was far stronger than he looked.

She glanced up, then away. This time, his physical presence was what captivated her, but honestly, he wasn't sure if it was due to fear, revulsion or attraction. Whatever, it was something. Rose Rydell felt something for him.

For God's sake, she bought him a life jacket and a rubber raft.

"No. And at least you learned to swim, so now you can go rafting with me." She smiled with a tilt of her mouth, her eyes sliding toward him and then away as a soft blush stained her face. God, it was the sweetest… and his heart slammed hard against his chest. Why the fuck was it her? Why couldn't he stand it?

He flopped unceremoniously inside the raft. His legs stuck out one end, but he fit. And he could move without getting wet. She blew his mind when she tied the rope of the raft to her inner tube and freaking dragged him after her. She was strong and sure. She guided him downriver this time. Far. They went through several high, rushing rapids before she pulled into the shore. She grinned and asked, "What did you think?"

Truthfully? He was frightened, but it was manageable, tolerable and not something he'd stop if it allowed him to spend this time with her. This odd, strange and unexpected time. She didn't say much as she floated in front of him, her legs kicking or pushing off the bottom, depending on the depth. "It was way better. Almost fun."

"It will be fun when your fear starts to diminish and you trust me and the raft and life jacket."

"Trust you?" His eyebrows popped to his hairline. Trust someone else? Fuck no. Never. He just didn't do that. Not with the lessons of his life behind him.

She turned to glance his way over her shoulder. "Sure. Don't you? You've seen what I can do in the water. I can maneuver you anywhere and rescue you if you ever need it. So yeah..." Her grin was uncharacteristically free and cocky, something unlike Rose usually. She was invariably cautious, prim, almost finicky and picky. A natural worrier until she set foot in the river and became the fearless Rose. "Trust me."

Fuck. He never had anyone ask him to trust them. Not his mother. His father. His brother. His friends. No one. Then again, who the fuck did he have in his life? Now, he had Shane and Iris, and they gave him some trust, but it was based on a job he did. And he did his job fucking well. All his skills, integrity and worthiness lay in that damn job. Doing it. Keeping it. Being the best at it. Being reliable and honest about it. They must have trusted him to honor that and his place here at Rydell Rides and even at the Ranch. They were perhaps the first people to trust him for more than a minute.

No one dared to expect it from him. No one dared to ask him for it.

He scowled. "I trust the life jacket to float me to safety if you fuck it all up and that's if I don't bash my head wide open on a craggy rock."

She shook her head. "None of that will happen. And you will trust me too someday."

Ha. No. He was there solely because he wanted to fuck her. And she was thawing towards him after spending so much time in her beloved river beside him. She even seemed to notice him. All he saw was how different he was from Rose Rydell's usual group. Maybe she would have a good fuck with him just to sow some wild oats. To feel something new and exciting. He clearly understood how temporary something with her would be. Which was fine with him. Excellent with him. Perfect. Rose's fear was mingled with interest that might allow him to fuck her. That was why he sprawled on the raft, trussed up in an ugly, wussy, bulky life jacket. All for the sake of fucking.

And maybe a smidgeon of fun. She might be that. Amusing. And the water relieved the endless afternoon/evening heat.

For days they followed the damn strange routine, like an unspoken code that assured they would meet up during the weekdays. He dumped himself unceremoniously in the raft and she towed him around. He sometimes hopped out so she could walk when the water got too swift or shallow to drag him but she still did it for hours. They spent a lot more time together. It was more often than not quiet between them, save for a random comment and small talk. It felt new and strange and so vivid in each second they spent together.

WHY? Why was she pursuing a guy who proclaimed to the world he was a damn gangster? Why did she buy him stuff to make his life easier? She didn't know. The urge to do so was overwhelming. After witnessing his panic and abject fear, she hoped she could alleviate it. She encouraged him to share the time that was usually hers, alone. She shunned everyone all her life when she needed time alone, but now she purposely dragged Mateo Alvarez after her?

She was the one who made it happen. She didn't know why. They spoke sometimes. Not all the time. She was glad of that. He could be quiet. She could let her thoughts drift and relax where others would talk and chat, thereby ruining a really good, relaxing float for her. So perhaps that's why she tolerated him.

Why the stupid life jacket and raft puzzled and confused him so much remained a mystery to her. They were nothing. She bought the cheapest life jacket they sold at the hardware store. She grabbed the raft as an afterthought and now felt guilty for being so cheap, considering how much her simple gesture impressed Mateo. God. Damn. She could only question what his early life was like. How he got here? Why was he sent to prison? She didn't know. She would never ask. She was too scared to inquire. Her tongue swelled with nerves whenever she had the impulse to casually ask. She couldn't make herself do it. So while they spent a lot of time together, she still couldn't speak openly or freely with him. She found it difficult just to unhinge her jaw and ask mundane questions.

But maybe… just maybe the shock factor she used to feel with Mateo was starting to fade and lessen. It seemed like she might even kind of look forward to seeing him. But only there. At the beach. In these circumstances.

CHAPTER 4

DAYS LATER, ROSE DRAGGED Mateo downriver. "Let me show you something." She scooted his raft into the small, pond-like alcove away from the rapids that she so loved.

"What do you think?" she asked as she parked them on the rim of a small, sandy section with a large willow tree to shade them. The canopy reached all the way to the ground and the tips of the leafy foliage created a tent-like effect.

With a spry leap, Mateo popped out of the raft and glanced around. "That's so weird. I never noticed this spot even though we swept by... how many times?"

She nodded. "Yes. Everyone is usually looking forward toward the coming rapids so they never spare a glance here. The only things visible are the willows and the rocks so people don't really realize this hidden sanctuary. Come. The water is sun-warmed and awesome."

It was very warm and shallow. It came up to their waists in the center and the sandy bottom was smooth as silk to her bare feet. Mateo sank down and sighed. "Yeah... a heated river is awesome. Why didn't you show me this from the start? We could have skipped all the freaking cold, deep spots and terrifying white water?"

She shrugged and looked away, sinking down too. "I never showed *anyone* before. I like to keep it my little secret."

"A secret spot? That's special to you? And you brought me here?" His gaze sharpened as he stared at her face. Without turning, she knew it. She didn't have to see it with her own eyes to confirm it because she could freaking feel it. The physical power of his gaze created an energy she never felt from another human being before. It radiated from one to the other.

"Mmmm…" was her only response. She closed her eyes and let her feet float as the sun warmed and buoyed her, stimulating her in a way no man-made heat ever could. She sighed and relaxed as she floated. The sounds were blocked out by the water covering her ears, but her breathing was evident as she dead-man floated on her back. For several minutes. In all honesty, she was too embarrassed to even try and explain her reason for bringing him here. She didn't understand why they hung out together, so how could she find words for it now? And so far, allowing it to remain unspoken seemed to make it okay. They met at the beach, so fine, they hung out. But making plans to do that? That was drawing a line in the sand she could never move past. That would make it weird. Or something equally uncomfortable. Right now, she didn't have to define it and most certainly didn't want to. What words would she use? And would that put pressure on her and him to… what?

So no. No words. No explanations. No plans. No acknowledgement of whatever this time represented. No.

Without any warning, his fingers touched her. Softly. They were on her leg. His one hand slid on her calf, getting her attention. She lifted her head as her legs immediately dropped and the world came back into focus. She blinked at all the colors and sounds, which nearly overwhelmed her.

He stood close. Way closer than he was when she had shut her eyes. She didn't realize how much she appreciated her space. He didn't usually crowd her or make her feel awkward, but why was he staring at her? His gaze was unreadable. Guarded. Eyes fastened right on her. Way different than they usually were since they'd started meeting on these afternoons.

"Why? Why did you bring me here?"

She swallowed. Her feet touched the river bottom. She stood up to her full height, and less than a dozen inches separated them. He was still asking that? Why? He'd discarded the life jacket. His hair was swept back with water that beaded down his clear, glorious skin and dripped off his nose, eyelashes and ears. He was so beautiful. But in a different way for Rose. Non-traditional. Her tatted-up, biker father was normal to her but Mateo seemed almost dangerous. The criminal element was stupidly sexy and she gasped when her stomach pitted out as she stared right at him.

"Why not?" She shrugged. She wanted to return to whatever they had cultivated to date. Casual. Easy. Not too close or complicated. Never looking so intimidating or so deeply into her soul. Her skin prickled. Saliva filled her mouth. She gulped down the lump of nerves that lodged in her damn throat, making it a chore. What in the hell was this oddly intense moment?

"Rose…" Her name hung on his lips. Not the usual *Rosie*. No teasing or mocking. Was he saying he knew she was afraid and nervous of him?

Nearly breathless, her heart thumped hard. "Yes?" She sounded strained and high-pitched.

Without answering her, he stepped forward, the water swallowing his legs and splashing slightly as he stepped toward her. Captivated by his gaze, her entire body seemed to ignite, despite the coolness of the mountain river.

His hand touched her shoulder and his fingers squeezed the back of it as his thumb slowly, but seductively strummed over her clavicle. Just an inch of movement made her entire core pulse and burn. She held her breath.

His gaze freaking impaled her, like a drill boring into her forehead.

She gulped and her mouth opened to say something, but she had no voice to say it. No words came to her. She could do nothing.

Her gaze was wide-eyed and almost stupid as she stared dumbfounded at him. Touching her. They didn't often touch. No. Never before. But there he was. His thumb was rubbing her. His hand was nearly scalding. Then he said the most surprising thing.

"I went to prison for shooting a man during a robbery. I was a minor at the time but they wanted to try me as an adult. I got a plea deal and a lighter sentence than the crime deserved. I did three years."

Shocked he told her that, fear made an unwelcome resurgence in her mind. The words were so ugly and evil, clashing with the moment. The sun. The warmth. The gold and lightness. The very definition of innocence and beauty. But he told her his crime.

She stared, held hostage by his dark eyes. Dark eyes that saw and did dark things? Why were they fastened on her? Compelling her? Not disdaining her? Why wasn't she throwing his hand off her? Should she simply laugh to defuse the intense looks and emotions roiling inside her? Should she turn and go under water to get back on track to where they were? And where they were was not here.

She replayed the words Mateo just said. He shot someone. Shot another person. Shot. As in a gun. Violence. She almost wanted to kick herself for hearing the words he was saying.

"Did he die?" The words emerged like a gasp that she forced out. It was hard for her to even talk.

"No. Barely grazed his arm. But…"

"You were so lucky. It could have grazed his heart or his head." She whispered the evil words like the shocking things they were. He nodded, still holding her captive.

She licked her lips. "Why tell me this? Why now?"

"So you know the truth. The reason why I went to prison. You can't come back later and be mad or angry."

"For what?" Her gaze didn't move but her forehead furrowed, and she seemed more than confused at what he was referring to.

"For us fucking. It is entirely your choice."

Her eyes popped. Her eyeballs nearly dropped out of her head into the water at her shock and astonishment. He just said that? Her mouth opened, closed, and opened again, like a baby bird eagerly waiting for its mother to drop a bit of food inside. "What?" she gasped.

He didn't answer and his hand stayed put. Then, very slowly, inch by tiny inch, he pulled her closer until she was right there. His face remained impassive as his lips hovered above hers. She stared up and the darkness she saw in his eyes ripped her in half. It pulsated through her core and extremities. The lust. The need. The desire. All of it was so shocking and new. She'd never experienced it. Never before. Not even during sex. Not ever. She didn't know what to do with it.

She licked her lips. "I…"

"Don't talk. Unless you don't want this to happen," he warned her. He didn't ask. He wasn't nice about it. He was harsh, which should have offended her and yet, she shut her mouth and didn't talk. Which was so unlike her. She did nothing but stand there.

His lips touched hers. She felt his butterfly-soft breath and tender touch. Her eyes were shut as if to block out all the stark, bright sunlight; as if that could deny the reality that she was standing in the river with Mateo Alvarez whose hand lay on her shoulder with his lips touching hers. Lips. Hers. Mateo's. What the fuck was she doing? Alarm bells started zinging in her brain. No. Never. What the hell was she doing? What was *he* doing?

His other hand came up and he palmed her face so soft and gently, as if she were a newly hatched baby bird. The soft tenderness he showed was astounding to her. She didn't expect him to be capable of it, let alone, do it. His hand was rather large and calloused. Her brain registered every last detail of his caress, even when his lips barely grazed hers.

She leaned forward, a hair's breadth of slack in her rigid stance but creating enough of a signal for him to respond. Like a tuning fork, he noticed the small tell in her posture. He brought his other hand to her waist and touched the skin, running his fingertips and palm over the curve of her hip, up towards her armpit before descending in a long, slow, sensual slide towards her lower hip and butt. His hand was half over her swimsuit, half on her bare skin. She shuddered at the seductive tenderness.

Then she remembered the lips that touched, brushed and tangled with hers. He suddenly tightened his grip around her middle, flexing his fingers and squeezing her flesh as his mouth pressed down with fierce pressure and she opened her mouth to him. He dipped his tongue in the tunnel created by their sealed lips.

She let out a small sound like a breathy, almost hungry moan. His tongue slid into her mouth and stroked hers at first. As if he were testing her out to see how welcome he was. She felt an immediate tightening deep in her guts. Her eyes flipped open, and the sights she saw filled her startled and confused brain. The bright sunlight, the searing blue sky, the lapping of sun-laced river water, the huge shade tree shifting in the delicate afternoon breeze.

What the hell was she doing? By then, both his hands were on her waist, his mouth was covering hers, and her eyelids were slammed shut. She allowed herself to fully succumb to the kiss.

She was spiraling down a long, dizzying tunnel. A vortex that drowned out the rush of water near them, along with the glaring light, colors and sounds. All that was left was Rose. Rose inside her head. Rose feeling every single cell of the person touching her. How often did she sense his gaze on her, or over her, or through her without ever physically touching her, not even coming close? Not this close. He always maintained a healthy distance. Respectful. Observing the boundaries.

Until now. Until this happened.

Her arms finally began inching up his bare chest. He shuddered at her unexpected touch. Maybe it was the wet coolness of her hands. Somehow, she didn't think so. She believed it was the effect she had on him. Her ability to have such an influence on him was like a strong aphrodisiac for her. Then his lips and tongue nearly swallowed her as she lifted her arms to hold his neck, preparing for the deluge of emotions that were stirring up her blood. A radiant warmth seeped from her core and started to invade every cell of her body.

She leaned towards the wall of his chest, straining to close the gap of space as she whooshed out the air that separated them. It was instinctual. The oldest, basest reaction. She wanted Mateo. Her attraction was sharp, deep and strong. Her unrelenting desire for him was unlike anything she could remember. It nullified all previous crushes, attractions, kisses and sexual escapades. After this, Rose knew she never had any true sexual chemistry or attraction toward the other men she'd dated. Not like this. This was the passion that she longed for.

She had it now.

She could never settle for anything less again.

But how could it be Mateo? The man she feared so blindly? The man who covered himself in dark lines and symbols she didn't recognize, except that he was dangerous. She knew his history and his crime. He'd done plenty of bad deeds. Violent acts. If Rose ever witnessed him doing them, she'd have instantly hated him. She would have hidden herself from him. Never allowed him to hold her tight, or let his steel bands for arms fall on both sides of her shoulders and torso before landing on her waist. Yes, he had complete control of her.

Something rippled through her. She was alone out here. No one even knew where she liked to go on the river. No one knew she was with Mateo. What if…? What did she know of his past? Of his women? Of sex? What if he…?

She jerked her head back and his eyes opened. He'd been shut-eyed during their kiss. His gaze met hers, drifting over her face to her mouth.

"I… I sometimes feel afraid of you."

The words came out in a soft whisper. She licked her lips as her nerves now replaced the burning desire. Caution won out over the simmering hotbed of coals in her guts that was seconds away from spontaneously combusting into flames.

He nodded. "I know. Are you afraid of me right now?"

Her eyebrows quirked down and she bit her lip. Her head jerked back and forth. He knew that? Yet he still approached her? Why now? She had no idea what to do with that. "No…"

"It's all up to you. You control this, not me." His hands left her waist and he held them up by his ears as if she just told him he was under arrest.

His eyes didn't flash with anger because she'd halted their progress out of fear. He didn't seem surprised by it even. "Step away from me, Rose, and I'll never come near you again."

Never?

Wait. Why would that idea distress her so much? She'd never wanted him near her before now and here she was disappointed and almost fearful he threatened that? She didn't move. Or look at him either. She didn't want to go through life and never feel the way his kiss made her feel again. She'd never experienced anything like it before. "I just…"

"Realized you were all alone with an ex-con and you wondered if I got aroused, would I force you? You wondered if you were safe. And since I look nothing like someone you can be safe with…"

"No…" She shook her head. Why lie? He wasn't. He didn't hedge around. "Yes… you don't look like anyone else I know. I don't think you'd hurt me but also…"

"You questioned me. It's fine. I don't care. Ask me and I am happy to tell you my answer. Your decision. You get to choose what you do with it."

He was so honest. Blunt. So out there. She lifted her face, her eyelids feeling extra heavy over her eyes. She could barely sustain the darkness of his gaze. It was hot, angry and also something more. Was he on edge over her answer? Was he vulnerable? Toward her? Did he really care what she said or believed about him?

Yes. She was entirely sure that's what she saw in his gaze.

"I'm not very… sexual as a rule. I just want you to understand that. Prim Rose is what everyone calls me for being

67

such a prissy prude and growing up so sheltered and all that... it's true. It's definitely me."

His face morphed from showing caution, defeat, and defensiveness to shock. She what? She didn't shut him down but shared her vulnerability? Her insecurity? She trusted him with something new that was very hard for her to admit?

His hand lifted a fraction of an inch from his side before he flopped it back and she watched his chest rise as he inhaled a deep breath. Was it for courage? Was he planning to touch her? Something odd melted her heart. She gazed up at the man, staring right at the tattoo stamped on the delicate skin of his neck. His dark, dangerous look and heavy-lidded eyes were exciting to her. Yet he seemed so unsure and hopeful, as if he were seeking the courage to touch her. Something rippled through her core.

Wow. It felt pretty powerful.

Then his hand shot out as if he would quickly do it before he could change his mind. His hand cupped her face. She was startled by the gentle gesture as she lifted her face to gaze past the tattoos on his chest, his arms and his neck. Her eyes studied his lips and nose as she moved towards his eyes. They sparked with hot, unmasked interest in her. Desire. All for her. It was intoxicating, like drinking a forbidden nectar she never heard of before. His hand slid along her jawbone and his eyelids fell over his eyes. She stared at them, lost and intrigued by the effect her straitlaced, proper demeanor seemed to have on him.

She leaned towards him and his mouth descended on hers. This time, there was no hesitation. He was demanding, fluent and mobile. They tongue-danced. They tangoed. They lip-fucked. She never before that moment, even thought of such things, or could have understood such terms. But she did now. This was lip-fucking. Their lips moving and sliding. Touching and caressing. Their heads turned this way and that, and their hands grasping each other's faces as his long fingers traced her hairline to rub the fine, soft strands that flew freely around her face. He slid the silky hairs in his hand; and for the first time, her entire body responded to the most benign contact.

She moaned into his mouth. He pulled his lips off hers and his gaze landed on her eyes. Hard. Demanding. Wanting her far more than any words they could speak. Something shivered in her spine. He wanted her soul. It freaking felt like that, the way he stared into her eyes. Then he dipped his head towards her and dived into her mouth. Their tongues clashed in a tangle of saliva and lips and teeth. Plenty of moans and groans as her entire body felt as if it could burst into flames Only moments before, she was quietly interested. Now? She was dripping wet and amazed by her own response.

She didn't understand it. Overwhelmed, she couldn't think but only react and demand and want. She wanted him. She'd never wanted a man before. It felt almost animalistic. New. Exciting. Foreign. She didn't know how to handle it.

Mateo fully grabbed her waist with both hands, wrapping his long fingers around her, which made her feel small and tiny and protected. Never before did she seek such things. He pulled her against the solid wall of the naked muscles on his sinewy chest. He bent closer to her until he was drowning in her mouth as she strained towards the heat and silk and him. Water flowed around them and the hot sunlight warmed them. But her eyes were shut to the world. She was blind to all but his embrace.

She dragged her hands up his chest, and it shocked her that she had the guts to touch him. Her hands glided over the scripts and pictures and symbols… God, they went on forever over his torso and up his neck. She chastely wrapped her arms around his neck and held on.

Rose had never experienced an orgasm before with another person. By herself, yes. Partners, of which there were three? No. Just pleasant sex. It never hurt. Or traumatized her. It was pleasant, but it never burned or stung.

It never ached.

Her passion never devoured her.

His hand slid to the side of her boob and he pressed it. She sighed into his mouth as she conveyed a not-so-subtle message that he should touch more of her. Take her. Relieve her. The overpowering, overheated, overstimulated sensations were nearly too much for her. Please. She almost begged him to do more.

Then… yes. He slid the straps of her swimsuit down her arms and allowed her breasts to pop free, her perky C cups all pointy, capped by dark red nipples. She half-masted her eyes as his hands reached for her and he held her. Her eyelids fluttered shut when his fingertips grazed her eager breasts.

She didn't open her eyes, but moaned. She was actually scared to see herself against him, like this. She was so vulnerable, naked in the bright daylight that hid nothing. There was nowhere to hide. And she didn't care. She needed, wanted, and desired everything he did to her and so much more.

The air moved and he lifted her chest upwards. Yes. Oh, yes! He took her tight, taut, pebbled nipple into the warm, wet, luxurious depth of his hot mouth. She never knew anything could feel so good.

She grabbed his head of thick, black hair and displaced the band he used to pull his hair back. Her fingers combed through the straight strands, and she tugged and held him as she pulled his head hard against her.

She was on the verge of exploding Her head and heart thumped.

Her insides were spinning.

She cried out. "Oh, God! Oh, God! YES!"

She never cried out during sex before. She never tugged or pulled someone's hair and head or forced her mouth on him. But she did now.

His hand slid to the front of her swimsuit and he pulled the gusset to the side. Her body, now wet and swollen, almost exploded like breasts when freed from a too-tight bra. And oh. OH! He was slipping his finger along her exposed lips. One side, then the other, in a tender, soft explorational touch. He could not ignore the dripping, warm, moisture of her body's desire that his fingers were stirring up. He ran his entire hand along her vaginal lips, without delving inside her. He was rubbing her so gently, tracing the seam of her lips until she cried out and pulled herself harder against him before bearing down to ride his hand.

"What do you want, Rose?" His tone was soft and low as his lips kissed and licked her ear. Right against her temple, he whispered it, which seemed oddly disparate with the chaste kiss he planted there.

"You. This. Now."

"Are you sure?"

"Yes…" She moved her hips to emphasize what she wanted. "Yes…" She was nearly sobbing.

He held her up in the river and she stood up in the knee-high water. Shameless. Begging. Dying.

Holding one arm around her waist now, he tightened it and held her closer to him. He turned her so she was against his chest, solidly by him, her back to his front. She could feel the pressure of his erection against her back. She almost flipped around to touch it. She couldn't wait to explore its immensity and her stomach bottomed out while imagining it coming inside her.

His mouth peppered kisses on her hairline, soft kisses and licks as he pushed his fingers inside her pulsating core. Hard. He kept rubbing her as she responded and cried out, nearly sobbing under the pressure. Finally, she felt relief from all the aching, tugging and endless desire. Jerking her hips forward and back in a purposeful rhythm until she was whimpering, she had no idea where she was. Time and space and pride and propriety were lost to her. Gone. She was reduced to a throbbing, hormonal response that needed this more than anything she ever needed before.

She felt herself being lowered and she wasn't ready to lose it. This joy and ecstasy. Whatever her feelings signified. Her want. Her pulsing, aching need. This was the white-hot answer to all of it. She pulled on his shoulders as he carefully set her down on the dry, soft sand. He started to pull back but she lifted her head and captured his mouth with hers. She aggressively stuck her tongue inside his mouth. His body leaned closer until she could feel his hardness against her. She opened her thighs wider and let him press against her. He pushed repeatedly, but the clothing kept him out. Still it was heavenly excruciating. She gripped his shoulders as her legs stretched apart before cradling him fully inside her. She kept her eyes shut and clung to her former orgasm while wanting more. An aching propelled her, one that was so rare and unusual, she didn't know how to handle it.

Pushing her swimsuit to the side with his hand, he hovered over her. She gasped and her eyelids snapped open as his body nestled into her wet, ready, steaming, swollen, needy vagina. She gripped his back hard when his body moved and he held her under him just as hard. She was shocked to find him fully inside her. Pressed as far and as deep as their groins would allow, her mouth opened in a shocked "O" and she had to clutch his shoulders for better leverage. Her eyes all but rolled back in her head and she screamed out as she raked his back with her fingernails, embedding them into his shoulders before he pushed himself fully inside her again.

Her body shifted with his movements. Reciprocal undulations. She expected to be a bit abraded from the friction of the sand on her naked back. She cried out. She shifted and her hips slammed back into his. She met his next thrust too. Her body was fully engaged and accommodating as it greedily welcomed his body.

She was lost to him. All the hormones and blissful sensations flooding her mind became exclusive and she soon felt nothing but her wetness and him. Sliding, thrusting and hitting that spot. Oh, God. That achy, demanding, greedy, ripe spot deep inside her. She'd never touched it before or even knew it was there. Not like this. She was a beast. Needy. Hungry. Her bare toes wiggled in the sand and she halted her hips until she was ready to take him as hard and as rough and as long as he was.

Nothing like it. No time. No way did she picture sex with him as hard, dirty, and rough, nearly splitting her in half, and yet it still wasn't enough. It verged on violence, but in the best way. Her entire body was on fire and he was the match, the flame, and the fuel.

His hand slid over her mouth when she began screaming and her eyes rolled back in her head. She tightened all around him and contracted her vaginal walls, milking him deep inside her as the heated fluid entered every cell of her body and brain. He held her hips up and she knew she'd have bruises from the firmness of his grip. He had to hold her still to help her handle the slap, slam, and slickness when he buried himself deep inside her.

She loved the way he held her like that. No one had ever done that before. Not anything like it. Being sore and marked and bruised didn't matter; the feelings he released from inside her were more powerful than any nuclear explosion. She was sure of that. It was incredible. Endless. Her nerve endings were still zinging.

And then…

Quiet.

She opened her eyes.

That quickly, the magic of feeling she was lost in another world, vanished. She was back to reality. Just Rose. On a beach. On her river. Mateo Alvarez was buried to the hilt, deep inside her body. No one had ever been so close to her. No one could be. He orgasmed before dropping on top of her. His head was buried against her shoulder. She stared up at searing blue sky above them. His thick, black hair, free and tangled—all by her—kept his face obscured from hers.

His naked front was lying on hers. Just the bottom half. Her bathing suit still covered her. How did they avoid taking it off? How long would that have taken? A second? They were so eager they couldn't remove her swimsuit? She shut her eyes and the reality inundated her as hard and fast as the sex did.

What in the living fuck did she just do? And why? How did it happen?

He claimed he would fuck her and she thought, no! No way… and then she did?

But how could she have ignored the constant onslaught of those feelings? They were so new and shocking to her. She had no idea. None at all. She was almost appalled at herself. She didn't know what to do now.

She hurt and couldn't breathe. The sand prickled her back; instead of being soft, small granules, it felt like a thousand pinpricks, sharp and unrelenting. His weight trapped and suffocated her. Her sore lower half began to protest the unusual activity and in all honesty? Being used like she never imagined using it before.

Hard. Harsh. Rough. Sex? That was what she wanted?

She became anxious about what she felt and did and with whom. She bit her lip. What could she say to him now? His head would lift and she would see those eyes, those soulful or soul*less* eyes, that seemed so deep and knowing whenever they stared into hers. What words could she say? How to say them? How could she share her joyful experience with Mateo? Someone she didn't trust or even care about? Someone who made her anxious and nervous? Something so mind-altering and unparalleled... and she shared that life-changing moment with him? Could Mateo even understand her feelings about sex?

She wasn't comfortable enough with him to casually or affectionately rub his back or hair. She didn't want to touch him now. She didn't know where to put her hands. They fell to her side instead of gripping his shoulders. She wondered how to feel and think and act. Other than... oh, crap. She felt awful now.

Rose never had sex with someone she didn't know. Or trust. Or care about.

Mateo was really a stranger to her.

She squirmed as he finally flipped his head up. Yep, that cold gaze and neutral scowl were heavy on her face. His mouth was a flat line and he had no expression on his face.

No words from either of them. Staring vacantly, his mouth dropped open and he glanced down between them.

Setting his hands on either side of her head, he put his weight on his arms and hovered over her. He stared right down at her, only inches from her face. She locked eyes with him, gulping, and feeling confused. The moment became so intense, she had to shut her eyes to soften it or she couldn't handle it.

He lifted his chest off her and slid back. Her eyelids flipped open and fuck if she wasn't staring at his naked body. He knelt and leaned back over his feet, still between her legs. His face was right there, beside her suddenly shameful female part.

Jumping to his feet and unconcerned by his nudity, he merely grabbed his penis and pulled the used condom off. Shit. Her eyes widened as she realized he wore one, which only now occurred to her. She had been fully ready to take him bare and raw. She would never have noticed it, she was so lost and overwhelmed by his touch and her response... well, hell. She proved that.

Mateo dropped the condom in the sand and grabbed his shorts before tugging them on. Rose scrambled to sit up, her gaze darting from him to her. She quickly tugged her bathing suit straps back into place.

What about tenderness? She needed a gentle hand on her back or shoulder. A kind word. A delicate inquiry as to how she felt. Anything to calm the tremendous feelings tumbling through her. She felt almost dirty. But also, relieved to the point of being languid. She never came like that.

She needed something more from him. But when her glance rose to where he stood, she encountered only neutrality and indifference, the old Mateo.

Okay. No words. No tenderness. No comment even? That was... well, frick. Definitely worth commenting on, that was for sure. Words like *glorious, magnificent, mind-shattering, mind-shaking,* and *life-altering* came to mind.

She wondered if they could share their thoughts, but she was instantly tongue-tied with his unreadable look. He casually turned to bury the condom with handfuls of sand. She bit her tongue and did not tell him he couldn't bury it on the beach. It was latex and non-biodegradable garbage so he was littering and... no. No comment. Rose could not imagine grabbing the dirty used condom and what? Packing it back upriver with her? She wondered who might be visiting the family beach. Shove it somewhere? She had nothing to carry it in. And neither did he.

How did he happen to have it? she wondered.

"How…" The word slipped through her lips so she pressed them shut. She wanted so much more from this moment and him. First, just to understand why it happened; and second, what it meant to him and her… They were so different and yet this happened?

"Pocket."

"Oh." She didn't look up. *He'd planned this?*

"I told you I wanted to fuck you and you could have said no. So no…"

She tilted her head up. The sun was behind him and it blinded her. She shielded her eyes and squinted, frowning. Softly, she said, "It never occurred to me to say such a thing. I mean… yes. I… we… it was consensual."

He nodded. "Long as you understand that."

She tilted her head, then glanced away. Not the soft pillow talk she expected or wanted or desired or… hell, *needed.*

Mateo was a white-hot ember in a burning fire during sex and then he became a cold lump of coal afterwards.

She got to her feet. "We should go."

"Yeah." That's it. His cool gaze was neutral, mild and as uninterested in her as if they had just… what? Finished a game of chess? He wasn't even lukewarm towards her now. Her heart dipped and tears filled her eyes. She tilted her head so he could not see her face. Her heart freaking hurt and she realized she made a huge, terrible mistake. Worse still, he lived in the area, worked with her family and she could never fully avoid her huge, terrible mistake.

She watched him enter the water before grabbing the rope to tug his little raft behind him. He glanced back at her, still neutral but with his eyebrows up as if to say, "Coming?" Rose licked her lips and stepped into the water, taking her own tube. She followed him. Plodding through the water, they strode against the river current. Her thoughts wandered. Her distraction was so complete, she barely noticed where she stepped. She hurt. She felt sore, and it wasn't due to a delicious secret between her body and his. No, she hurt and she was embarrassed about it. Glad when the cool water slipped between her legs. Washing away the evidence of sex and allowing her body to be soothed.

When they finally hit the beach, Ian, Kailynn and their son were there. Mateo didn't say anything as he got out and barely patted his wet body with a towel. Rose was greeted with the usual pleasantries and chit-chat. She wished they would all go away so she could grab Mateo and talk or say something... anything... to make this more tolerable. Not so gut-clenchingly awkward and awful.

Then, without a glance back or a single word, Mateo left.

Did it really mean zero, nada, nothing to him? Or was Mateo the worst sexual partner in existence? Rose could only wonder if he was awful, nasty and sociopathic or... maybe he was really just awkward, lost and unsure?

He might not know how to act, but right now she had no idea why she had even done this.

CHAPTER 5

ROSE WALKED INTO THE shop and found Mateo behind the hood of a car. He heard her and glanced up and his gaze crashed onto hers. She was pinned. Frozen. Trapped. Then, something very much alive and sharp, traveled down her spine before it almost zapped her in her gut. What in the hell was that response? His eyes were dark and unreadable as they traveled over her. Taking in every detail of her outfit: mid-thigh khaki shorts and a lavender tank top. There was nothing revealing. Neither cleavage nor bra. Her hair swept back in a ponytail. She seemed so wholesome, the polar opposite of his looks. He didn't say anything. His gaze first chilled then heated her. It pinned and then freed her. Yet nothing was said. He set her on fire before turning back to dive into his work.

"Rose? Rose, did you want to go tonight?" Iris's demanding voice snapped Rose back to attention. She whipped around, her face blooming with color. Crap. She didn't hear Iris because she was so entrenched with Mateo who showed zero reaction to her. He had to feel something, didn't he? What she felt? Was sex always like that for him? He didn't think about it because it always ended this way? Lucky man. She never heard sex described the way he made her feel. Yet… now there was nothing. Curious looks. Silence. No smiles. No tenderness. No idle chit-chat about her day or how she was. Never a date. Why would he not want that? What *did* he want? Why did he kiss her that day? Why did he do that? Why did she? And why didn't it continue? Why didn't they discuss it or something? One question begged another and she only became more confused and paralyzed since she honestly didn't know what to do now. She was terrified of how she felt for him both during and after what happened. How could she allow it to take place?

Rose went home afterwards and simply banished it from her brain for the remainder of the day. She kept herself stupid busy with trivial stuff that didn't matter, trying to erase the memory of what happened. She tried to convince herself it had no real meaning but when she went to bed, she thought of nothing else, so it did mean something. At least, it meant something to her. Every moment was replayed like a slow-motion movie on a loop. She relived his first touch and his last. She relived every kiss, every movement, every word. The fantastic way each caress, word and movement made her feel. Inside and out. How she reacted. Why she reacted. After analyzing it long and hard, she still had no idea why she did it at all. She regretted the way it all went down and then suddenly ended. How could she live with it? But she was honestly grateful for the fantasies he provided that started to percolate and overtake her brain. Images started to drift through her mind that were new and unusual. She was more aware of her feelings and desires and all because of the things he said and did. She recalled how quietly he began before he started commanding her in an almost rude tone. His brutishness sent odd shivers of longing through her body.

But nothing happened. Three days passed and Rose had

no clue what happened or what to do. She could only wonder if they were an item or still just strangers. She had no idea how to process it, but it wasn't working for her. She feared seeing him again.

Mateo did not return to the beach after that day. If this were truly nothing, why did he disappear? Rose wondered if he regretted it or hadn't like it. Maybe it *was* something that he didn't know what to do with either.

Rose waited patiently because she was so unsure how to approach him. But when her mother told her she had some items to give Iris, Rose quickly volunteered to run them over to her. She and her mom were hanging out much more often, starting to integrate Rose into the business and tutoring. Allison was gathering material for Rose to review and sharing her ideas. But the errand to Iris was something Rose pounced on. Gladly. The reason she needed to go there.

She couldn't wait to go to the shop.

Once, it was the place where she always looked first for her dad and sister. It never had any other significance to her than that. She entered it eagerly and without hesitation. She would bop in and out at will with little reflection in between. Whether she ran into Jeff or Chan or Iris or Dad, who cared?

Then Mateo showed up. Now, Rose paused before entering the shop out of caution. But never until now did she react with panic or hyperventilation at the thought of simply seeing his face. His gaze. His neutral look. His eyes on her. Him standing near her. Her sweaty palms and tight lungs made her shove her images of him to the back of her mind. How to prepare for this?

After spending too much time in the bathroom fixing her hair and makeup, she rechecked her outfit... All this fuss to go to her dad's greasy shop. Not a big deal. Until now.

After she delivered Iris's stuff, some crap Mom bought for her, Mateo realized she was there. Out popped his head and he studied every last detail of her careful preparation. What did he think? What did he feel? Interest? Annoyance? That she was too preppy and conservative? That she was nauseatingly prim and proper and goody-two-shoes? She was. She felt that at first, until he came on to her. No doubt about that. But her other doubts were staggering. Her insecurity was insurmountable and she couldn't even find the words to speak. Simple words. A greeting. That would be the obvious start. She felt her tongue thickening under his merciless stare. A vault that held whatever he thought and felt. She used to believe he felt nothing, certainly not for her. But what about their swims together and the way they ended? Why did they suddenly end? And why did all of it have to happen?

Mateo's head popped down behind the hood, hiding him. She no longer could see him. He didn't say a word or smile or even lift an eyebrow to acknowledge her. The hurt was sharp and real in her chest. She didn't like it. She felt unsure about him and what they did together, but she definitely didn't like that being the end of it all. A look? And then he ignores her?

As if she wasn't there?

She refused to allow that to be the end. Or the beginning. Or whatever the hell it was?

"Earth to Rose." She snapped around at Iris's voice.

"What?"

"Tonight? Want to go hang out with Pam and me for a while?"

Pam was a friend they both liked. "Oh, no. I have plans. Maybe another time."

Iris shrugged, lying on the rolling dolly she used to scoot under the car. "Whatevs, no worries. Catch you later. I'll be out late then."

"Sure. Yeah, catch you later then," Rose replied, although

her thoughts were totally preoccupied with the person hiding barely one car-length over. She planned to see him. This was asinine and she refused to let it be this way for long.

She ducked out of the shop, realizing she had to face it. It was the only course of action that made any sense to her, and his hiding from her gave her the strength and courage to do just that. Tonight. He was in her plans.

Even if she had to ignore her body's reaction when it immediately got wet and she felt like singing and thumping and doing all kinds of other weird and new things at catching a fleeting glimpse of him. Mateo. He drew her to him like a magnet.

SHE SNEAKED BACK into the shop later. Her dad was there and he started chatting with her. She told him she was merely saying hi, and when he got a phone call and stepped out, she almost did somersaults of joy. She quickly ducked into her dad's office, pulling the employee files and snapping a picture of Mateo's application and address. She only hoped it hadn't changed.

She returned to the main part of the shop when her dad finished his call. She smiled and said she was meeting Iris and would see him later. Shane bought it with a smile and a hug.

Rose drove to the main road where she got decent cell service before putting the address into her maps and following the voice's instructions. It started with a "turn left and go point eight miles towards Amber Mills Road." Rose turned her car and started down the valley towards Pattinson. She followed a sloping driveway that was graveled and then drove through an abandoned orchard in disrepair. Some of the trees were uprooted and piled together, prior to being burned at some point, she assumed. Other fields were wild with weeds and overgrown old trees. Sorry to see the orchard in such a sad state, Rose followed the road down another incline that dipped below the orchard towards a flat spot that fronted the river. It was below one of the popular rapids, about seven rapid sets down from their swim beach. Rose often floated past this spot.

The row of red cabins had been redone over the last few years. That was his address? She parked at the bottom lot and found number five. It had a front door with a window beside it. A small awning covered the concrete stoop. The back overlooked the rocky beach and swiftest part of the river.

Her hands were sweating. She rubbed them on her shorts and sucked in a breath of warm air. It was well past seven and the sun was hanging low in the sky, but the heat clung to the ground and wafted up towards her. She took a deep breath and forced herself to knock. Her heart pounded louder in her chest than she could knock on the damn door.

Mateo swung it open with a sharp jerk. His expression was kind of annoyed and then... for once, the neutrality left. Raising his eyebrows to indicate that her face wasn't the one he'd expected, she realized she'd startled him. No... maybe she'd just surprised him.

She sucked in more air for courage. It didn't work. She pushed her hands on her thighs. "Uh... hi."

"What are you doing here?" His voice revealed the dismay she saw in his facial expression. He was annoyed as hell to see her.

"I—I... wanted to speak to you."

He leaned a shoulder on the door jamb with no indication he wanted her to enter. One eyebrow lifted this time. "Yeah? What?"

"Um... could I come in? Maybe... I mean... I don't know..." Her words drifted off as her thoughts fled her mind.

She didn't know what to say. But after intimacy, the partners should talk. The most personal act... and the wildest, harshest, hardest, bruising and best all-around orgasm she ever had and he wondered why she was there?

"How did you know where I lived?"

She grew hotter under his stare. "Um..."

"Fuck." He straightened his lazy slouch on the door jamb. "You didn't ask Iris, did you? Or even worse, your dad?"

She swallowed, oddly relieved by his passionate, but scary response that she had not done so. She retreated half a step. "Uh... no. No. I didn't ask them. Why would that matter so much?"

Perplexed. Confused. Offended. Hurt. The warring feelings clashed inside her. Why was she being relegated to feeling those things?

"Because your dad is my boss and your sister is his daughter, so do the math. You could get me fired. You didn't consider that?"

Her mouth flapped opened and then closed. She'd never considered anything like that. What was he talking about? They weren't living in the dark ages when her dad would have demanded a dowry before allowing his daughter's precious chastity to be violated. Hell no. She chose to do it. She was fully in charge of her body and her needs and wants, her emotions and behavior. What was Mateo so angry about?

"Consider what?"

"That your dad warned me to stay away from Iris when I started working here. What do you think he'd say if he discovered that I fucked you? His precious Rose? His other daughter? He's definitely not going to play favorites."

There... he said it. The word. What they did. So out there. She glanced around to see if anyone heard, but no one else was visible. Puzzled, she wondered what these cabins were used for now. She couldn't catalogue what happened between them or how she felt about it or what she felt about him.

"Could I please come in?" she asked again. Her tone was firm, but polite. Maybe… yes, a little prim and proper and sharp, but she couldn't help that. That was how she was.

He puckered up his lips and made his cheeks hollow. Indignity fueled her courage as she realized he was actually considering not honoring her request. He might not open the door to her. She glared and pushed the door. "Mateo." She said his name sharply, in a chastising tone. "You owe me a conversation."

She started to slip past him but he leaned in and trapped her in the doorway. Ready to intimidate her, his gaze was cool and heavy-lidded as his eyes roamed her face before landing on her lips. Her pulse raced in response. Her lower half also reacted to him. With unmasked desire. She hated herself. She wished she could scold her traitorous body. Stop it. He was awful.

His hand gripped her bicep. The gaze that was so intent on her lips lifted to meet her eyes. "I don't owe you or anyone shit. Just so we're clear, baby girl."

There wasn't one thing sexy or tender about what could have been an endearing nickname. Not when he uttered it like that. She swallowed hard and jerked her arm free. "I—I actually prefer not to be called that." Then she pushed past him. Getting into his space. His domain. Was she crazy? Suicidal? Maybe.

But despite the tiny bit of trepidation that crept through her, she refused to be intimidated. He might talk tough, and even seem like a gangster, but she didn't believe he was. She also observed that when he felt cornered or unsure, he usually did that. She fell right into his hands and reacted to her fear. Maybe, and she wasn't one hundred percent sure yet, but maybe he was just a frightened kitten who tried to sound like a cougar poised to attack. But he wasn't really any cougar. That was just his armor. His face to the world. His image suggested it, but she saw plenty of other things in their time together. Things that attracted her enough to do what she did with him.

She could be wrong but she knew she wasn't.

"You don't prefer..." His voice drifted off as he shut the door and shook his head, ostensibly puzzled by her statement. "It wasn't a nickname of endearment, baby girl," he added with a smirk.

She shifted and turned so she could gain her equilibrium. The conversation wasn't going well for her and getting so far out of her control, she wasn't eager to continue it. She took in his place, which was very small. Dark now, with the door shut and both windows covered with shades. The heat was stifling in there. Not even a fan to blow the hot, oven-like air out. It was worse than outside. At least, outdoors had little breezes that cooled down her heated skin.

Light came from a bedside lamp. The bed took up the whole right side of the cabin and the kitchen was directly opposite. The nightstand was next to it and about three feet from the small refrigerator that hummed away. The kitchen consisted of a fridge, a small, one-burner stove, and a farmhouse sink with a counter that was barely two feet wide and long. There was a microwave on a table beside the counter. A dresser stood in the corner and one lone recliner with a small side table occupied the main room. Rose saw a shoe rack and miscellaneous items tossed about.

It was pitifully small and not very nice. Rose was truly surprised. She'd never been in anything like it. But she concealed her astonishment and privilege although she immediately realized it. She had no right to judge. None whatsoever. The reason why she was there was unimportant.

She only came to talk. Communicate. Understand. Clarify. Maybe... well, who knows why?

She turned towards him. He stood up, folding his arms over his chest, but this time without the neutral soul-staring. No, it was outright snarled-up lip and glaring eyes. He hated her being here. He expected what? Her to sniff the air with disdain? And say something horrible? Probably, if his defensive stance and the energy emanating off him were any indication.

Several beads of sweat dripped down her back and her brow. It was so hot.

She cleared her throat and threw her hands up before finally being totally honest in her confusion. "I don't know what to do or say to you."

"Why do you have to say anything?"

"Because... because we... we... I can't make sense of it. And we should talk about it."

"Fucked. We fucked, Rose. Is that what brought you here? You want to do it again? No worries, baby girl. Do a face plant over that table and drop those shorts and we'll get it over with."

Her stupid body reacted to his cruel words by clenching with need and weeping in her southern parts. Yeah... apparently, she became insatiably horny whenever she was around him. Good thing her brain was in control.

She was crestfallen by his words. His actions towards her. His attitude.

Didn't it matter at all to him? She was no more than a joke?

"No. No, that's not what I want at all." Her voice was quiet, her words faltering. She lifted her eyes to his cold stare, and it took every ounce of her strength to keep them there in the face of his callousness. Shocking lack of regard or care. Was that how he lived his life? "Why would you say such a thing to me?"

She kept her arms loosely at her sides, trying not to cross them over her chest or mimic his indifference. She did not want to grow angry. She was more hurt and confused than actually angry. If this were really him and she missed it all the times they spent together, then she deserved what she got and whatever he said about her to others. She cringed with dread at the thought of him ever using those off-color words about her to others. Anyone who might know her. But it was done. And she did it, and he had the knowledge. She could not control what he said about it or how he said it or whom he said it to.

She seemed to perplex him, by her lack of anger. His gaze darted around. To her, the bed, the door and then, back to her. "Was it a joke? Was I a joke to you? The time we spent together? I believed it wasn't a joke. That we had a... a connection. Might have mattered to each other even. But if you think that's what I want, how I want it and worse, how I want you to speak to me, then no. No, that's not at all what I want. Or who I am. Did you really not understand that about me?"

His entire expression dropped and for the first time she saw Mateo Alvarez looking uncertain. He didn't know what to say or do. He stepped back. For the first time ever, he really did. He stepped back. Did she have the power here? She didn't know. But somehow, she suspected she was reading this right finally. He wasn't sure what to make of her for the first time ever.

"I don't like the word fuck." She started there. Might as well be simple.

Again, puzzled at her turn of conversation, he scowled but snapped, "You say it. I've heard you."

"Sure. If I stub my toe, I might curse and say 'fuck' or 'shit' or if I'm messing around, I might say… I don't know… 'this hamburger is so fucking good' but when you refer to what we did? Never. I don't like it. Said to me or about me."

"Well, what do you prefer to call it then?" he inquired with his head tilted. He truly seemed miffed. She all but groaned. He thought that was the only word to call it?

"Umm… I don't know I guess calling it 'it' or… 'sex.' But not what you call it."

"So you want me to call it, 'it'?"

"It describes two people with a connection. With a… a reason for doing 'it' together."

"It again." He shook his head. "You got me, Rosie. I don't know what the fuck to say to you. What do you want?"

Her eyes widened. He really didn't know. Didn't see any need to even talk. She shut her eyes as she realized how remotely apart their impressions of what they did together was.

"Want? Just to talk about the changes between us. Now that we…"

"We did it?" He let out the smallest smile. Just the side of his mouth lifted but only a fraction of an inch.

But he joked about it. He relaxed. And he would have done the same with Iris. She nodded optimistically. "Yes. We did that. And I've been… unsure."

His entire body stiffened. "You could have stopped me any time. There was not a moment when you said no or paused or whatever. So—"

She held up her hand to say halt. "Oh, my God, you are just impossible. I did not in any way come here to discuss this regarding my consent. Or lack thereof. Of course, I wanted to do what we did. All of it. I was willing and glad to be with you. I just… there's… an emotional side that I'm struggling with."

His shoulders started to release in obvious relief but he simply blinked. "The... the emotional side of things?"

He wasn't deliberately being obtuse. She almost shut her eyes and faded to the floor. He really didn't get this. That they weren't just... well, to use his words and obvious frame of reference: he thought they fucked once and were done?

Frustrated, she turned and flopped on his bed. "You don't get this at all, do you?"

"No."

"You don't like me at all?" She finally asked what felt like the simplest way to start.

"I... yeah, I like you. What... why?"

"Then why would you think we'd do it and not talk afterwards? Or discuss it? Or connect over it and figure out what happens next?"

"What happens next?"

"You don't follow?"

"I don't. We fucked." He winced. "Sorry. We 'did it' and agreed it was consensual and I'm not being redundant, right?"

"So you don't want to do it again?"

"I do. Sure, but I didn't figure you would, not with me. It's not your thing."

"Why wouldn't it be my thing?"

"Fucking just to fuck. That's what I mean, Rose. You get that. Right?"

"Of course, but that wasn't what happened. We didn't just do that to do it."

"Then what do you think happened?"

Circles. They were talking in circles and not moving forward. Time to turn around and try another tactic. "We had fun together? Right? I mean, with the raft and playing on the river together? Or did you fake that? You didn't enjoy the time you spent with me?"

His eyebrows lowered and his head shook. He didn't know what to say. For real. He didn't know how to answer her question. "Did you?" She pressed. "Or were you faking all of that to sleep with me? Did you just want to fuck me?"

There, she said it. She put it out there. She restrained a wince of horror.

He stared at her and slowly let out a breath and a laugh. "You might be right, but you don't sound right saying it like that."

She pressed her lips tightly. "I know. Slang never fit me. Or even cursing in a way that had any meaning. I just can't pull it off. I'm not cool at all, Mateo. You surely must have realized that before we… you know. I'm no Iris."

She stared down at her hands, which she clenched on her lap in discomfort. Now that she revealed an insecurity she never told anyone else, at least not in words, she wondered, *why Mateo?*

He dropped beside her. To her surprise, he didn't glare at her. "You think I ever thought you were like Iris?"

"She's your best friend and all. Of course, I thought that. But I'm not like Iris and you'll be disappointed if that's what you expected."

"So you… you think you could disappoint me?"

She sensed something in his measured words and tone, but she wasn't sure what it was. "Yes. Of course. Hence, the reason why I'm here."

His lips twitched and he touched her face. A gentle, quick swipe of his finger on her cheek before he dropped his hand and immediately turned his head away. "Only person I know to use the word *hence*." His small smile thrilled and confounded her. Why did that word amuse him so much? In that moment, he was more like the Mateo she recognized from the time they spent together on the river. "I can't believe you'd worry about what I might think."

Puzzled, she rubbed her fingers together to distract her nerves. "You're the most intimidating person I ever met. We did something I rarely do with anyone and now you won't look at or talk to me. Of course, I'm confused, intimidated, and wondering about you. Of course, I care what you think of me."

"I never thought you were like Iris."

"Is that good or bad?"

His mouth twitched. He did that a lot with her, she suddenly realized. "Well, I never wanted to fu—" He stopped his words. "To be intimate with her," he swiftly amended his statement. "And I can't believe you're worried that I was disappointed in you."

"So did our time together matter to you at all?"

"Yeah. That's why I…"

"You kissed me?"

"Yeah. Why I kissed you."

The miscommunication hung between them. She gripped her fingers together. "Is it always that way for you? Is that why you ignored me and never talked to me or sought to do it again or whatever?"

"What? You mean sex?"

"Yes. Is it always that way for you?"

"What way is that, Rosie?"

Her shoulders almost slouched in relief at hearing the trace of lilt and teasing to his tone when he used the nickname he liked to call her.

"Well, the words don't fit."

"Is that good?"

"Yes. But… it was exponentially better than that."

"Exponentially?" He shook his head and lifted his hand to ruffle her hair. God. It was incredible, even more thrilling than when he entered her. He was being playful and innocent, showing affection toward her.

"Another word you don't often hear used?"

"Not when someone is describing the best fucking I ever enjoyed."

She winced and blushed, which made her smile as she stared harder at her thighs and asked, "Ever?"

"Yeah." His tone was husky.

She lifted her gaze and gave him a side glance before looking away. "Me too. But that wasn't surprising if you knew my history. Back to yours... is it extensive?"

"Yes."

She chewed on that for a moment. He didn't elaborate, thank goodness. Or add anything crass or decadent and she hoped the need for doing that was safely stashed for a while. She couldn't take it and manage to keep her equilibrium.

"Does that make you think it has no meaning?"

His shoulders fell and he released a long breath as he leaned forward, placing his elbows on his knees. "Oh, fuck me, Rosie. You just aren't like anyone else, are you?"

Perplexed, she simply stared in disbelief at his profile. *What? What did she say?*

"Well, I used to think I was pretty ordinary but from your reaction to me shall I assume I'm not?"

His head shook and he buried his face in his hands. "You're not. And it never had any meaning to me before because I've never been with anyone who wanted it to have meaning. Okay? I'm not trying to hurt you or do this the wrong way... I've never had a relationship that went beyond a day spent fucking. That's it. Done. And I thought... no, I truly believed that's what happened. Especially as..."

"What? Tell me, Mateo. Help me have a starting point."

"Especially as... it's you, Rose. Rose Rydell. God, don't you know?"

No. Her heart nearly screamed it. No, she didn't know. She had no idea what he thought. Or what she thought of him. Or why she was sitting on a threadbare, single mattress in a stifling heat-box trying to understand a man with a neck tattoo, a crass vocabulary and a prison record... But now? She invested all of her hope and aspirations in his answer. Even if he articulated nothing with a string of pretty words. They were raw and honest and truer than anything she ever heard before. "Know what?" Her tone was as breathless as her hollow lungs.

"I never wanted anyone like I wanted you. How could you not realize it?"

His frustration seemed to seep out of him.

She swallowed hard and a series of thrills excited her. Her mouth felt dry. This man... this very hot, scary and mysterious man wanted her? Seriously? Rosie Rydell?

"Honestly, no, I never can tell if men want me. It's never been part of my experience at all. Never. Men want Iris. But me? Never."

He didn't reach over and touch her or say anything else so she sucked in a breath of the stifling air and tried to pry him open again. On this attempt, she tried using different words. "Mateo, did you stop wanting me? Was your desire for me only sexual?"

She clasped her hands together primly on her uncrossed legs. She was wearing shorts and Mateo glanced at her white, freckled legs. Staring down at them, she saw the polar opposite of sexy or interesting. She couldn't imagine how anyone could want or be passionate towards her. She saw why: she was too prim and practical.

She watched his profile as he turned his face just a fraction of an inch towards her to let her see him. "I—I don't know. I guess... it's more than that. It just never occurred to me..."

To ask? To think she might want him back? Of course, she didn't before. But now? Maybe. Just maybe she did.

"Did you ever think to just… ask me out?"

His head jerked as he whipped around to look at her. She lifted her eyes and pressed her lips together. Judging by his dramatic, startled reaction, he didn't.

"Ask you out? To do what?"

"Maybe you could say, hey, Rose, why don't we grab dinner, or lunch, or coffee? And go on a drive or something? Anything besides nothing and then crazy sex."

"No."

Simple. Straight to the point. Okay, she would throw it right back at him with total simplicity. He was so different from her. "Umm, why not? Why did that never occur to you?"

He shook his head. "You were always so scared of me."

"Yes, but after I towed you all over the river in an inflatable raft, my previous misconceptions about you changed." She shook her head. "Well, okay. I was and I am still a little unsure about you… but most of my preconceived notions about you changed."

His hand flopped up and down. "I don't know what you expect me to say. Okay? I don't know anything about this. Or you. Or women like you."

She snorted. "As if I know what to do or say with guys like you," she said, volleying his anger, annoyance and uncertainty right back to him.

He bowed his head. "That never occurred to me. You have all the power here."

"How the crap do you figure that?" she exclaimed.

"You're beautiful and smart and you come from a caring family who pays my salary. You'll never be discriminated against in any job opportunities or money ventures. You aren't an ex-con with a neck tattoo. Right?"

"Well, no. But you did that to your own body. I didn't. So don't use that as the only reason why I initially had a negative reaction to you. Isn't that the real reason you did it?" She nearly slapped her hand over her mouth. She sounded bitchy and rude. It was so unnecessary and besides, she didn't know how he'd react to her attitude. Something about him made him appear almost feral and volatile and unpredictable. How dare she taunt him!

Despite all of that, he thrilled her formerly sedate, middle-class heart and soul. Apparently, her desire was stimulated and fueled by his alpha-male bullshit that was borderline sexist and completely rude. She nearly sighed at the soul-shattering, shocking revelation. It was a discouraging thing to discover about herself.

He laughed. Startled at his reaction, she turned, bringing her leg up and bending her knee while resting her foot on her other thigh. "My tattoo. It all came down to that for you. All I had to do was say boo and you would have swooned."

"Which you did quite often to me. But it was more than that. The way you looked at me for instance. I had to wonder if you hated me and were plotting to kill me or you were somehow like..." Words escaped her. She couldn't say that. Not out loud. She withheld what she really thought.

His gaze finally captured hers. Cool. Soulless. Dark. The same mysterious eyes that always thrilled her to the bone. "Like what?"

"I can't say it."

"You should try being honest more often. You don't always have to be so polite."

She bit her lip, then shrugged. "But I like to be."

"You like to be polite?"

"Yes. It makes me happy when I have good interactions with others. I don't like to cause strife and I hate conflict. Don't get me wrong; I'm no pushover. I will always stand up for myself, but I prefer to start with politeness and self-restraint in what I say."

He tilted his head as his gaze probed her. "I've never known anyone like you."

"You seem to say that often. Is that a positive or a negative?"

"It's… it must be a positive. Because I can't stop myself from liking you."

Her heart nearly slammed into her ribs. It was the most he ever revealed about what he thought of her. It was a nice thing to say.

"So what did you want to say that's not very polite?"

"Oh, this is not impolite, it's… just embarrassing to me."

"Well…" His eyebrows rose.

"I used to think you could look right into my soul and read my thoughts. I thought you saw past all the fluff and politeness. I wondered what you saw, and it disconcerted me. At other times, I was sure you hated me for all the reasons you listed: my privilege, my family, my years in college and everything else that I have. But once or twice, I thought you saw the real me. When…" Her head bowed. There was only so much she could say under the same gaze she was describing.

"When what?" His tone was husky. Different.

"When maybe no one else could. Not my parents or Iris or my other sisters. Not my friends from school or anyone else in my life. But that didn't make sense. You don't know me and I don't know you but I felt like you saw me clearly."

"I do know you."

"How?" she whispered. Her strength was gone. Her ability to face him while baring her soul took a toll on her and she felt very vulnerable.

"I paid attention to everything about you. Everything you said or did, I watched. No matter how small or insignificant. So what you saw was just me observing you. I saw your father ignore little things about you. I saw Iris overlooking the reasons why you often got hurt by her relationship with your dad. I knew you were smart and interesting and nice. So fucking nice. Yeah, even when it came to me. When you didn't know how to deal with me. Or what to say to me. I saw you clumsily trying to figure out who and what I was. River's End and all your college years and experiences in life never mentioned or included anyone like me. Yeah, I saw all that."

She held her breath and released it slowly. Owl-eyed, her gaze widened even more as he spoke the true words. He said more words now than she ever heard him string together before. For once, the conversation did not revolve around car-fixes or rude, crude jokes with Iris and the other mechanics.

"Why don't you want to go out with me?"

"I don't know what you mean. I can't say I don't want to. I just don't do that, I guess."

"But you do want to have sex again?"

He snorted. "Duh."

"But you didn't even speak to me. You didn't even try. How could it happen again? You were mad when I showed up here."

"It didn't occur to me you would want to with me again. I thought it was a one time, whatever. You'd consider it a mistake and ignore me or pretend it never happened."

"That's what you were counting on?"

He shrugged. "Sure. Yes."

"But why? If you knew me so well, you had to know that I don't do anything casually. I certainly don't indulge in sex like that. How could you think I'd ignore you? Us? This?"

"Because of your basic fears. Because you don't know what to think of me. You don't know if I carry a weapon, in case I get the urge to rob the next store I see. There is some niggling part of your brain that always warns you I might just do that."

"Yes." Brutally honest. "If you saw that, then how did you not see me coming here?"

"It never occurred to me that you'd acknowledge it."

"But you did it anyway?"

"I thought it was my one chance. I'd have you once and that would be it. Enough."

"Is it enough?" Breathless, she stared at him. He stared back.

"Never," he muttered in a tone so low, it was more of a breath than a word.

Her heart skipped a beat. Then he moved so fast, her thoughts and perceptions failed to capture or process what was about to happen before it did. He reached around her, putting his face near hers and his lips on hers. His mouth felt hard and determined as his tongue boldly addressed her sealed lips and demanded entrance into her mouth. His tongue thrust inside hard, with little question he was stealing her response, taking what he considered his. He slid his tongue along hers and that quickly, her nipples hardened into pebbles while a need much deeper and darker tugged down lower. Her body was swift to respond. The sliding of their tongues opened her entire body to him; it seemed to say, *come to me, come inside me, make me come.*

Her traitorous body responded as if her heart was as wild and rebellious as Mateo, not the staunch, prim, provincial person she really was.

She let his tongue spear her repeatedly. Her response seemed so easy. Maybe the first easy thing between them. For Rose, Mateo was easier to be with than she ever felt with the opposite sex. She opened her arms and let him press her onto the sleeping bag placed over the bare mattress that served as his bedding. His weight was on her top half and his hands slipped up her back to comb his fingers over her scalp. She let her lips tangle and twist and turn with his frenetic movements. His other hand slipped down the front of her, over her ribbed tank top and bra-covered breast. He stopped briefly to rub and squeeze and appreciate her body's tight response before slipping towards the seam of her shorts. He firmly pressed into what was already hot and bothered and wet.

She whimpered and her hips thrust as she...

Crap. Again. Lost. So fast. Emotions morphing into raw hormones. Desire. Lust. Chemistry. Pheromones. Words vanish. Thoughts only of her body's pulsating needs.

No. She couldn't let it so quickly eclipse what she really wanted, and how she was. And yes, oh, yes, she loved the way he felt on top of her, and how she felt under him. But there was so much still to sort out. She had to figure it out. Talk about it. And this was the fastest way to stop all of that, something he didn't want to do. It was the thing she most needed anyway. She wanted it too, but the need to figure out what they were (or weren't) and her feelings about that and what she wanted to do next consumed her.

Meanwhile, she let him continue kissing and rubbing her until it was almost too late. Her skin heated up and her eyes all but rolled back in her head. No.

CHAPTER 6

*R*OSE RIPPED HER MOUTH away from his. Pushing against him, she whispered. "Mateo… no."

No. The one word he understood and reacted quicker to than any other. No. He especially knew what it meant with women. With sex. And to get the fuck off and away from whoever uttered it.

He was not a rapist and would never be accused of it if he could help it. He was sensitive about his looks and reputation and what people assumed about him. It was too easy for someone like him to be accused and later caught. Most people would probably believe it.

He released her, letting her body flop back on his mattress as he jumped off her as well as the bed. He backed away from her as soon as he was on his feet.

Rose was a rich, well-known, small-town girl from a prominent white family. Shit. Fuck. He ran his fingers through his shaggy, loose hair. "I thought… I should have asked. At the moment…"

He stuttered and stammered, hating that she caused it. He

hated all the things she said and the words she drew out of him. He didn't understand why she insisted on analyzing it and talking about it. The easiest way to stop her was by ramming his tongue down her throat. And just like the first time, after one second of touch, they were one. Their contact seemed to milk and nurse and sustain each other. The coursing blood and heat were just as strong from her side.

But… Mateo, no.

So, no.

She lay back as if stunned for a moment, slipping her elbows underneath her as she struggled to sit back up. "It was. You didn't do anything wrong. I was about to let you have… I mean, let us have sex again. I don't want to do that, so I reluctantly made you stop. But you can relax. God, Mateo, I was just as interested as you."

Relax. Easy for her to say. She wasn't a tatted up ex-con in this small town.

He didn't know what to say or do now. It was obvious when he'd opened the door to his hovel that she was angry and probably intending to bawl him out for fucking her. Unless she wanted a repeat performance after she'd orgasmed so hard, long and fast. He felt more choking in his chest and a desperate need to get her away from his hovel. His glorified tool shed. Most of all, he didn't want her to see where and how he lived. He didn't want her to even get a glimpse of what and who he really was.

But Rose demanded entry. With no outward disdain or disgust, she never once complained of the stifling heat even when the sweat ran off her forehead and he felt it on her skin when he touched her.

But her response to his question of more sex was: *Why would you say that to me?*

Her words astounded him. The hurt and uncertainty almost made his knees buckle. He was chastised by her and also turned on; but he felt bad. He really did. He actually hurt her with his words, his ways and his assumptions.

She'd said a lot to him. So much that his brain ached. He'd never conversed so long before about… what? Their feelings? Who cared? Feelings just were. They existed. Why talk about them or give them breath and life? They were not concrete or real. They changed so often, they only served to confuse and lead the way to one's downfall. No, Mateo didn't give them much credence. He didn't acknowledge his feelings for Rose while hoping she would notice. No, he was direct and pretty concrete when he said he wanted to fuck her. He did. It was over. Unless she wanted more. But then came the words. So many. And then… Maybe fucking and no. Not.

She rubbed her mouth with her hand, not to wipe off the taste of him, and she seemed almost surprised he was there.

Her pink tongue licked her lips then and his entire body tightened as his hot blood surged. He wanted her.

"We have incredible chemistry. I have never felt this way before. I didn't know I was capable of it. But it's not what I want, or at least, not like this. I need more. I can't do casual sex. If you think you saw the real me before then you must have noticed that. I can't do this just to scratch some urgent hormone release. I need more."

Okay. Mateo all but escorted her out. More? Him and her? Fuck no. What the hell was she describing? How could that be? No… just no. His brain steamed when he tried to imagine it.

"Mateo, you said sex wasn't always like that with other women, right?"

Okay, his sexual performance was a subject he could tap into and discuss. "No."

"Me neither. But there was one part I hated."

She was surprised to receive his undivided attention now.

Performance problems? Fuck no. She was screaming. Full on screaming her lungs out while writhing under him. She was so open and wet he… fuck. It turned him on every time he relived it. She was so open to him and lost and gone. "I had to cover your mouth to keep the white water rafters from hearing your moans of ecstasy. No way were there problems with my performance."

She turned a bright, feverish pink. Her entire face was swallowed up in it. It almost made him laugh as his heart did something weird. It kind of twisted up and he didn't want to fuck her for being so cute, he just wanted to touch her. "People were rafting past us?"

"You didn't wonder why I covered your mouth up?"

"I guess I was too gone to think anything except maybe you didn't like screamers." Her voice lost its volume. Prim little Rose, a hell-cat in the sack, was so prim and proper in her daily life, she didn't know how to talk about sex.

Mateo could fuck and talk about it just fine. It was all the other subjects she spoke about that he didn't get or understand.

"I loved your noises. Your screams, Rosie. You were screaming."

More blushing. Then she shuddered at the memories of what made her scream. "Did they see us?"

"I don't think so. We were blocked by the bushes and I never saw any heads straining our way to look; and the constant roar of the rapids would have hopefully drowned you out.'"

She shuddered again. "Anyway, that would have been horrifying. But I didn't like… afterwards."

"After what?"

"When we were done. And you were lying on me…"

"I got off as soon as I realized I was crushing you."

"That's just it. You got off me. Like you didn't… care."

"Care?" He stuck his hands on his hips. *What the fuck was she talking about?*

She sighed. Her bangs flipped up at the air brushing past. "Could you sit down? It's hard to discuss something so difficult when you're standing above me, glaring at me."

Chastised, annoyed, and yeah, grumpy, he flopped back beside her. "We could be fucking right now and skip all this talking."

She groaned out loud. This time, he lifted his gaze to her and wanted to laugh. She was ticked at him. But it was non-threatening and almost amusing as he tried to figure out what really upset her about the best sex that she and he ever had.

"What do you mean, I didn't care? You came first. I wasn't mistaken on that. I wanted you to come before me."

She freaking scowled back at him. "Oh, be still my beating heart."

Puzzled at her sarcastic answer, he threw his hands in the air. "What did I do wrong?"

Shutting her eyes, she dramatically flopped back on his bed. Then she half-screamed into her arm before slowly rising back up. "Frick. You really don't know? You don't see it? Or understand?"

"No." All the former glaring, scowling and being tough vanished. He answered honestly, unsure of what she wanted from him.

She slowly released another long breath. Dropping her shoulders, she began to relax and the next time she spoke, her tone was even and far more controlled. "Okay. So usually after sex, even with a new partner and when it's spontaneous and kind of inappropriate, I don't like feeling like I was no more than a convenient receptacle."

"A convenient receptacle? What the hell are you talking about."

"A caring gesture would have been nice. Some tenderness. I wanted... no, I *needed...* and I deserved a kind word, a caress, hell, even a pat on the shoulder would have probably worked at that point. But no. You got up, stared down at me with the same scary stare I have to wonder about before you littered the beach with the condom and... that was it."

The images flashed through his brain and his temples started to throb. "I don't know what you mean..."

"If we ever have sex again, it can't end that way. Not for me. I don't do casual sex. That's why I'm speaking to you now. I'm trying to understand all the things I don't. We should have done that first. You should have freaking asked me out. But fast forwarding past all that doesn't mean it's over or suddenly resolved."

"Why talk about this now? It's over. Done. We aren't...."

"Don't you want to do it again? I thought we agreed it was that good and special and the chemistry isn't something either of us can deny. So..."

Special? The word evoked all kinds of connections in his brain. It repeated over and over. Rose thought something about him... she thought they were special? He stared at her, flabbergasted. At a loss. His brain had to be firing wrong. Blank and dumb, he asked, "You want to fuck again?" He repeated the very first thing he asked her at the beginning of this conversation.

"I want to figure out what happened first and whether to end it now or go forward. The chemistry is so strong we should consider... and yet... I really didn't like how it ended. It hurt me."

He hurt her. Those words stuck with him. He would never hurt her intentionally. Not knowingly. Or cruelly. He messed with Iris and Rose on occasion but never in a serious way. It was always joking.

He leaned forward, resting his elbows on his thighs and

staring at the old, cracked linoleum floor below him. It was beige and white with a pattern of framed flowers in it. Repetitious. Old-fashioned. Hideous.

"I didn't mean to. What? What would you want?"

She sighed. "You really didn't know? Or mean to hurt me?"

"No. Really. It's how it always ends for me. It just ends and we part and go our separate ways or whatever. I rarely do it with anyone twice. Maybe not at all in fact."

"Oh." Her tone conveyed nothing. Disapproval? Disgust? What? "Okay. Then perhaps we could try being honest and discuss what you want and what I want. Maybe we could... I mean, I want to have sex with you again. I do. But I know it won't be enough for me. Guilt sets in. Justified or not, I'm hard-wired that way. I need a connection. I need more than just that."

"Have you ever had sex for sex's sake?"

"No."

"Maybe you could."

"I felt guilty and weird and I didn't like that part. So I could not. Is that all you wanted? One time and you're done with me?" Her eyebrows quirked down. Puzzled, and looking almost offended over what his answer might be, she nudged him with her hand. "Mateo, please tell me that wasn't all you wanted. One time and we're done?"

He smirked, unable to resist the obvious answer. "Well, maybe twice and we're done?"

"No." Her lips twitched. It was final. There was no negotiation. "If that is what you want and I can't change your mind, then tell me and we'll both be done right now. No more awkward talking for either of us."

He sighed softly. "I never thought it out this far on my end. But no, I guess I don't want it to be just one and we're done. But why would you feel guilty if we did do that?"

She shrugged. "Honestly, I don't know. I just do. When you walked up the beach without a second look or glance at me, I felt dirty. Ashamed. Hurt. You just walked away after doing what I consider the most intimate and important act two people can share. Without even a smile. Or a wave. Or a look. Anything to make me feel connected, or noticed, or appreciated. I did not like it one bit. I can't tolerate any more treatment like that. Just so we're clear."

"I never imagined you felt anything. Let alone, dirty or hurt. I don't know my thoughts about it, but they were never intimate or important to me before. But…"

She shut her eyes as if to hold in a scream. "Please tell me you're going to say, *but it feels different this time.* Please."

"Yes," he answered simply. He added no words to explain what it meant to him now or what he wanted or how to go about it. But he didn't say he felt weird after sex with Rose and it remained on the top of his mind constantly. It was all he could think of.

Her eyes fluttered open and she shook her head. His reply seemed to pacify her for now. "Why do you feel guilty though?"

"I can't imagine it's owing to my parents' upbringing. Iris never suffers from it. She's just fine. And my dad is Shane Rydell. He is pretty vocal and out there about sex, including his encouragement to both of us to enjoy it. But I always felt oddly embarrassed, and I blushed while wishing he'd be less vocal about it. I guess I like it more subtle. I like to let it simmer on the back burner, even in the way I discuss it. Crass and dirty are not for me. I struggled with it during my teen years and college was even worse. That's all people our age can talk about and making it as crass and curse-filled as they can. I detest that."

That might have been the reason why she always held Mateo's interest. She made him smile. Her prissy ways were kind of antiquated and annoying, but also, cute as hell to him. He never met anyone who was so guarded with herself, let alone, her words, true intentions and thoughts as Rose. He figured she could never emit a bodily noise in front of anyone or anything unless she were dying.

"I can try but... it's always just been fucking to me. It's balling and getting laid and getting sucked off and..."

"Yes, I understand your frame of reference to it."

He nodded. "Right. Yes, doing it. I can say that?"

"I can't stop you from saying anything. Tell anyone anything you want, but I would request that you don't, if you respect my wishes at all."

"I do respect your wishes," he answered softly. He respected her perhaps more than any female he ever met. As much as he respected her dad. "I won't tell anyone because no one can know. Your dad. Remember?"

"He really warned you to stay away from us?"

"No. Just from Iris. But I can still have my ass kicked and get fired over a technicality. I know what he meant. Don't go near his daughters in a physical way. So..."

"So quiet now. Is it just us?"

"Yeah." What? Did she want to do it again? But how if she wouldn't give it up? What did she want? How did she want it? "But what is it between us?"

She shook her head. "I don't know. But what happened was powerful and strong for me. I don't want to ignore it, that doesn't feel good either, does it?"

Damn. Rose was so forward and direct, she didn't let anything go. Nothing was skipped or glossed over. He never suspected Rose would seek him out to talk about what they did. Talk so openly and real. She didn't mince her words. She didn't act coy or play games. She wasn't at all what he expected or was familiar with. She was both refreshing and shocking to him.

"No. It felt even more awkward and harder to figure out. I just assumed you'd never want..." He let his words trail off. He didn't dare utter the obvious word he should have: "me." He didn't say he assumed Rose Rydell made a mistake and would never want him again. She only wanted him for a handful of moments because he caught her in her favorite spot and her guard was down to allow what happened to occur. But how could he admit the simplest and most meaningful point of his entire life? He didn't think she would want him.

"The thing is, Mateo, I don't even know you. So I can't say. I know there is a physical connection, duh. But that's not enough. I'll walk away and ignore it if that's all you want or if that's how it ends up being. But..."

"But what? What are you saying?"

"I'm saying I think we should simply spend more time together."

His face morphed into lowered eyebrows, scrunched up mouth and darting eyeballs. "How do you want to spend it?"

She swiped her hand over her forehead. "I'm hot, Mateo."

He all but closed his eyes, back to the thing he offered before the conversation. "I know. That's how we ended up... doing it."

"No. I'm hot as in sweating." She shook her head, rolling her eyes. "No offense, but I'm suffocating in here. Could we just go outside? Maybe take a quick swim in the river?"

"Uh... now? Here?"

"Why not?" She set her feet on the ground. "Lucky you, I'm wearing my swimsuit as I so often do this time of year."

Mateo tried not to picture what Rose wore under her clothes. Bra or swimsuit he was uncomfortable.

"A half dozen guys are down at the beach right now. Work is done. It's hot as a..." No crude language. "...Well, I

111

don't know but it's hot and they will be cooling off. All my neighbors will be there."

She shrugged and blinked. Her neutral expression waited for the reason. Why not? "And they'd be right."

She didn't seem to realize they would also stare and snicker and make remarks about her. Women just didn't hang out here. This wasn't a camp for families or couples. It was a bunch of rough-assed workers that worked out in the fields, orchards and alfalfa pastures of the valley. This time of year, even a few worked the cattle herds that roamed far from the range lands. For the most part, only crude, young guys like Mateo lived in this small enclave of rental units.

"You'd be the only woman."

"So?" Blink. No stress appeared on her face. She rolled her eyes.

"Really? You had to say that to me? As if what? I can't go there now? I'd somehow not be allowed to use the river? Please don't say that to me again. I don't care. I'm hot. It's so hot in here that we should swim. That's how we should start."

Still unsure and frustrated, Mateo's anxiety grew from not knowing the rules, and he pressed, "Start what?"

"Getting to know each other."

"That's it. That's all you want?"

"Yes. Don't you?" Her head tilted and her eyes were big and beguiling. She wasn't teasing or being sarcastic. She meant it. She would be hurt if he said he didn't want to get to know her. He knew he was right about that. It both pleased and surprised him. He was also uncomfortable under the pressure to do and be something he just didn't know how to begin. But she waited for his answer. And she seemed to freaking care if she got it.

He nodded, gulped and said simply, "Yeah. Okay."

She smiled, turned and headed for his front door.

Opening it, she inhaled deeply as the air was a smidgeon cooler outside than in his shack.

He followed her as she crossed between the two buildings to the obvious river trail. It was short and rocky and they passed through a small gully filled with bushy willows. Their "beach" was merely a rocky bottom. But it was always cool, clear water and the only thing to do on evenings like this. Bottles of beer and pot were often passed around. Sometimes food. Mateo didn't know what to make of Rose Rydell so casually marching up there. She seemed fine. Not worried she was stepping into a world that wasn't the least bit familiar to her.

A few noticed her so she stopped and smiled. "I've rafted past here many times. Looks very different from this angle." That's all she said as she slipped her shorts down and pulled off her tank top.

A few more gazes slipped her way. They stared. Nobody was subtle about it. They all but licked their chops at her little strip show. But, for Rose, it wasn't. She didn't move her body in a seductive wiggle. She was modest and economical with her body movements. She was always in such a hurry to get into her beloved river. And tugging off her shirt or coverup was part of it. She didn't realize the unexpected reveal of slim arms and round, full breasts and hips were something Mateo long awaited each time he went to the damn beach, which was mostly for her. To see her. Never did she realize his fantasies were stocked by Rose's urgent desire to quickly duck into the water she loved. Like now, she was hot and ready to swim. She didn't see it as anything sexy or revealing or showing off. Just wearing the right gear for swimming. Over her shoulder, she smiled at him.

His dead, black heart stirred to life. Her damn smile. It could stop the next world war.

He'd put on a black pair of nylon shorts when he got home

but never expected a knock on his door, or to find Rose Rydell standing there. He never dreamt she'd visit his glorified tool shed without raising her nose in the air with disgust, much less, sit down and talk to him. They truly talked. A deep discussion. But what he found most alluring was the honesty with which Rose spoke of herself and her feelings toward him. She had no clue how he felt because he didn't know. He certainly never shared such things with anyone. So what she said was like telling it to a blank wall. She was brave and smart and her courage dripped off her, while he stood mute and stupid in the corner. Never knowing how to say anything. Never sure of his feelings.

The only thing he would admit was his constant need to put himself in Rose's sphere. He befriended her sister. He came to her beach. He kept coming when he saw what it meant to her. He fed her tidbits about him, things he never told anyone else. Ever. He surprised himself by doing so. He lay awake many nights wondering why he felt so compelled to tell her small facts about him. Why? What was he after?

And the only answer was: SEX. He wanted to have more sex with Rose. That must be why he tried to be so honest and kept seeking her out. That was why he said things out loud that his brain told him not to.

Sex with Rose was better and hotter and deeper and all the wonderful things he never felt before. So he ran away from her and was far more confused than Rose thought she was. Because in his mind, of course, Rose wouldn't feel anything like that about him. No way could she.

But she did.

She came to him. Here. And here she was.

Voices called their names as they stepped to the river's edge. Words were spoken that Rose didn't know the meaning of. Good thing she didn't and Mateo blew them off. He dismissed them with a wave and snarled his response. Rose didn't know a word of Spanish. She took French in high school and college. She'd told him that. He remembered everything she ever said.

She let out a soft groan as her bare feet touched the river bottom. The rocks were rounded, and the size of a man's hand on average. Shoes were needed, but she didn't have any. It wasn't even close to her family's section of the river. She didn't care as she got to the deepest point, which only came up to her mid-thighs. She sunk down anyway.

She made him smile. It was so her. She was visibly enthralled with the water in the river.

She blinked and stared at him as he joined her. It felt really nice. Mateo was used to the absence of AC despite the extreme heat of the shed. So it wasn't quite as relieving for him as for Rose.

"What?" he asked when she kept staring at him, tilting her head. Her expression was strange.

"You're smiling. It's so rare. I don't think I noticed how rare it really is before. You tease Iris so much. You laugh, but I never see you smile. Not like that."

"Like what?" He sat on the river floor, sinking his shoulders down. He grunted his response, unsure how to speak to Rose now.

"Like... affectionate. Like you were amused with me and you liked me just now."

There was something beguiling about her tilted head and sparkling eyes. Was it because of his damn smile? She seemed to see him when no one else really did. No, he didn't smile much. He joked and teased and easily threw shade. He could be sarcastic and mocking. But a friendly smile like she described? Rare indeed. Never much need to smile in his experience. But she was right. She did amuse him and he was feeling affection. But having someone read him so clearly, when he didn't even know how to label it himself, was disconcerting and strange.

She bobbed closer to him. The urge to grab her around her waist and drag her against him crossed his mind but he simply stayed still in the cool water. "Did you?" she pressed.

"Yeah. I guess. You and the water are funny. You're so reverent about it. You react to being in it like other people react to having sex."

She punched him on the arm kiddingly. "I don't look like I'm having an orgasm."

She'd shrieked it. Loudly. And hearing the word orgasm swiveled five heads around with avid interest towards them. She realized it too late and shoved a hand over her mouth. "I can't believe I yelled that." She kept her face tipped towards the water as her pale, fair skin turned the same shade of pink to match her hair. He... well, fuck, how could he resist the adorable mess that Rose Rydell became when she was embarrassed? About the words *she* said. He leaned forward and instead of crushing her mouth with a hard, unrelenting kiss, like he wanted to give her, he knew she'd hate having an audience so he did something new.

He took her hand in his.

She stared down, somewhat startled at his unexpected touch and the way his fingertips clenched hers. After a second, he felt strange and dropped her hand. He wasn't one to seek or want affection. In all honesty, there'd never been anyone to give it to or receive it from. His mother? Never. His brother? Ha! No. His dad? Maybe he was the closest thing to giving and getting affection. From a bitter, hardened father. But his dad's way of showing love was by teaching him mechanical skills.

Mateo cleared his throat after the quick touch and glanced towards the opposite shore. "You do look a little orgasmic in the water. But it's also what drew me back to the beach for the whole month of July. Just to see that look."

She replied, "Mateo?"

He had to look back or be rude.

"You… you're not comfortable with affection, are you?"

"Uh… I don't know. Never thought about it before."

"Maybe you could think about it."

That's all she said. She smiled and dived under the water. What was that all about? Was she tucking it away for later? Part of her understanding him? How could she when he had no understanding of himself? He never spent any time examining his inner self so why would she? Her body wiggled and squirmed under the clear water and she didn't come up for air until she was well downriver, in the thick of the other swimmers.

She smiled and started swimming with them. She was frolicking with the same guys he no more than exchanged greetings with now and then. The few filthy words they'd implied about Rose when they'd walked up provided more interaction than all of the months Mateo had livedalongside these men.

But Rose had several of them smiling and talking to her. Her warm smile and twinkling eyes showed a kindness, the same warmth that drew Mateo to her and they responded too. First, they stared at her alabaster-white skin and curvy body; now they were enthralled by the warmth that she projected.

Mateo wandered downriver to be closer to her. He listened and spoke and interacted. He joked and even laughed a few times. Rose made him interact with her. And them. At this place. It should have been an odd environment for her to be in. Amongst men who lived in cheap, tight, small housing for a month, or a season, or longer. There was nothing pleasant or neighborly in the homes that existed here.

Rose was the only woman and the daughter of the family most of them worked for. The wealth and privilege that characterized her life, said she should have had nothing in common with any of them. But like Mateo, her charm and warmth and Rose-essence managed to win them over.

Finally, the sun began its descent and the breeze cooled the stifling air. Goose bumps broke out all over her body and she finally emerged from the water as she rubbed at her arms. "I'm getting cold."

"Finally? Are you sure you aren't half mermaid?" he teased. Mateo retreated from the cool water more than once only to rejoin her as she talked with guys he only now learned the names of.

Rose struggledto cross the rocky shoreline, for there wasn't a foot of sand there. Mateo quickly walked after her, his steps surer than hers. They entered his shed and she quit shivering and laughed. "It's still stifling in here but now it'll warm me up." She was dripping wet. Her hair sent rivulets down her slim shoulders and back. He stepped forward, fighting the urge to lick the streams of water. And to cup her breasts outlined in her wet swimsuit. But no sex. No rules. He had no idea what she meant and no history to gauge it by. He dug around the bottom drawer where he kept a few towels and handed her one. She gratefully took it and wiped her skin dry, toweling off her hair. Her face was free now of makeup and she was natural and glowing and beautiful. Inside as much as out. Her kindness and warmth and honesty were qualities he was totally drawn toward, but it was so unusual for him to find all of them in one person.

"So can you handle that?" she questioned. She was bent over, towel-drying her hair.

"Handle what?"

"What we just did. You and me together. A little getting to know each other. That's it. It's a start."

"It was… doable," he finally answered her in a monotone. He looked bored, but she glanced up and straightened her spine to see him clearly.

"Doable? That was insulting. You can do much better."

His lips twitched. Could they flirt and be casual and funny? He didn't know. He never felt it with anyone but friends. Like Iris. Not Rose. But now, he felt things. Mixed up things. Things he had no words for. New things. Big, new things. "Tolerable?" His mouth twitched.

Her gaze narrowed and her lips pursed. "Yeah, that's even worse. Lord, you suck at this. Try again."

"A degree less than torture?"

Her eyes shut and her shoulders fell forward. "God, grant me the serenity to accept the things I can't change…"

"What the hell are you doing?"

"Praying for divine help in dealing with your narrow-minded, chip-on-your-shoulder, clueless ass. Duh." She scoffed. A smile teased her lips. Her head was bowed and her eyes half closed, but she couldn't resist the grin that overtook her face. "You're going to make me insane before we figure this out."

She was right about all of it. His face closed up and her teasing froze him. She noticed it. "I still want to do this. It was fun tonight, right? Easy? Like the times we spent in the river before we…" Her lip caught on her teeth as she finished, "…started doing it."

It was fun. Not easy because it was so odd, but every word she'd said was etched into his mind. Every movement was memorized. Every little gesture, sound and nicety she said to strangers was appreciated and categorized by him. So yeah. He noticed her. He liked her. It was fun. And intense. And fuck yeah, he wanted more from her.

And she wouldn't say fuck. So he recalled the edge of her that was so serious that made him smile.

"God, grant me the patience to deal with a grown woman who won't say sex or fuck or getting laid or anything remotely accurate but *doing it.*"

She laughed and swung her wet hair back. Leaning forward, she slid her legs into the shorts she'd hauled up from the beach and pulled her tank top back on. Her wet swimsuit stained her dry clothes with dark marks. His gaze devoured her and he loved the view.

"I'm going home."

"Okay." He was at a loss. What was he supposed to say or do now? Was it over? Have a nice evening? A great fuck. Another lost opportunity to fuck again? What did he do or say?

"You're worried about my dad knowing about us?"

"Yeah." Us? Her casual use of the word and subsequent assumption about it pertaining to her and him confused him. It made him stiff and unnatural and blustery. Kind of mean almost.

"Then we'll keep it quiet." She shook her head with a small smile. "Between us and… well, the ten orchard workers who all know my name. But I doubt any of them have a burning desire to run out and tell my dad. We'll have to come to your place. Because… well, duh, Iris lives at mine. But what about tomorrow night? Dinner?"

"You want to come here for dinner?"

"I want to come here. Yes. And perhaps you could open the window? Let some fresh air in?"

"Uh… okay. But what should I make?"

"Nothing. I'll bring it. So it's a date?" she pressed.

Date. Him and Rose? It nearly suffocated him. It made his heart beat so hard like it could hammer out of his chest, fly off, and hit the horizon. Suddenly, he wanted nothing more than Rose Rydell coming over to his place with a meal. Tomorrow. No one ever willingly made him a meal. Or sought him out. He hated his desire for it. That he wanted it so badly. He hated himself for being so damn vulnerable to her. To that. Because it stirred up something he long ago banished from his life: hope. He now hoped to see her. If she cancelled their date or changed her mind, which was very likely, he'd be disappointed. And he detested giving her that power over him.

After he went to prison, he lost his relationship with hope. He ignored hope. He survived. He thrived. He saved money and sent it home. He made sure he was never caught unaware. And it was the toughest, brightest, boldest lesson of his young life: never, ever trust anyone. Not Iris. Not Shane. Not even himself.

His mama tried to teach him that at a very young age.

As for Rose? Trusting her to come back? No.

But his heart counted on it.

"Mateo?" Her voice was soft. Questioning. Wanting affirmation.

"If you want to. This is all on you, Rose." There. He banished the hope from the equation. She could do what she wanted. He refused to invest anything into her plan. This was most likely a new toy for Rose and she wasn't serious.

"Then six o'clock. Tomorrow." She smiled softly, but there was a gleam in her eye. It said something; he didn't know what.

CHAPTER 7

$\mathcal{M}$ATEO'S LEVEL OF DISTRUST was so deeply ingrained, it startled her. He let it slip more than once. She had a steep hill of resistance to climb and surprisingly to her, she was intensely interested in doing so.

She showed up with dinner the next night. His gaze was as dark and intent as ever before, so she didn't know if he wanted her there. But he let her in. The window was open too. It wasn't much cooler than yesterday but at least some fresh air wafted through, riding the mini-breezes that randomly moved the hot air around.

Dinner wasn't anything special. She picked up a pizza from the River's End diner and hoped it would still be hot when she got to his house. She took some pop and beer and salad out of a bag. He had no food and no cooking space and she wasn't comfortable enough with him yet to haul a stack of dishes and utensils. This was all so new and relatively tentative. It might last now, or a few days. A week? Maybe longer? She couldn't even picture that... but she had no way to gauge it. No benchmarks. Nothing. They had sex and he aroused some feelings inside her she had no idea she harbored towards him, which led to an almost insatiable curiosity. Intrigue. Wonder.

The man with the firefly tattoo. That was her subject of interest. Once, she believed he was a dangerous gangster. A criminal. A man to avoid. Now? She saw glimpses of raw fear when she touched him. Confusion that almost broke her heart. She didn't know which persona was really him. What if there was much more to him than she ever dreamed? But he had a tattoo on his neck. She felt ashamed because that's what had stopped her from knowing him in the past. That's what had triggered the judgment. The cataloguing with unfair assessments. Distrust. All the wrong conclusions. She did that subconsciously.

But after a real conversation with Mateo Alvarez, she met someone who amused her and made her relax a bit. He taught her how to be sarcastic when she wasn't comfortable. And she saw vulnerabilities in him. Confusion. Things she wanted to explore. What did she really want to do? Cuddle him. Yeah. He needed a lot of care. She was certain, deep in her gut, that affection and caring and all the things that she suddenly felt the impulse to do to him were necessary. Hug him. Hold him. Smile at him. Make him smile. She realized how seldom he genuinely smiled. But when he did, it softened his whole appearance. His face. His cheeks. His eyes. His intent gaze. It made him so much younger and uncertain, and she loved to see it.

So there she was, standing at his little house with her arms full, kicking the door in her attempt at an awkward knock. He flung the door open an she grinned widely, showing all of her teeth. With a tepid contortion of his mouth, he grabbed the pizza box and guided her inside. She set the drinks down on the small table and he put the pizza on the counter that was smaller than the box. "There're some paper plates in there. It's still hot, I hope."

"Yeah. Thanks. Smells good. This from the River's End café?"

"Yes. It's a lot better than the pizza made on the ranch but don't tell anyone that." She began opening the box and took out a few pizza slices before dividing up the ready-made salad and setting it beside each slice on a paper plate. She slid his plate to the opposite seat. He stood there awkwardly, unsure of what to do next.

They sat in his warm oven-shack. The window over-looked the river and mountains. The lovely view and fading light supplied the ambiance. She took a bite and let the cheesy, loaded toppings melt over her tongue. "Ahh. Hell, yes."

He was watching her and his eyes did that glittery thing. That hard-to-read thing where she had no idea if he thought she was stupid or wonderful. "Go ahead."

"No way I can make it as sexy as you just did."

She pressed her lips. "I wasn't being sexy. I was starving. Don't stare at me. Anyway, how was your day?"

"My day?" he repeated, caught off guard.

"Yeah, your day. This is how it works. We eat. We talk about big things and small things. We mention little specifics about what happened during the day to each of us. And that's how we get to know each other."

His eyebrows lifted. "Little specifics?"

She bit again and the cheese dripped onto her chin. She stuck it back into her mouth and sucked on her fingers. His gaze was fastened on her lips and tongue. She rolled her eyes. "God damn it, Mateo. I am not doing this. I'm eating pizza. Quit looking at me like you'd like to—"

"Like to what, Rosie?" His lips curled up at the corners in a soft, mocking smile.

"That…"

"Like I'd like to fuck your mouth?"

She almost choked while sipping her drink. His words made her sputter as she tried to keep the soda inside her mouth and nose. She grabbed a napkin and held it over the lower half of her face. She was burning up. Her entire face was an angry red. Crap. Then Mateo let out a laugh. It was a short, sharp snort and chuckle. Barely audible, she slowly lowered the napkin. He was shaking his head. "I might have been thinking that, but I said it for your reaction. You're so easy."

"Easy…"

"Easy to fuck with, Rosie. Not fuck. You can't possibly think I'd say you're easy about sex. Ha. You're the opposite of whatever that would be. I just like how pink you get when you're shocked. It's kind of—"

Angrily, she smacked the napkin down on the table. "Kind of like a sport making fun of me?"

"No, you're adorable when you blush and get flustered. You wanted to get to know me. Here I am. Sorry but I'm rude and crude and you make me laugh. I like it."

She rubbed her hands together. Was that a compliment? At least he found her adorable… but… well, crap. She did ask to know him. The truth can floor you sometimes.

She tilted her head. "We are completely opposite."

"Lord, Rosie, I would hope you noticed that already."

She glanced down, staring at her fingers that were interlacing. Her nerves made her so unsure. "Yes. Do you think we can find enough in common to make anything work?"

"No." His tone was as harsh as his expression. "But I… it's fine if we keep… whatever."

She darted a glance his way. It was like pulling teeth to get anything out of him. But when she threatened to leave him, it was actually a subtle request to stay near him. She had no idea what to do next. Where it could lead?

As long as she was careful not to get sucked in by those hot, sparking, dark eyes that promised so many things... things she barely had a taste of. And crap if she wasn't eager for more.

OVER THE COURSE of several such evenings that began with her bringing dinner to his place, Mateo started to talk a little more. Literally, he offered her little morsels of information. She'd ask him a series of questions and he'd answer each question exactly as she asked it. No more and no less. It was so frustrating for her. She could not coax him to elaborate or explain and he could barely participate in an ordinary conversation, guarding everything he said or did in his history. The most innocuous of questions like, *where did you go to elementary school?* made him squint at Rose with unmasked suspicion. He seemed to be looking for an ulterior motive behind what she asked. Something dark and manipulative. He honestly never hung out with a woman, or anyone else it seemed, just to get to know them.

"How did you become friends with Iris? You let her talk to you?"

"We had to. We worked together so we had no choice."

"So you think someone needs a reason to want to get to know you?"

"Uh... I don't know. Just... shit, maybe, yeah."

Her eyebrows nearly crossed in the middle of her forehead. "Except for Iris, have you ever just had a good friend?"

His entire torso straightened and he bristled. "I know a shit-ton of people."

Eye-rolling him, she shook her head. "No... I'm not

talking about just hanging out with them but really knowing and seeing and interacting?"

Sadly, that made him squirm and fidget. He looked at her as if she'd stripped off her clothes and started singing "Cabaret." He felt weird and uncomfortable. "It's just talking and caring about what the other says. It's not that hard." She tilted her head. "At least it's not supposed to be."

He bristled and crossed a foot over his knee. "I'm not scared. I always answer you."

She gritted her teeth. "Ask me something. Socialize with people. I've heard you do it with Iris. Do that with someone else once in a while."

"But Iris and I discuss the cars and how to fix them… it makes sense. We don't sit around confessing our feelings and shit."

"Okay." She released an exasperated breath. "Let's start by talking about things that make sense to you and don't involve feelings and shit."

He perked up, but kept eyeing her with skepticism. "For real?"

"Yeah, for real. Tell me what you and Iris are working on? What did you do today? Tell me in the simplest terms so I can understand."

"But you don't fix cars. You know nothing about them. What do you care? Why would you want to know about that?"

"Um… because it's a starting point? Conversation. Work with me here." She smiled. "Relax. Just start there and let's see if we can't find something new to talk about that doesn't involve me grilling you as if I'm reading you your Miranda rights."

"And if we can't?"

"Then we'll know we should quit wasting our time together and we won't sleep together again so it's all done."

His entire face contorted, then relaxed with surprise. "Huh."

She had no idea what it meant.

He leaned forward and rested his hand on the table. His long fingers were almost elegant and her gaze landed on them. Maybe she was thinking about things she shouldn't have.

"So a couple came in and the wife was trying to explain the noises her engine was making. But he kept talking over her and correcting her like an asshole. So I finally just started the car and low and behold. The woman was spot-on. I told her that and she gave me a relieved smile before they left to sit down and wait. He never quit grumbling about how wrong I was, and what a stupid place this was. But they waited for me to fix the car."

"What an asshole he was, but at least his wife appreciated you."

"Exactly." He nodded and Rose almost clapped, nearly grabbing his hand to cheer, yes! Just like that.

He was finally talking about his day and she could ask, "Does stuff like that happen a lot? Where the women drivers are ignored by their husbands?"

"All the time. Guys are such assholes, to be honest. So many times, and if I was the wife, I'd kick the guy in the nuts. But whatever."

She giggled and laughed, liking him all the more and they started talking more. Just talking about inconsequential things. Nothing. Getting an idea about what they both wanted. Getting an idea if they could stand to spend more than a few moments together. The part that scared and thrilled her was she could not only stand it... she overly looked forward to it. But could she trust him? Date him? It seemed incredible and strange to imagine but... here they were… doing what exactly? Almost dating? Oddly… she thought so.

~

ONE WEEK LATER, he was stuffing the pizza box, for she bought a lot of them, into the small trash can. He was trying to make it fit while pushing his hair back. It was down, falling long and untethered around his shoulders. "Stupid hair," he muttered.

"Why don't you cut it off if you don't like it?"

"Cut it?" He straightened up and glanced her way.

"Well, if you don't like it, change it." Had that never occurred to him?

"I got the ugliest haircut when I was growing up. My mother did it to me. She didn't give a shit how I looked so I was often ridiculed for the haircuts she gave me when I was young. I vowed I'd never get a stupid haircut again."

Her breath hitched. That was so much information. So much more than he usually divulged about himself. Including his opinions. A glimpse of his childhood and a mother who didn't care and how angry he was. Wow.

"I can cut it. I do Iris's anytime I'm around. She always wore short hair and I have a knack for doing hair so I can do it."

"I don't want Iris's haircut."

"Well… duh. No. How about this?" She grabbed her phone and brought up a series of men's haircuts, scrolling down until she found what she believed was ideal for him. "This?"

He took her phone and looked. He glanced back up at her and tilted his head. "You think you could cut it exactly like this?"

"Sure."

"For real. I can't go around looking like Iris."

"I swear I won't make you look like my sister." She grinned as she got up and shoved him playfully on the shoulder. "I really can do it. I'll bring my comb, razor and shears tomorrow."

She showed up the next day with dinner, which they ate, before taking out her electric razor and sharp shears. His eyes followed her as if he worried she would stab his neck with them. Gulping he asked, "You sure you know how to use those?"

For a moment, she bristled but ignored it. "Yes. Now, slip your shirt off." He gave her a suggestive eyebrow lift of interest. She rolled her eyes. "For the haircut."

She stepped back and grabbed the scissors. She had to hold her breath when he tugged his plain white t-shirt over his head. His long torso was smooth and dark. He was strong, but slim. Muscles were visible on his strong arms and stomach, but everything was skinny. Like he needed to eat more. She also saw the collage of his life. Tattoos swirled from the waistband of his shorts to his stomach, climbing over his abdomen to continue around his pecs and shoulders. Pictures, symbols and letters. Sayings and scripts. There were so many. She didn't know what any of it meant. The tattoos were mostly black lines and words. Most of the actual colors were absent. Her gaze wandered around the words and illustrations on his skin.

He turned and slipped into the kitchen chair. She smiled and went behind him.

"Do you hate them?"

"What?" she asked as she grabbed the elastic band that held his silky hair back. She tugged and he flinched. She gently unwrapped it from the strands, but many of them were caught and it hurt him when she undid them.

"I feel like you know what I'm asking."

"I hate these more." She stuck her freckle-covered arm in his face. He flinched back to see what she was showing him.

"What?" he asked.

"Freckles. White, pale, ghostly skin that never tans but stays either white or pink and then goes back to white again but not before being sprayed with brown splatter dots that number in the thousands."

He tilted his head up to stare at her. His neck tattoo was nearly covered by the long hair falling around his shoulders. He looked dark and dangerous and her throat was parched. She regretted confessing her hatred of freckles to him. "You think those are worse than my tattoos?"

"I never said anything about your tattoos. But yes, I hate my freckles. I didn't stick them on my skin. You chose those tattoos so you must have wanted them. It's not the same thing."

He ran his long fingertips up and down her arm. "I love these. They are what make you, you."

She touched his shoulder, following the line of a circular image there. "And these are what make you, you," she said softly. He stared up at her. She gulped down her nerves and a soft smile touched her lips.

"And these don't disgust you? Or turn you off?"

Her tongue slipped out and she licked her lips. "Mateo, I think my reaction to you on the beach was evidence that they don't."

His severe, fierce look relaxed when his lips tilted up in a smile. "Yeah. Hmm, if that's how you show stuff… You showed me a lot."

"Then don't ignore that." She blushed furiously, turning to relieve her embarrassment as she took the black comb and brought it through his hair. She did that several times. She grabbed the spray bottle of water and quickly doused his hair. He shuddered as the cool, fine mist hit his bare skin.

Taking the towel from her shoulder, she wiped his neck and shoulders before letting the towel rest there. Stretching his wet hair out with a comb, she snipped off a hunk. "You sure?"

"You said you knew what you were doing."

"Your voice sounds like it's trembling," she replied, biting her tongue to keep in the smirk.

"It's… I'm a little worried I'll look like Iris."

She laughed and only when she quit laughing did she snip. Then she snipped and again and again. In only a few seconds, most of his hair lay on the floor in wet chunks. He stared down, then said, "Wow, that's a lot of hair."

"Just wait." She grinned as she started styling it then. She worked from the top. Then she blended the sides and shaved his neck and around his ears. She came directly in front of him and stared right at his forehead to get his bangs right. They flopped over his brow, so they were still long, but now they made him look breathtaking. A haircut changed his entire appearance.

She snipped and snipped again to layer it, standing back to check that the ends were straight and even. She was so busy concentrating on her task, she didn't realize he was staring at her until she lowered her gaze.

She gulped. He'd been watching her face as she worked so intently on him. But he wasn't smiling. He wasn't interested in the end result. He was devouring her being so close. She licked her lips, physically affected by his proximity.

Dark, solemn gaze. How long did they hold eye contact? Ripples of energy flowed down her spine. Shivers broke out on her skin. He meant so much to her. She felt so intense. She couldn't hold it long. She was unable to be sultry and sexy enough to keep this dark angel interested. In her. But he seemed to be. Her gaze lowered and she focused on the place where she used to stare to avoid his gaze. She couldn't hold it now. Not anymore.

Instead, her gaze drifted to the delicate illustration on his neck. It had the most detailed, intricate wings under almost translucent skin. She never realized the design was so exquisite. His Adam's apple made it move. She released her fingers and the comb dropped. She lifted her fingertips and brushed them over the design. She felt the warm, smooth skin of his throat. She rubbed his neck. She was entranced when she felt his pulse through his skin and it fluttered like she imagined a firefly's wings would.

Her gaze lifted to his when he sucked the air through his nose. His eyes sparked. With annoyance? Lust? Emotion? She didn't know. She never could be certain when he was like this. Her dark angel. He really was. So hard to read, yet what she discovered under his demeanor wasn't dark or hard to be around. That still surprised her.

She set the scissors on the table. Her gaze was still riveted on his neck. She licked her lips. "Did it hurt?" She rubbed it as if she would smudge the ink.

"Yeah."

"How old were you when you got this one?"

"Sixteen."

She lifted her startled eyes to his. "So young."

"Was it? I was never really young, Rosie. Not like you."

Why? What was he then? Where was he from? What happened to him? What? She had so many questions. But tight lips and closed eyes were his response. She kept rubbing over the firefly. He swallowed and she could feel the vibration. She smiled down at him as he sat, making her taller than him. Just barely.

"I would like to know why you were never young. Why you got this tattoo. Why you work here. Where you came from. Everything. I want to know you, Mateo. All about you."

His gaze scanned over her face. "Why? We could just fuck

and end this. There is no need for so much talking. We are so opposite that we don't have to do this."

"This? As in what?"

He shut his eyes, closing the window to the most churning, intense soul she ever imagined.

Eyes open now, he grabbed her wrist hard but not hard enough to bruise her. "You're so gentle. No one's ever touched me the way you do."

She sucked in a breath. "You don't like it?"

"I didn't say that. I don't know. It's strange for me."

She lifted her other hand and ran her fingertips over his. He tightly gripped her wrist. She raised a finger and said, "You don't have to hold me so tight."

He released her immediately. "I'm sorry. Force of habit. I… usually only touch out of…"

"Not from tenderness. I'm getting that."

Her gaze studied his forehead, his nose, his full lips, the sharpness of his chin and the long column of his decorated throat. She leaned forward and he flinched at her proximity, which made her heart ache. Was he that startled or that afraid? She could only wonder. She was sorry to see how unfamiliar a gentle caress was for him. He became so suspicious of her desire for simple affection. She ran her hand from his neck to his shoulder. The muscles beneath his skin were smooth and she flat-palmed her hand over the slope of his neck to the round cap of his shoulder. She softly cupped the other side to match. His gaze drilled into hers. His mouth puckered and she leaned forward to place her mouth on his.

Warm, smooth lips. Holding onto his shoulders, she pushed forward towards the heat of his mouth, and just like the first time, she was drawn into the vortex of something new and singular. A special chemistry with all the sparks and energy of passion. They created it. Rose never imagined such a feeling ever happening to her.

She leaned forward, holding his shoulders tighter as she tilted her head to change the angle of the kiss. Her tongue gently rubbed his closed lips. He finally opened his mouth and she moaned as she kissed him. He resisted her. His mouth was open and his tongue engaged with hers, but he didn't fully respond. He reserved part of himself from her. She didn't know what or why exactly. She couldn't explain it. She just knew that he did it.

With one last kiss on his lips, she pressed her forehead on his. "I want to be comfortable with you. I want to kiss and touch you without worrying do you want me? Do you like this? What do you think and feel? I just don't know, Mateo. I can't read you. I can't figure you out. You have a cool, even gaze that conceals what you think and feel. But I can't get comfortable, at least, not until I'm sure of you... and myself with you. You have to let me in. You have to open yourself up to me, just a little. If you want to... that is... See? I don't know. Do I leave you now and let you have a good laugh at the stupid girl who keeps showing up here? Do you think I'm lame or stupid or what? *I don't know.*"

She sucked in a breath for courage and lifted her face from his long enough to stare into his eyes. The *cool, even* gaze.

"Please tell me. Am I crazy or do you feel the same way too? I know we make no sense. But that doesn't stop what I feel. Am I alone in that?"

Finally. Good crap, he could hold a stare and the moment far longer than she could. He did it without flinching, turning away or filling the silence with awkward words, movements or twitches.

The weird tremors slid down her body, which she found both sexy and intimidating. He was probably feeling hatred and annoyance at her. As always, she didn't know.

"You're not alone." The words were low and soft as he

pinned his gaze on her. "No one has ever shown up for me. Just for me. I don't know how to handle it. I tend to distrust it. But I like how it feels. And I like how I feel when you're around." He slowly rose to his feet, making her step back to accommodate him. He towered over her. She stared up at him, gulping down all the words that filled her heart and hung on her tongue. She was good at expressing herself with words. She talked a lot. A lot more than he did. But she had no words left to say right now.

Shaking his head, the springy, short hairstyle made him look sexy and dangerous. He embodied every fantasy a woman could have for a man, but he came with a warning: look out or your heart could get broken. "I don't know how to tell you the things I think and feel. Often, when I'm with you and when you're near, I can't breathe. I can't explain it. I keep thinking I'll blink and you'll disappear. I wonder why you're here, in this shack, with me. On purpose."

Her breath and heart stilled with astonishment and hope. Wonderful hope at what he said. Made all the more poignant since he rarely expressed himself so eloquently. She didn't realize how much she wanted to be in his shack with him until that moment. Kissing him made all the insane chemistry churn and stir, but his words? God, his words offered the hope and light that made their physical relationship feel even stronger.

If it were anyone else, Rose would have finger-combed his freshly coiffed hair—that she cut—off his face. She would stretch up on her tiptoes and reach around his neck and pull him down to kiss him. If he were anyone else... Any other boyfriend or casual date would have easily received that kind of treatment. It was nonchalant, pointless, fun and interesting, but never deep or meaningful. Now her heart was lodged in her throat and nearly choking her with undeniable feelings. Hope. Nerves. Confusion.

The only thing she could do was be honest. So she told him that. "I am here to be with you. I'm not a figment of your imagination. I'm not special or different from you. I'm a woman, and I feel all the things you're saying you feel. But I'm nervous and I want to do something right now. I have trouble reaching for you casually or with affection as I often do with my friends. What I feel for you is so deep and strange that it's far more than friendly. But at the same time, I can't force myself to breach the wall you insist on building around yourself. It's that intimidating to me. It's why I first came here. I thought I could jump or climb or crawl over it. But apparently not because it's still there."

He stared down and his eyes were again unreadable. She sucked in a deep breath. *Honesty* was her only technique with him. "You're doing it now," she whispered.

He nodded but his face didn't change, although his head tilted. "I want you to do all those things. I don't know how to respond to you. I freeze up. Every single time. No one has ever wanted me to respond. Don't you get that? No one. No one has ever asked me to touch them or wanted to touch me. It's just sex. Fucking. Not what you're talking about. I don't know those rules. I don't know *how*. It's so easy for you. Your warmth just oozes out of you. I feel like a block of ice. But I don't mean to, I just don't know how to melt it."

She smiled. Brightly. Genuinely. "That was a good start. Just say your thoughts. No matter how hard or strange it feels. It opens you up. There's a lot I can do with that." She stepped a few inches closer to him, setting her hand on his chest. She did not fail to notice the contrast of his bare, tattooed, busy and very different chest. She stared at her white, freckled hand against his dark skin. It looked so pretty. It felt so right. Their personalities were symbolized. His dark intensity against her wholesomeness and light.

She could feel him breathe. His physical reaction to her

touch. He was speaking to her through his body language. He desired her. She slid her hand over and made a trail up the right side of him. Sliding her other hand from his stomach all the way to his neck, she looped her hands and stared up at his face. His expression was blank and harsh and she remembered his face never showed his heart, his wants, his needs, his thoughts or his feelings. He didn't know how to show or tell her those things, but she knew they were there. He was trying to open himself to her. It was a start.

"You can put your hands around me now." She kept her smile small and warm, and resisted the affectionate teasing she wanted to do with him. His body seemed taut, so stiff and tight. He didn't react, but his hands moved to her waist. She pulled herself right against him when he failed to do it. Her hands drifted down his back, following the curve of his spine. She loved his silky skin and sinewy muscles and she shivered when she felt him underneath her hands. So much for her to explore. His was new and uncharted territory and a strange bubble of excitement thrilled her. She imagined conquering and exploring him. It was so new and strange when it came to sex and a budding relationship. She'd never felt like this before.

Rose was better equipped to process and deal with the novelty and strangeness of her feelings. Mateo's coping abilities and even his frame of reference were impeded by his lack of familiarity with them.

Sucking in a sharp breath for courage, Rose rested her hands around his waist and pulled herself against his chest. She pressed her head right against his illustrated chest. Right under his collarbone, she lay completely against him.

He hesitated, but finally put some strength behind his hold and hugged her back. She smiled because he couldn't see her face. She closed her eyes and rested quietly. Content to feel fully against him.

A hug.

She wasn't sure he understood what hugs were for. There were so many indications that his life was lonely and lacking in affection from his childhood to his youth. Then he went to prison. He found no caring or nurturing there. Things like swim lessons and even bedsheets were suddenly luxuries for God's sake. That defined Mateo's life until now.

After he had sex with her, he withdrew literally and figuratively because he didn't know any better. The thought of reaching out to hug her, or take her hand, or say a kind word to her were beyond his cognition. No one did that to him.

She wanted to have sex with him but learning more about him seemed more important to explore. The undeniable chemistry she felt only heightened the magic.

For long minutes they stood embracing. Hugging. She noticed a subtle change in him. His biceps tightened. She could feel them near her ears. And his grip on her waist was more evident as his fingers dug into her. He was engaged. Fully. He suddenly grasped her next to his body, and *plastered* her to him. She felt like a life preserver being clutched by a drowning man. When he moved his head and rested his chin on top of her head, there wasn't an inch of space between them. She wilted against him and let her relief wash over her. Something so new and different, even desperate and needy, but he was showing her something he felt. He was sharing with her. Words might still escape him. But this was a start. And she dared to believe he might be feeling all the wonderful things that she did.

God… was it ten minutes? Yeah, at least that long before she pushed off him just a little bit. She stared up at his blank face and said, "That is quite a hug. The kind that I want to have more often. And I want you to initiate it sometimes too. I don't want to be the only one doing it. And I especially want you to do it after we have sex."

His mouth twitched and he sounded amused. "We get to have sex again? When? And I do know what a hug is."

Her head shook. "Sex comes after you learn proper hugging. And you don't really know how to yet. Do you? Who was the last person who hugged you?"

His mouth tightened and she gave him the same grim look. "Someday, you'll tell me who hugged you last. You'll eventually tell me all those things. We will talk and hug and yes, have lots of sex. But it has to be all tangled up in us, Mateo. I mean it. And I won't be deterred by your absence of skills. I'm going to coach you through this and you're going to take my advice and guidance. You're a fast learner so I know you can do this."

"Who said I'm a fast learner?"

She rolled her eyes. "Your quick intelligence was something I didn't fail to notice when I first met you. Now who hugged you last?" she repeated, ignoring his surly response and the strange grimace of pain that clearly shone in his eyes.

"I… I can't answer you. Because I don't honestly know."

"That's what I feared." She tightened her arms. "Well, you can hug me now. Okay? All the time even. You get that?"

He chuckled and lowered his mouth to her ear. "You're a bossy, little thing."

"Oh? You don't even know yet." She looked up. "You said you felt things about me?"

"Yeah. I can't describe… I don't know how to say what you want to hear."

"Do you feel lots of things for me?"

He hesitated and seemed to be scanning his body. Then he nodded, and his face became more serious. "Yeah."

"Okay. Then that's how you begin. You know you feel lots of things for me. And now you can hug me when you feel them. Remember this: your face often doesn't show me that you want to hug me or that you feel things for me. That's what I see so I don't always know what you feel. So you'll have to work at improving that for me. Make any sense?"

He laughed and she knew it was because of his nerves, and he was trying to hide them. He wasn't comfortable with intimacy. Obviously. Never being hugged for years, how could he be? His head tilted back and he replied, "Makes sense."

He didn't release her but pulled her back to his chest and she stayed there. She wanted Mateo Alvarez to be fully cognizant of what it felt like to be held and loved.

"Rose?"

She was almost asleep, cocooned in the warmth of his muscles and flesh. "Yes?"

"I like this. I like how this feels."

She smiled and didn't laugh but sealed her lips. She was gravely serious and caring when she lifted her eyes to meet his gaze. "Me too." More than a million flowery words could have been added to her reply, but that seemed enough for today. She did not want to overwhelm him. His feelings and emotions existed and that's all he seemed ready to say about them. It must be disconcerting when you can't express your own thoughts and feelings. Was it because no one cared? Not ever? Was it due to his chronic childhood pain and trauma? What was the source of it? Or was it simply neglect? She didn't have the full picture of him yet, but she caught a glimpse of a tiny corner of it today. And she was ready and willing to let it slowly reveal itself to both of them.

CHAPTER 8

ROSE BROUGHT A FEW small amenities to
Mateo's place. She got there early so when he
came home late from work, as he often did, he would be
greeted by her and a hot meal. She finagled a house key by
claiming she wanted to pick up the dinner early because he
inevitably worked late. He never got home at the same time
twice. Whenever he finished his work for that day was when
he came home.

He walked in and froze, his gaze panning around, the
usual strained look on his face. "What did you do?"

He took in the line of candles that she set on the lone
windowsill. They were the kind that ran on batteries and
could not burn down the small wooden hovel. There was no
chance she'd take that risk. The flicker and glow against the
fading sunlight streaming through the window was lovely,
homey and sensual as the last of the daylight seeped out. She
previously cleaned the window, scrubbed the floor and all
the other surfaces, including the bathroom. The fresh scent
of natural citrus cleaner pervaded the air. She also lay a
clean, fluffy rug along his bedside, providing softness and

warmth to bare feet when one slid into bed. The space was so small, it also served as padding when standing at the small sink to wash dishes by hand.

She put her spare set of sheets and a comforter on his bed. It was a lavender quilt she used in her dorm at college. Her dorm bed was the same size as Mateo's so everything fit snugly. She expected him to furrow his forehead when he saw the freshly made bed in lavender sheets... It was probably warranted. Rushing to explain, she said, "I used my old bedding. I'm sorry it's lavender but it's all I had. I didn't pick them up from town or choose that color."

He examined the room all around. No words yet. He noticed the obvious cleaning and a few niceties. Two fans now cooled the once stifling, stagnant air. One stood as wide and round as a bicycle wheel. The smaller one was clipped to the bed and adjustable. They could aim it to hit their faces or anything else with a heavenly swirl of cool, moving, fresh air.

"You... what did you do?"

"Just a few things to make it more comfortable."

"It's a shed. It's not supposed to be comfortable."

"No... it's a shack. And making it more pleasant makes me feel more comfortable. Far more comfortable than the first time I was here."

His dark eyes blazed on her. "It's not good enough for you."

"That wasn't true for one moment. It was too hot before. Your sleeping bag is made of nylon and flannel, which is stifling when it's hot... so yeah, I brought some creature comforts. I can easily remove them all. I just thought it was nicer this way. We can't go to my place with Iris there and you want to keep this on the down low—right? You can't accuse me of being a snob, because I'm here. You can't say I'm hiding you either, since you're the one who insists on that. I'm simply working within your parameters. And since I get way too hot when I'm here, I wanted to improve the accommodations. Now it's pretty pleasant… right?"

"My bed is purple."

"Actually, it's lavender," she corrected him, wincing when he scowled as she took a step back. "Okay, purple. You think I went too far?" She grew quiet. "I wasn't trying to establish my presence here. I just thought a few niceties could make it more like home."

"Home? Why would I ever claim this piece of shit as my home? It was cheap and easy and there was no you at the time. I never planned to stay here."

"But if you do, now it's okay. That's all I was trying to create. A few small comforts. That's all."

His arms were folded over his chest. He pinched his nose and lowered his head as if he were so exasperated he could not find the words to express himself. Finally, he lifted his gaze and said, "You gave me your old bedding?"

"Yes." As usual, she had no way to read his take on that.

He suddenly approached her. One moment, he was grumbling, and his body language clearly warned, *Don't touch me!* and the next, he was standing right in front of her. His gaze was blazing with fire as he suddenly lifted her clear off the ground and took the three steps to the freshly made bed. He set her on it and his mouth came down on hers. His lips devoured hers, his tongue diving so deep and long into her throat, her stunned body instantly reacted. She instinctually met his thrusting movements and his probing tongue, even though her brain short-circuited while trying to keep up with him. First, he seemed annoyed and now, they were lying on the bed he was so displeased about?

He lifted his face off hers, using one arm to hold some of his weight. His gaze shifted and he scanned her. He seemed to drink in her features as if he wanted to memorize her face.

"You're angry," she stated when he didn't speak. It was the

only explanation she could find for why he suddenly grabbed and kissed her so harshly. It was so out of character. Except for the first time he'd kissed her.

"No." His eyes roamed over her again. "No one ever bought me a life jacket or a raft or made my bed for me or gave me their own fucking bedsheets."

Her breath hitched in her chest. His words were so raw, like skin being peeled off, and she knew how hard it was for him to admit that to her. "It was nothing. Honest."

"Yeah? Then why did I never sleep on sheets before? Always in a sleeping bag. Never occurred to me..."

Her heart skipped. "Even as a child?"

"Yeah. Even then."

"Why? Why did you never have any of the basics?"

He leaned forward. "Later. Right now?" He started with her lips and peppered kisses all over her face that were soft and deep, tender and gentle, until her heart was fluttering. His breath was warm when he spoke into her ear. First, his tongue traced her outer ear and her entire body shivered and reacted. "Let me fuck you, Rose. Like only I know how. I can't give you the pretty words you want to hear but I can make you feel everything I want to say. Let me, please... just let me fuck you."

Her entire body flushed and she reacted by getting very wet. She leaned closer to him. His tone was so sultry, sensual and steamy, she nearly swooned. Her stomach pitted and her body wept. He lifted his face, his deep, dark eyes staring straight into hers. She nodded, swallowed, and suddenly became mute. "Oh, well, okay..." she barely gasped out.

HER BREATHY REPLY ONLY MADE him more eager to have her.

She was so funny. So sweet. To him. For him. He wished he could somehow repay her for all of her kindness.

He had to tell her and show her how he felt the only way he knew how to.

He didn't smile as he suddenly covered her lips with his. He sucked and licked and caressed her lips before diving into her mouth with his tongue and wrestling and dancing with hers. His hands slipped down her sides as she writhed beneath him, sighing at his touch. He grabbed the hem of her shirt and pushed it out of his way. He released her bra clasp and freed her breasts.

He watched them settle as her nipples stood out like twin beacons on tiny ice cream cones. He kissed her stomach and she moved towards his lips as he trailed kisses to the base of her white mounds. He kissed and licked both of them in turn. He showered the round base with kisses on one breast while his palm caressed the opposite nipple. Without pressing, he gently tapped and rolled the flat of his hand over the nub. It instantly responded by hardening and straining for more. That's what he wanted. He sighed as her body followed the dance he was choreographing. He rolled his fingers repeatedly over the soft nub, adoring the way she emitted telltale sighs with his touch. Then, he took the whole nipple inside his wet, hot, greedy mouth. He held her prisoner, grazing his teeth across it, using his tongue and lips and saliva to bathe and titillate it. His hand worked on the other breast and mimicked his mouth. She cried out after several long minutes of this sweet torture. Her gasps and cries aroused him, and he got so hard, it was painful because his clothes were still on.

Finally, he eased her back and her eyelids fluttered with surprise when he rose up and discarded his shirt. Her gaze devoured him. Their styles and personalities were so opposite, their ways of expressing themselves like night to day.

Nature knew that when it made her pale and pink and him dark and brown. They were never meant for each other.

Yet here they were. Staring with hunger that seemed to be equally shared by the other. They paused to catch their breaths, heaving as they stared in serious contemplation ateach other. Then, his hands slipped under her waistband and he grabbed her shorts and tugged them off her hips with her assistance. Her thighs were so creamy and soft, demanding his undivided attention to the fine red patch that was trimmed and groomed for him. He loved her softness. Her naturally red hairs against the whiteness of her skin. Alabaster white.

He unceremoniously pulled off all his clothing and she stared at him, for the first time with leisure and seeing him fully naked. She sat up and hissed through her lips. Impressed? Evidently so.

She smiled as she reached towards him. Her touch made him shut his eyes as her cool, soft hand slid along him almost reverently. He shut his eyes and ground his teeth in his overwhelming feelings for Rose. The same Rose he admired from afar for the past three years and fantasized doing exactly this… She began tugging on him. Exploring him.

Then, her hands slid to his backside and she grabbed his ass cheeks. She began kneading them and his body nearly exploded. She pulled his hips towards her and his eyes shot open. He was shocked to behold the magical, beautiful, unexpected sight of her head bending over him. Her white scalp was clearly visible from his viewpoint. But he was more aware of her lips than anything else, because they were wrapped around the end of his dick. He sucked in a breath of air and his eyelids slammed shut. The sensations were overwhelming. Her mouth seemed shy, soft and tentative as she chastely kissed him. Pre-cum eagerly welcomed her perfect, hot, juicy mouth. She was kissing him and opening her mouth slightly wider to graze him gently with her teeth before timidly sliding down his length with her tongue.

His hands held her head which she buried in his crotch. He played with her thick, silky tresses of hair. He fought the urge to grab it into a ponytail and shove her face as hard and as fast as his greedy dick demanded, strained and begged for. But this blow job was different... For the first time, he heard a new and surprising voice. From what? His heart? Maybe. It was definitely something inside his chest. Something that made him want to cradle her head gently and reverently. Something that softened his touch and made him notice how her hair tickled his fingertips. Something just as sensual as the heat building in his groin from the magic of her manipulative mouth. She started out soft and gentle, hesitant and unsure.

Had she never done this before? He suspected not. But he gave her the space to figure it out. She kissed and fondled and sucked him, albeit a little clumsily. Despite the awkwardness, it was hot and sweet and raw and pure. She didn't have any moves down and that proved it wasn't familiar to her, which turned him on more than anything.

He let himself sink into the unparalleled pleasure. She slowed down her movements and began building him up, rationing the delicious sensations until finally... yeah, she got him there. He couldn't think of anything hotter than Rose Rydell with her mouth full of *him,* and his hands snarled in her hair as she did her best to please him. All of him.

He used to scare her. He wasn't the man she ever thought she'd desire. Knowing this, it made it all the more epic and special for him.

"Rose?" His tone was strangled. It was obvious he was ready to come. Inside her mouth or all over her. "Stop..."

But she didn't.

And he came into her waiting, hot mouth. Stunning him. Shocking him. Totally enrapturing him.

After, he fell back on the bed, bringing her with him. He was a mindless, boneless, gooey puddle of tenderness and gratitude.

She cuddled him and nuzzled his neck. She licked his firefly tattoo and peppered little butterfly kisses on his carotid artery. He imagined she was christening his neck tattoo. That's what it felt like. Her seal of approval. Fuck. Things were heating up.

He loved what she was doing. His heart swelled until it was about to explode. He wanted to say things to her but he choked on the words. How could he possibly express what her touching him like that meant? She handled him with ease and never seemed repelled by him, from giving him a blow job to kissing his neck tattoo. He could never say how much her touch meant to him. No one else used only their fingertips to glide over his chest as hers did now. No one else caressed the muscles of his back or his ass or above his heart with the care and tenderness that she did. He didn't think he'd ever been touched that way before. But now that he was, he had to admit he loved it. He wanted to place himself in her hands, trusting her gentleness, protected by her fierceness. He remembered how she came to his place and pursued him, drawing things out of him he never knew he had and still, she demanded more. And then... this?

He had to repay her kindness to him. Show her. Tell her. But he didn't know how. He only communicated with sex. He could give her that.

He set his hands on her waist and pulled her upright, settling her on top of him. He slid down on the mattress and pushed her towards his face. She gasped and realized his intention. She resisted and he simply lifted her up, easily pushing apart her legs until she was over him as he pulled her towards his mouth. Out of necessity and panic, she grabbed the headboard and tried to avoid crushing him. But he already pushed her on the roller coaster of ecstasy.

"Mateo… oh!" She started to admonish him when his tongue plucked her clit. Her exclamation was long and drawn out as her hips rocked and she dripped with joy. She was all in physically.

Rocking herself over his mouth, she moaned and clung to the metal headboard. Draping her arms over it, she tried to hold on while her mindless body fully responded to him. Without thought, worry or reason, she was pulsating in a glorious display Mateo never expected from the reserved, prim Rose Rydell. Not like this. Not rocking and heaving over his face, sliding her body back and forth in unbridled desperation to feel his mouth and tongue and fingertips. She was grinding on him with her teeth clenched and shouting his name.

"OH! Mateo! OH! Ma-tayyyy-o!" With a final scream, she deflated and her body collapsed after its explosion.

Embarrassed, she immediately ducked down on the bed, almost burying her face against his armpit. He stroked her hair, a first for him with a woman. He thought about the ease and speed with which she went from being hot and bothered, so eager to come, to being tender, caring, gentle and needing his support. It kind of amazed him. He could give her hot, fast, incredible orgasms, while she asked for his gentleness and comfort, two things he never had inside him, let alone, gave to anyone. His heart swelled with something big and new that filled his chest until it almost suffocated him. He liked returning the tenderness.

She lifted her head up and her entire face was flushed from her orgasm and subsequent embarrassment. "I can't believe we just did that."

He smiled. "First time doing it that way?"

She nodded. He slipped his hand over the curve of her waist, loving the way she tapered in before her hips flared out. He kept touching the curve, petting the sensual lines with unconcealed appreciation. He slipped his fingers between her legs and found her hot and wet and more than ready.

He rolled her onto her back and grabbed a condom, which he quickly put on before easing himself into her. This time it was gentle and unhurried. The heat, speed and pseudo violence of their previous mutual orgasms were being replaced by leisurely time, deliberate slowness, and general ease. She gripped his neck with her hands and held him closer as his body filled her up. They rocked together gently, their hips colliding and rappelling. She stared up at him. Her eyes seemed like huge blue lakes filled with uncharted emotions and unrestrained ecstasy. He was accustomed to giving women a moment of ecstasy but not the... what? Awe? Was that what she felt?

Their bodies as one, they held onto each other, staring into each other's eyes, their mouths open and their groans synchronized. She leaned forward and their foreheads met as they gasped together when he suddenly moved deeper inside her. It was slow and hot... he imagined a ladle of honey being drizzled over them. Each movement was exaggerated and in that slowness, heat, depth, and darkness, their emotions were exchanged and explored. Their eye contact was a record breaker, overwhelming both of them. Rose was ready to blow his mind. She held up her hand and he gripped it, their fingers clasping like teeth on a zipper before her hips started devouring him. He rocked to her rhythm as they held hands, their eyes and gazes fastened on each other as they finally came together at the same exact moment. They both strained, moaned and whispered each other's names as their foreheads met and their hands remained clasped.

The profound moment lasted for a long time and it was the most connected Mateo ever felt to anyone, anywhere. Originally, his only intention for Rose was to give her a good fuck, but now they had a deep, heartfelt connection. Now, she had the power to steal his breath and his heart, and he almost trembled with fear at that knowledge. Rose kept showing him things he never knew about before and this time, she did it with just a few words.

CHAPTER 9

ROSE WAS STILL THERE. Mateo never had anyone stay overnight with him, let alone, in his bed. He felt strange and he couldn't sleep. He couldn't even relax or move. She hogged the whole bed. For real. Lying on her back, legs spread, her elbow poking his chest, she shoved him into the wall and he curled up on his side. Granted, twin beds are only designed for one person to sleep in. But after he'd moved away, she'd dropped off to sleep. It was almost comical how quickly it happened. She was kind of adorable next to him. Soft breathing. Even and steady. Her hair spread all around her, in tangles now, and her bangs pushed up.

Mateo didn't know how to be close to anyone. Even eating with her was strange for him. He never ate meals with anyone consistently. And talking each and every day…? Kind of mind blowing to him. People really did this shit? Daily? Yes, she'd informed him when he'd asked her one time.

Sex, however, was fantastic. Her constant coaching of him was kind of… he didn't know the word. He wasn't used to having someone listen to what he said so carefully and he couldn't believe how much Rose cared. She was a caring woman. He knew that from Iris, whom she often hovered over like a mother hen. Iris complained about it, and Mateo almost told her she was the luckiest person alive if that was her only complaint about her sibling. But Rose's fussing came from her abundance of kindness and wanting the best for the people she loved. She wanted to be close to him and a part of his life.

They were cuddled in his bed, bathing in the afterglow. His body was stiff and unnaturally withdrawn from her just because he wasn't used to it. Holding someone after sex, before sex, even during sex, was not Mateo's customary pattern. Not like Rose insisted upon. He was too scared to broach intimacy after the first time, when she'd said he'd hurt her feelings… He wasn't confident he could fix that.

She suddenly started to stretch as she flipped over towards him. She blinked and jolted. Taking a moment to orient herself to being awake and her surroundings, she rolled over and rested her head on his chest, wrapping her arms around his sides. Then she snuggled against him as if it were the most natural, easiest thing in the world to do. It wasn't natural for him, and it certainly shouldn't have been for her.

"What time is it?" Her voice was hoarse from sleep, lacking her usual peppiness.

He glanced at the lone alarm clock. "Two."

"And why were you lying there wide-awake staring at me so strangely?"

She flipped her head. The illumination from the single yard light above the row of sheds provided enough light through the front window that she could see his face between the shadows.

Slipping away from him, she sat upright. "Let me pee first. Then you can tell me."

Tell her? Pee first? His head was muddled by all the

154

strangeness. She was so very strange. Easygoing. Open. Why was she so damn open with him? Nothing about him or his demeanor would encourage anyone to open up to him. Rising, she took the four steps to the small bathroom that was added on to the original cabin. The bathroom was small. Standing before the sink, you could turn around and take a step to the toilet or one to the side if you wanted to go into the shower.

The uninsulated walls were thin and he could hear her pee before she flushed and let the water refill. Moments later, she popped out and sat on the bed, turning towards him. He was still frozen on his back, pushed against the wall. He was studying her ease and grace in her movement inside his shed. His hovel. His embarrassment.

The same one she'd cleaned. And cooled. The two fans wafted the air back and forth, providing freshness and relief. He sighed. She'd made it better, but it was still an embarrassment.

She pushed her snarled hair back—after his hands had messed it up—and it fell heavily over her face and shoulders. Seeing the extent of damage caused by his wandering, frantic hands in her hair as she gave him a blow job turned him on. He easily recalled his orgasm. She swallowed him whole. It didn't compute.

She sighed, studying him before simply lying down and facing him, only inches away.

"Tell me why you never had sheets to sleep on."

"We were poor. This shack would have been an improvement on our apartments over the years. We were that poor. As long as I can remember, I had to sleep in a sleeping bag. Then I went to prison. Not exactly a country club. When I got out, the sleeping bag was a luxury."

She asked, "We? Who was we?"

"My mom and my older brother."

"I didn't know you had a sibling. Are you close to him?"

"No. Nothing like you and your sisters are."

"Your mom?"

"I send her money." There. He finally told her the one thing that was on the tip of his tongue. That was the reason he lived like this. The reason the money he earned from her father, which was pretty decent, didn't allow him to live a decent lifestyle. Most of it went to his mother and therefore, his brother.

She watched him closely. He didn't flinch or smile. He kept all the details of his life to himself with a neutral face. It had kept him out of trouble with his mother, his brother, the hood rats of his old neighborhood, and especially when he went to prison. But Rose hated it. Not knowing his history made her afraid and unsure of him.

Mateo wasn't sure he could drop it yet. He didn't really trust her, not completely, maybe not ever. So he kept the wall up and kept her at a distance, despite his need and desire to smash it.

But she smashed through it—yet again—by simply reaching forward, and placing her fingertips over his jaw. "There's a story there."

"Isn't there always?" he muttered, but his tone was too sharp. Mean. It matched his look.

"Are you close to your mom, then?"

"No. Not at all." Harsh again. He couldn't disguise his utter dislike for the woman who gave birth to him and raised him.

Fingers stilled on his face. "But you send her money?"

"Yeah, I send her all of my money."

"Where? Where was your home? Where did you grow up?"

"Not in the country. Nothing like this."

She grinned. "I deduced that. You remember the incident with the water snake?"

"El Paso."

"Texas? Really?" She tilted her head and thought it sounded so exotic. It might be for some people but not at all for him. His memories were mainly dirty floors and concrete prisons. "How did my dad get involved with you?"

"He usually dropped by on his way down to Mexico. You know his marathon rides in his youth? When he met enough people across North America to sustain his business for the next twenty-plus years? We were one of those contacts. My dad was known all over for restoring rare bikes. Fixing them and finding original parts. When your dad needed something, he hunted down my dad and they collaborated. It led to an enduring friendship. Anytime Shane came down through El Paso, he'd call my dad and stop by. I knew him for years. But not very well. Not well enough that he should have hired me."

"Why not?"

"You realize what my dad did, right? Iris must have told you?"

"Iris? She doesn't tell me anything. You might have noticed my frustration with her? We live together but dragging the most basic information out of her is like pulling teeth and excruciating in its slow pace. No. I don't know. Just as I don't know more about you, other than she cares for you and you guys act like two sixteen-year-old boys who still snicker at penis jokes."

She made him smile. "Yeah," he confirmed. "That's why Iris is so great. Unusual. Especially for a chick. A boss's daughter chick at that."

She play-punched his arm. "Because she doesn't make you talk? Or relate like a human?"

He rubbed his arm melodramatically before reaching out

and taking her hand in his. Damn. He was holding it. Why? He didn't know. It felt natural.

"So what did your dad do?" She brought the subject he was avoiding back to the forefront, because it was time to rip her blinders off.

"A chop shop, Rose. I worked for him."

"Okay. What does that mean?"

He almost shut his eyes at her clueless innocence. "We stole lots of cars. And took them to the shop and removed the license plates and filed down the serial numbers, any other identifiers. We sold them to a local gang who smuggled them out of the city and re-sold them. We stripped down other cars for parts and did the same with motorcycles. That's why we always had the parts your dad needed. And cheap. He liked our prices."

Her mouth popped open and her gaze was riveted on him. "My dad knew?"

"Yeah. Duh. When he hired me."

"Okay…" She swallowed. "So you worked in this shop? How old were you when you started?"

"Crap, as long as I can remember I worked there. It's why I knew so much about the makes and models of cars and bikes, I've always done it."

"Your dad didn't think it might not be… appropriate?" She struggled to understand a father not doing right in his kid's eye. Not like Shane did with her and her sisters.

"No. We had to work. We had to earn money."

"But you were still poor."

"In my later years, I was not as poor. In my younger years, my dad wasn't around. He showed up when I was about eight or nine. He had the shop so he had a reason for keeping me around. He saw my long, adept fingers and he knew I wasn't stupid."

She touched his face again. "No. You're definitely not

stupid. So he didn't raise you? But he showed up just to put you to work in his illegal chop shop and then he sent you out to steal cars?"

He steeled himself for her rejection and locked his jaw. "And bikes."

"Right. And bikes. How old were you when you were doing that?"

"I started when I was twelve. It was easy. No one suspected a gangly kid. I could barely reach the pedals or the steering wheels. But I was fast."

"Right. So did your brother work there too?"

"Not the same father. My mom actually *loved* his father, so she settled with mine and then mine ditched her too."

"That's harsh."

"Nah. I kind of get it. She's not an easy person to live with."

Rose didn't reject him. She didn't turn away or seem repulsed. In fact, her eyes were wider and bluer, and something sparkled in them. What? Crap? Sympathy? Pity? Was she sorry for him?

"Rose, I jacked cars all during my teens. You get that, right? Like tens of thousands of dollars' worth of vehicles. I learned how to turn them, flip them and sell them to gangs who resold them. You get the reality of that?"

"I do," she said quietly. But her hand cupped his damn jaw. His locked, rigid, angry jaw. His stone-cold look said he was prepared for her rejection.

"Rose?"

"Mateo, do you still do that now? Do you steal cars? Use my dad's shop to turn them around? Or whatever the proper term is?"

"No. Not since I got out of prison. Too risky when I was on parole. And your dad..."

"Trusted you not to. He'd have forbidden you from going anywhere near Iris. So he knows you won't. Right?"

He frowned. "Yeah. But why would you know that? After what I just told you?"

"You just told me your father showed up late in your life, but you were still a needy, impressionable little boy. Eight years isn't old, Mateo. You wanted his love and attention and you did what your father said to get it. He taught you how to steal and hide and defraud people. You were ordered to do it. What choice did you have? What other option? You were a child. I don't know what role your mom played, but it doesn't sound very influential; and yet you still send her your hard-earned, honest salary? And she considers it something you owe her, instead of being grateful for it, right? I find it tragic you were committing crimes at age sixteen. Crimes you ended up going to prison for."

"That's your summary of my life?"

"Yes. I glossed over some of it. But did I get any of it wrong?"

"No. I guess not."

"Your brother? He was the contact in the gang?"

"How did you—"

"Just an educated guess. You weren't in a gang, though? Because you're not now. I imagine a prison term would have only hardened you into doing more gang-related stuff. I honestly don't know but wouldn't prison simply exacerbate what you were already doing? Instead, you came here to River's End to work an honest job for my dad so you can live the way you don't like, just to send money home? I have that part right too, don't I?"

She did. He was so puzzled when she deduced the main trajectory of his life and it wasn't what most would assume. "What about all my tats?"

"Your dad's and brother's influence. You did what they

did. You were probably ready to get initiated into the gang next but something held you back. Something that is better and more solid inside you. Your intelligence. I feel like that sets you apart from most people. So you might have looked the part as a teen, but your heart was never in it. Because you're not really in it."

"My intelligence?" he scoffed.

"I hear it in your voice and it's what attracted me to you. Your sense of humor and intelligence. Your vocabulary. You have to know that. I'm not a total sap for physical attraction. I need some intelligence."

"I'm so intelligent, I got popped for a felony. Imagine if I had to pay for all my crimes. Don't sugar-coat this, or me, or what I've done. It colors the rest of my life and how others receive and perceive me. I'm a felon and I deserve decades in prison for all my many crimes. I can't even count all the cars I stole, Rosie. I didn't keep track. My dad did."

She snorted. "I'll bet he kept track. I'll bet he saw a large profit along with your brother. Allowing a minor to do the work. And they didn't contribute any money to your mother, did they? You did. That's why you never had any money."

She nailed it. He didn't expect her to understand so quickly. "None of it changes that I'm a criminal. You can't wash that away, Rose. Not with all my sad childhood stories you want to blame it on. At one point, I was old enough to know better and stop. I had the skills to earn an honest living. But instead, look where I ended up. It's forever, Rose. It's my stigma in this country. Felon. Ex-con. I look like a gangster. Just today, Iris pulled over to help a guy who was stranded, and he took one look at me and stepped back. Is that what you want?"

She slid up to lean on him as she pushed him flat on his back and slid on top of him. Straddling him, she stared hard into his eyes and pressed her forehead on his. Again, with the eye-lock.

"I don't want any car-jacking, Mateo. Or prison sentences from being a gangster. I believe that's what predisposed you to the crime that sent you there. But you came out, stayed clean, came here and worked for my dad and you're best friends with Iris. You chose to change. You chose to be honest. And you moved away from the influences that would have destined you to a life of crime and struggling. Instead, you're here. You're making eyes at me. You noticed me. Long before I ever noticed you. So yes. I want the gangster Mateo, the ex-con who committed multiple felonies Mateo. I want you just as you are now."

She leaned forward and her lips captured his. "The looks you give me. The hot and cold vibes you send my way. It's all from you, your own push and pull. You wanted me and you liked me but I wasn't familiar with you so you erroneously assumed that I didn't want you. You assumed that, and now you don't know what to do with me here."

He glared up at her, then he smiled slowly but it got wider to hammer his point.

"I figured it out pretty well. You weren't complaining."

"Sex? That's what you want this to only be about? No, Mateo, you feel something as deeply as I do and you're scared shitless by it. Well, so am I. But not because you're a gang member or I expectyou to steal from my dad eventually. Or me."

She was impossible to scare off. And the worst of it was: she was right.

"But everyone else assumes I'm an incorrigible criminal. They always do. And they always will. I'll always be the one who gets blamed if something goes missing. I expect that. I'm surprised it hasn't happened yet. It's just the reality of my life. My past determines how I'm treated in the future. My sixteen-year-old decision to tattoo my neck raises red flags, and it keeps most people like you away. Your friends don't like me. Little old ladies will just wonder what a nice girl like you could be doing with someone like me. Hell, I wonder why. Guys are scared of me and no one trusts me. Do you really want that?"

"I want you. So yes. And I don't care what my friends think or little old ladies that I don't know. Why should I care about them? I trust you, Mateo, with my life. I trust you. I don't think you'll ever steal again, especially from my dad. I trust you with my safety and my body, which I don't offer anyone that easily. I think you're smart and funny and you have so much to offer the world, but you've been categorized and rejected for the stupid mistakes your damn father told you to do. As for a few tattoos that are a little unconventional? No. I won't let them undermine us. It's why I'm here."

"A little unconventional? Most people assume they're gang signs and codes. You've seen it. The negative reaction I get everywhere I go. Even people who know me."

Rose flinched as she flopped her entire body on top of his. She wrapped her arms around his shoulders as far as she could reach. "I do. I know. But people like me are assholes if they judge you so harshly. Your tattoos are also sexy as hell and now it makes me feel funny inside when I look at you. You used to be so dangerous-looking but now that I trust you, the dangerous aspect has become a strong, intoxicating aphrodisiac for me."

Her way of speaking was like no one else. He never heard anyone admit everything they ever thought or felt or did. She was so open and honest; it was hard to keep erecting walls around himself. Ideas he once clung to in order to keep people like her from hurting him. Or worse, rejecting him. He could never admit that rejection was his deepest fear.

Rejection. By decent people he longed to be part of. After he left prison, he stayed away from his criminal family, becoming a low-key, easy-going, law-abiding guy. He liked to work. A lot. He loved it, in fact. The pride he found in being a mechanic for Shane's shop? He'd sooner die than break Shane's trust in him and he could never feel grateful enough for the second chance Shane gave him. He would do anything for Rose's dad. For Iris. But especially for Rose.

Rose accepted him before she fully knew or trusted him. Her words affected him and he responded. He slipped his arms around her, placing his flat hand on her bare back. He pressed her against his chest, hard. Then he began clinging. Yeah, fuck. He was clinging to her.

"You don't detest my outward appearance?" He was compelled to ask it. He hated being on the edge of his seat as he waited to know her answer.

"I find you hot, Mateo. I always did. Scared or not, you melted my insides until they were all molten. Do you know that feeling? White-hot, turned on. And now, I can't believe my luck that the person inside that package turns me on even more. Imagine all the boring men I've dated. They bored me intellectually. And their mundane personalities were so tedious. I thought I'd like their clean-cut crispness but that bored me too. You have to remember who my dad is. He's a tamer version of you. But it's not as if I was sheltered from the dark side of life. Who bought the bike parts from your dad's illegal shop? Oh, yeah, that'd be my dad. And if you think that's his first dubious choice before marrying my mom, you'd be very much mistaken. Just because I look like Pollyanna, which I can't seem to alter, doesn't mean I'm looking for a male counterpart. Sexually, that doesn't hit it for me. You do. I just didn't know how to reconcile that."

She said a lot and everything she said swirled in his brain. It wasn't anything that he expected her to say or think.

"That's how I felt when I saw you. I just knew we were

opposites, and I thought you'd never see anything beyond a thug. Deserved, yes, but not—"

"The person you really are? I see that, Mateo. I should have seen it simply from your conversations with Iris. But I was a priss so…"

"You are not prissy." He laughed out loud. She might have looked it, but her actions belied that theory. Her reaction to him showed courage, spunk and understanding; but damn, sex with Rose…

"Was…" Her head dropped down, and she buried it into his chest. He was staring at her white scalp and red hair again. God, he loved how she got embarrassed and burrowed against him. She trusted him. It was new. He wasn't sure he'd ever get used to it.

"Was what?"

"I haven't done that… that thing very much. I'm sure you noticed…"

Her vocabulary lacked any sex-words, but instead of being annoying, Mateo found it adorable. "Blow job?" Her head nodded in affirmation. "You were excellent, like a pro."

And damn if her shoulders didn't drop in relief. Her head popped up again and her face blazed in pink, soft, cute, blushing innocence. Over what he said?

"I had a boyfriend, my last one at school. He was president of everything and had short, blond hair, blue eyes, a rich family and he planned to be a lawyer. You know, what you'd expect from me. He also made me feel like shit all the time. I was never smart enough or accomplished enough, and he said my family were country hicks along with plenty of other insults. Anyway, when I tried doing that with him, he told me I sucked." She bit her lip. "That was not the right word. Yes, I sucked, but he said I was terrible. Every part of it. So I never did it again. I swear to God, the only time he got off was when he was morbidly embarrassing me."

Mateo set his hands on her biceps and lifted her up before rolling her under him. "You didn't bite it off, did you?"

She laughed. "Well, no."

"Then you did it right. He's a fucking prick. You felt me inside your mouth, right? Hot and pulsating until... I came right into it. You let me come in your mouth. You ask me if I liked it and if you did it right? Honey, you couldn't have been any sweeter."

"I felt awkward."

He touched her cheek with his finger to comfort her. For being herself. "You were awkward and I loved it. The fact that you were willing to do it with me when you were so nervous and it wasn't something you practiced? It showed me you were as much into me as I am into you. So it was a pretty powerful blow job. And fuck that prick."

She smiled, soft and sweet, which was also alluring to him. "I had sex with my high school boyfriend. Once, after we graduated. My first time and his. It was clumsy and I didn't come, but it was sweet. We broke up afterward because we realized we were just friends. There was another guy when I was a sophomore, but it's the same story. Not much chemistry. Lots of friendship. We had slow, deliberate sex. But I didn't come with him either. I thought maybe I was flawed. Compared to Iris, who had orgasms all the time, with herself or others, and so easily. She was always more confident and sure in that area than me. And I'm so far the other way. And then, when I was getting my master's, I met Benton Smith."

"I could have a told you he was a douche from his name. Benton Smith? He made that up."

"No. He didn't." She giggled and it made him smile. He liked to see her laugh. And hated anyone who could hurt her.

"I thought he was it. All that I wanted. He looked the part. Had the pedigree and a promising future. But Mateo, it was never right. I should have realized it then. I never felt the thrill I feel from one look from you. Until you came along, I never felt sexual attraction or energy. Or all that we share between us. I know you know, how could you not? We are amazing."

"So… Benton?" he pressed. Maybe this story could explain what she was doing here with him.

"He was overly controlling. An OCD asshole. And the priss I hate to be. I don't think I am for real though."

"No. Not if you want me."

"I do. Anyway, we dated for a year. When we had sex, it was strange. He was so controlling. And oral sex was forbidden. Can I tell you something that I find humiliating? Something that I tolerated and now I wish I'd punched him instead. But I was young and thought everyone should have a match and all that. All my friends and classmates said that I was lucky to have him. All the reasons you listed why we shouldn't be together were what they saw in him."

"You can tell me."

"He only had sex if I was face-planted on the bed, never looking at him and only… you know, like that."

He brushed his hand through her tangled hair. She all but purred at the simple affection and leaned her head into the palm of his hand. "Doggy-style?"

"Yes." Her face burned up. "I know, it's really hot sex and some people prefer it that way. But not when it's the only way you have sex. He refused to look at me. He didn't want me to touch him and my body disgusted him. He'd tell me to get naked and assume the position. Then he'd stick his tiny dick inside me. Nothing romantic and no foreplay. Never mind if I was ready or not. After he'd orgasm, he'd slip out of me and that was it. He all but slapped my ass before getting dressed. That was my sex life. I didn't orgasm with him. Not once. And then you came along… Dear God, you discovered entirely new parts of my body I didn't know existed. Hot, hungry, needy parts. I've had a few... you know... alone."

He tousled her hair and his heart swelled with emotion. Her story wasn't what he expected. His anger churned at hearing how she was so used and abused without enjoying the full potential of her glorious body. He remembered her skills and how she'd responded to him. It was organic, raw, wild, and hot; so far beyond rehearsed or prissy... And still, even the most ordinary word remained unspoken from her mouth. "You masturbated."

"I hate that word. Anyway, so I knew I could have orgasms. Just not during sex. And when I did, you walked away from me as if it were the most blasé experience in the world. So I found it very confusing and hurtful. You literally rocked my world and then you dismissed me and I thought you didn't feel it."

His heart hurt in his chest. "I felt it. My world was rocked too. I just didn't, and still don't, know how to describe it. I can't put words to sex. I can't put my feelings into words."

"You just nailed our differences perfectly. You can't use words to communicate. And I can't strictly use sex. I vowed after Benton, sex would be on my terms. And only when there was loving and kindness and caring. Affection. All the things I never had and lacked in a relationship. That's why I was so weird at first."

"Well, I was weird too. I thought it was all my fault."

She rubbed his chest and his entire body reacted, but the strongest organ to react was his heart, not his dick. "It can't be all your fault. We both have to figure this out. Please don't doubt that or the future."

"Future?"

She slid her hand in his. "Yes. Please, say you want a future with me. I can't imagine giving this up now."

He never felt so excited before. Was his heart growing?

Blipping and skipping heartbeats? And something else was swelling in his chest. What was it? Hope? Joy? Rose? The future? He never looked forward to having one because he didn't deserve one. But a future with someone like Rose Rydell? God. It was a dream come true.

"Please…" She was begging him? Hell, no. He should have been begging her.

"Rose, I'll continue to want you for as long as you want me."

Her body relaxed under his and she stared up at him. Her fingers dipped into his hair and ran along his scalp. "I've never had it done to me either, you know."

"What?"

"Umm… what you did to me."

"Oral sex?"

She blushed to her neck. "I never imagined it was like that…"

He couldn't help his cocky grin. "You liked it?"

"I…I almost passed out it was so overwhelming and strong and oh, yes. Yes, I loved it. But don't you mind…"

"Mind what, Rosie?" An amused smile appeared on his face and for the first time, he couldn't wait to hear what she had to say. He loved her funny thoughts and distracted wondering. Her uncertainty with sex words and her prissiness about saying them, even though she turned out to be quite adept at *doing* them. She loved doing them, even if she couldn't talk about them.

"Me… my body… you know…"

"On my face? In my mouth? Tasting you?" he teased her. Lifting his head, he laughed out loud at her furious blush. She threw her arm over her eyes and he grabbed it. "Oh, hell no. You don't get to hide from me. You'll get used to my crassness eventually. When it has to do with sex, I can't help it. I loved eating you out. I'd do it every day. I'll make you come as often as you like to compensate for Benton fuck-head. Whatever that jerk's problem was, it can't be you. You're the hottest piece of ass I've ever had. And before you hit me for my words, think about what I'm saying."

She had been about to sock him in the arm for referring to her as the *hottest piece of ass*, but then he'd added, *ever*. "And I'm to assume you've had a lot of ass?"

He nodded, his expression completely solemn and serious. "Yes. So I'm prepared to comment and make comparisons. You. Are. Hot. Whatever issue he has, control freakiness or whatever… it wasn't you. It was all him."

Her entire face contorted into several expressions. First, he shocked her with his words, "eating you out," although she hoped he would and that sparked in her eyes; and then came her dawning realization she wasn't the problem in her former relationship. Benton was. That thought probably never occurred to kind-hearted, worry-wart, sweet, funny, quirky, neat, clean Rose.

His Rose.

"Do you think?" she whispered.

He smiled. "I know. You were lucky to escape his bad sex. You know not everyone is good at it. Just a sad fact of life. People can ruin anything."

It was impossible not to laugh at his dry tone.

"I'm glad you aren't with him now," he added, sweetly.

"Because it allowed me to find you?"

He almost argued with her. It was so new and strange that it still confused him. But instead, he nodded. "Fuck. Who would guess that?"

"Not me. But I'm so glad…" she whispered as she scooted down. She trusted him not to have sex and only wanted to cuddle up against him and lie in his arms. He responded by wrapping her up tightly in his embrace and hugging her back.

Moments of silence passed until she nudged him. "Mateo?"

"Hmm?"

"This is the Love Shack. This place isn't horrible anymore. It's ours. Our secret place to be alone. So I think we should christen it The Love Shack."

His heart flipped and did somersaults. He blinked with surprise and joy at her words. She fully accepted and embraced his hovel. This shack. So much that she named it something cute?

"The Love Shack?" His tone was incredulous.

"Yes." Hers was pleased and chirpy. She cuddled back against him, as open, honest and trusting as a small child. In a matter of moments, her steady breathing told him she contentedly fell asleep. With him. In his—no, in their—Love Shack. He fell asleep next to her, humming the old song by the B-52s, "Love Shack," in his head.

CHAPTER 10

ONE DAY IN AUGUST, Rose said, "Iris had a guy who stayed over the entire weekend."

"So?" Mateo rubbed his long fingers over her shoulders.

"Apparently, they had sex the entire weekend. He's a stranger. No one I've ever seen around here."

"Again, so? You and I had sex most of the weekend too." His voice was so reasonable, he almost sounded disinterested. "Iris doesn't need your supervision or want you monitoring her movements. She can take care of herself."

Rose sighed. "I just wish she'd talk to me. She tells me nothing. We live together and I don't even know who is in her bedroom."

"And she doesn't know whose bedroom you're in."

She lifted her head and replied, "But that's because of your job. Your livelihood depends on us not telling anyone lest we incur the wrath of my dad. Which is very different from not telling Iris. The guy's name is Quinn."

"Yeah, I know. I met him and helped with his car."

"He's also a billionaire, you know."

"I figured he was money. He reeked of wealth. But that's more than I guessed."

"His family is crazy successful. Larkin Group International is the source of the family fortune."

"Oh? Damn. That's not what I pictured Iris getting into. I gathered he wasn't struggling by the car he drove and his cocky demeanor, but never to that extent."

"No. I wonder why he's so into Iris? What does he want from her? A female mechanic from River's End? Look at all this about him." Saying that, she showed Mateo all the internet scuttlebutt she dug up on Quinn and his family, which was long and extensive. There was a lengthy dating history too and not a single one of the women he dated came close to being like Iris. "He's obviously using her."

Mateo coughed to cover his laugh. "For what? Good auto care? There would be no reason for him to use her. He's a rich, hot, desired bachelor and he comes here far more often than she goes to his place. Which means, Rosie, I think he likes her."

Rose scowled, staring at the rich bachelor's picture on the tablet, still suspiciously sure he had ulterior motives towards her little sister. "I just don't like him."

Mateo grabbed her around the waist and rubbed his nose on her neck as he kissed the back of it. "And that's why I like you. That protective, caring core under all your primness and propriety."

She elbowed his gut playfully, before falling against him. "I'm just worried about his true intentions. I don't want Iris getting hurt."

"Anyone who saw us together, would warn you of the same thing."

She considered that and replied, "But they'd be wrong."

"Yes, so perhaps you are wrong too."

She let it go. Without directly interfering, Rose kept an

eye on Quinn the Billionaire who frequented River's End for her sister.

Mateo hugged her and kissed her head. She got thrilled each and every time he did it. It was so unusual for him. She tried to keep track of every single kiss and valued each individual one.

There was so much to figure out. To celebrate. To talk about. To do together. The sex was unimaginable and now that she'd experienced it, even the thought of all the things Mateo did to her body and how he made her feel, caused her to squirm with discomfort, but in the most delicious way possible. Sex nearly became a drug she craved. An addiction. She'd watch him across the shop when she made excuses to visit her dad or Iris. Mateo always gave her his practiced neutral, deep stare and managed to keep his cool like no one she ever knew. She'd often blush and a small, dopey smile would form on her lips, no matter how she tried to appear unconcerned and disinterested. All that existed between them would spring up like new blooms in a blink of seeing his face, his eyes and his freaking arms. When he buried himself in his work beneath the hood of a car, that turned her on too. Every aspect of Mateo was an aphrodisiac.

He could hide it so much better than she could. She could barely contain herself. When she showed up later at their Love Shack, he'd grab her, kiss her and do wonderful things to her body. Their long make-out sessions often led to touching and licking places that still made her blush when she talked about them. When he entered her body, she felt instantly sated after a full day of longing for him. Then, with visible exasperation, he'd tell her to keep her cool around him. Quit blushing. Quit smiling as if they shared a secret. She usually replied that they did and she just couldn't stop herself.

She'd smile and kiss him on the side of his mouth or trail

little butterfly kisses down his neck, which always ended with him straining towards her. He couldn't resist her. She soon discovered his vacant, scary demeanor was just a show. He was sweet and kind and the only thing he wanted was her unadulterated happiness. He was uncomfortable being affectionate and talking or showing he cared, but that too was owing to his lack of trust in anyone. He hadn't overcome most of the negative things from his youth and it would take a lot of time before she could nurture him long enough to trust her to release it. She imagined herself on the receiving end of it and believed she was the luckiest girl alive.

She adored Mateo. Their relationship moved fast and easy once it started, like a lighter igniting gasoline. Despite the long fuse, their chemistry promised a marvelous explosion that was fast and wonderful and different for her. Like nothing she ever experienced or felt.

And much of it took place in the small Love Shack that Mateo hated and Rose grew to cherish. When they went to the river, they were always careful not to touch each other or exchange suspicious looks when they were on the family beach. They always staggered their arrivals and never showed up together. But after they disappeared down the river to their hidden sanctuary, they could flirt, touch and engage in sex without any inhibitions. Oh, that was one of her favorite pastimes.

Eventually, the leaves lost their green foliage as the weather cooled down. Occasionally, an oddball day in September would turn out to be too hot, but most of the time, it was achingly pleasant. The yellow, red and gold leaves gilded the valley, and the cobalt blue sky seemed crisper and clearer, like a high-definition TV screen. The beautiful autumn days also delivered the alluring aromas of dried leaves and spicy pines.

And every day, Rose felt privileged to either spend the

evening or the night with Mateo. She did not miss a single one.

When Rose started working full time for her mom, she came home tired most evenings. She was still getting accustomed to working with young kids. Just trying to keep their attention focused on subjects most of them didn't really want to do was a challenge. They complied but only after their parents demanded it. Rose had twelve clients, four came to her in person and the rest saw her via a face-to-face app on the computer. She saw all of them a minimum of twice a week.

She was exhausted, but thrilled at the work she was doing. She enjoyed building her own client list and tutoring for her mom one afternoon a week. That was when she could delve into a higher level of program that they used. It was far more intricate and involved, requiring different models to follow, depending on the needs of each learner.

One day, Mateo told her, "Your sister is acting weird. She clings to her phone like you do. Always mooning at it. I think her boy-toy is in constant contact with her. Never thought I'd see Iris acting so stupid," Mateo muttered.

Rose slid her bare leg up his and he reacted. "I act the same way about you."

He grinned and it was cocky and proud. "Yeah. But I like that. We're talking about Iris. She's not supposed to be that way. We talk about cars and paint colors… not how many times her boy-toy called or whatever. I hate to see her being so…"

"Womanly?"

"Yeah." Mateo sighed and she slugged him in the arm. Playfully. But not completely. She hated herself for the streak of jealousy she felt regarding Mateo's long-standing friendship with her sister. They shared a bond that she and Mateo could not share. Iris and he had a mutual interest that Rose couldn't understand no matter how hard she tried.

Rose remembered losing her dad's interest to Iris for the same reason. That's probably where it started. She hated feeling so small and petty.

In October, the first chilly mornings crept into the Love Shack. Rose shivered against Mateo and said, "We need space heaters."

"Yeah, these shacks lack any insulation." But Rose doubted Mateo ever used a space heater before and simply opted to freeze instead. Why Mateo couldn't take care of himself or his creature comforts remained a mystery to Rose. It never seemed to occur to him that he could be happier in more pleasant surroundings. He was allowed the basic comforts. No, he was *owed* them.

He tossed his phone on the bed when he got up. Rose picked it up to move it before making the bed. She glanced down at a reading app that was open and the words crossing the page. Glancing closer, she was surprised when the words computed and made sense.

Mateo was reading Shakespeare. Really. Honest to God, Shakespeare.

Rose set his phone to the side as he came out of the bathroom. She said, "Mateo? Were you reading Shakespeare's The Taming of the Shrew?"

He glanced at his phone when she pointed at it. His shoulders lifted, and he casually went to his dresser to find a clean shirt. "Yeah. So?"

"Why?"

"I told you before I like his work."

"You did. But you just read it for pleasure?"

"Yes, Rose. Surprise, surprise. The gangbanger can read." He turned away, slipping into his shirt when his sarcastic words hit her like a spray of buckshot. It hurt her when he did things like that. He defensively tried to lump her in with the others who misunderstood him.

She ignored his response and walked up behind him. "What else do you like to read?"

He sighed and stomped the few steps to grab his phone. He pressed some buttons, then handed it to her. A library of books. So here, too, was where he spent his money. Fancy shoes and ebooks. Lots and lots of ebooks. Most of them said *read* on them. The titles included almost every single classic she could think of.

"All those times I saw you on your phone... you were reading?"

"Mostly. I'm a very fast reader."

She set the phone down, taking in his complete library. She, like so many others, totally underestimated him.

"How were your grades in school?"

"I dropped out in my junior year. Remember?"

"But when you were still in it? Did learning come easy?"

"Yeah. I could have been a straight A student if I wanted to be."

"Didn't you, just a little?"

"Sure. But why all the questions?"

Sadness filled her heart but she didn't tell him that. She grabbed his hand and tugged him closer to her, wrapping her arms around his shoulders. He, as usual, hesitated at first. Every single time she reached out to him seemed to floor him. She lifted up on her tiptoes and set a kiss at the base of his neck.

"I bet if you'd ever been allowed to live your life without your family's inferior guidance, you could have excelled in the theater, acting, directing, or whatever. You could have also become a band nerd who got straight As and a full scholarship to any university in the country. I think if you had your IQ tested, you'd find out you were way above average, in the genius range most likely, and the saddest thing is that no one freaking noticed. No one in your life fostered it. No one cultivated or directed that insane curiosity you have about everything. You need new things to learn just to fill up the bottomless depths of your brain. Your brain is that beautiful and interesting; and you know it is. You know everything I'm saying is true. You were attracted to me for a reason and I think it's because you sensed I might discover it. I might see it. See the real you. And I do, Mateo."

She pressed her head under his neck, near his collarbone as she fully held him against her. At first, he was silent and did not respond. He reacted like that whenever he was unsure, or she was too close to him and he couldn't process it.

Suddenly, his arms dropped to her waist, and he brushed his lips over her scalp and kissed her, nearly knocking the wind out of her with the pressure he used to yank her next to him. "Yeah…"

She didn't expect him to reply, but he surprised her when he didn't argue. She was flabbergasted he admitted it. "So you do realize how smart you are then?"

His shoulders shrugged. "Sure. It's not like I never heard it before. I could read when I was four, two years before my older brother. I could do anything my teachers asked me to do and on the first time. I holed up at the local library, poring through stacks of books. As many as I could devour, usually at least one book a day. No one noticed or cared though."

Her heart crumpled in her chest. Rose was pampered and loved throughout her school years and everyone encouraged her and did anything they could to help her succeed. Once, Daisy had some minor problems and their mom was the one who noticed and corrected them. Her mom and Rose taught kids who were the opposite of Mateo; they were smart but unable to accomplish simple tasks in their learning. Rose and

Allison helped them read, and alternate ways to learn their multiplication charts rather than simply memorizing them with endless drills. They worked on spelling and sight words using different learning techniques, many of which were based on pictures.

"Imagine you as the band geek," she said softly. She was kidding, but not really. Her tone was too tragic for it to be just kidding.

"Imagine that. Think the neck-tat would exclude me?" He teased her too.

She reached up and rubbed the tattoo. "You would have done big things, huh? If anyone who could've made a difference ever noticed or encouraged or helped you… Instead of going to prison, you might have gone to a great university on a band scholarship or from the drama club."

"Maybe. It doesn't really matter now. I have a prison record. I am a felon. The neck-tat says it all. It's me, now, Rose. And hell. I also have a profession and a job that requires my skills and abilities. I have so much more than most of the people where I came from and used to know."

"That's not good enough now. No. You don't have to settle or be indebted and grateful. You—"

He set his fingers on her lips, gently shutting her up. It was the first time he'd ever done such a thing. "You don't know where I'm from. Or what I witnessed. Or how close I came to becoming it… yeah, this is very far. Now my life is freaking amazing and my successes exceed my failures. So I do have much to be grateful for."

She let his words filter into her brain. She wanted to argue but she understood he knew this part of his life better than she did. She nodded. "Why did you seek me out?"

He let her go and tossed his long, lithe body onto the half-made bed. "Your red hair caught my gaze the first time I saw you. You came in to tell your dad something. Then your blue, huge eyes widened in shock at me when he introduced us.

"Iris and I were still circling each other like fighting roosters and then I noticed you. You were starting your master's degree. Your dad was plainly proud as he introduced you and told me that. I never knew anyone who got a master's degree. You were as rare as a unicorn to me. Beautiful. Different. Smart. Naturally, you caught my attention. But you were also afraid of me. Disdainful too, I believe. I was all the things you tried to avoid, and no sane parent would advise you not to. That was my reality and it should have stayed it. The truth? You have no business here."

She flung herself at him and straddled his legs. He jerked back from where he rested his elbows on his knees to stare at the floor. Rose was knocking his arms away and he had to lean back even further to accommodate her as she straddled his lap. Her knees were bent and her feet were under her butt. She grabbed his face in her hands. "I belong here. With you. I don't care what you look like or what I look like. Strip all that away and we exist, Mateo, as two souls that connect and talk and our brains match. We love the same things. And we will explore those things. As far as the world can take us. We're not done. Your life and mine are just starting out together. You are my reality and I am yours. So deal with it, Mateo Alvarez. This is so far beyond money or appearances or histories or even prison records. This is the real us."

He gripped her neck with his hand and held her head still as he all but glared into her eyes. "Why are you being like this?"

"Like what?" she whispered as she licked her lips. Sometimes, albeit rarely, Rose glimpsed the harsher side of Mateo. The side that both attracted and scared her. That side was in charge, she believed, when Mateo held the gun on the clerk and shot him.

"Like… unbelievable." His face didn't lose its edge, nor his voice its meanness. But his eyes hungered for her. He liked what she said. And what she believed about him.

"Because I love you," she said softly. They were words she never acknowledged out loud or even in her head. But the moment they passed her lips, she knew they were true. Truer than anything she ever said or felt. Truer than her eye color. She loved him. Everything about him. His history, his body, his heart, his brain and his thoughts. She hoped their future together was just starting.

He slightly freaked out and let her go. He pushed her torso back, almost dumping her to the floor as he prepared to fully jump up, but she grabbed his shoulders to keep her balance. "God, Rose. Don't… Don't say things like that."

Grabbing her waist, he lifted her away from him. He set her on the bed and got up. He paced. The floor space was laughably small and his frustration appeared comical. But she didn't laugh or smile at his obvious distress. He wasn't ready to hear that. Or say it back. Or did he even feel the same? Probably all three. Maybe he didn't feel it. But he still needed for her to say it to start to believe it.

Pacing, he muttered. "Why would you say that? Because I'm the ex-con you like to rebel with who gives you a decent fuck?"

Ouch. She flinched. He hadn't resorted to foul language for a while. He was mocking what they had. What they found in each other. But she must have scared him because Mateo lashed out when he was scared. Or unsure. When he felt pushed into feeling something or being urged to talk or share.

"No, because you're an ex-con who reads Shakespeare and Confucius, along with every single historical event of any significance and about the people who were featured in those events. You challenge me and demolish my previously held beliefs. You changed everything I used to think and feel, but in all the best ways. You make me a better person. And when I make love to you, I feel insanely amazing and I treasure those times and feelings. And no matter how hard you try to cheapen or degrade it, you know in your heart you can't. Or change what it means to both of us and to each other. So yes, I love you. I'm not ashamed to admit I'm in love with you."

She got to her feet. "Please don't mock me. Or us. Or what we have together. I know I scare you when I talk like this. You think I'm playing with your emotions and that scares you. But please, don't ruin this."

He swallowed, looking like a feral animal that was cornered and scared. "I can't promise anything... I don't know... you don't know what this is or... or even what you feel."

"I do actually. But that's okay, if you don't." He ran his fingers through his hair. "Mateo, do you want me to leave?"

"You must want to. How do you know I don't still pinch cars? After you leave, how do you know I won't run out and knock over a few convenience stores? You can see I'm not rolling in dough. What makes you trust me to be the law-abiding citizen you want me to be?"

Sigh. Crap. He was still pushing. Rose recalled the first few days of being together with him. She smiled softly. "Well, now I trust you."

"That's it? Your criteria? Do you know how naïve and stupid you could be to trust me? I could make a total fool of you. I could use you. Or abuse you. How do you know I won't do that? You haven't known me long enough to successfully predict my behavior."

"I know that Iris trusts you with her life and she isn't naïve or stupid, is she? And my dad? He's the least naïve person I know, besides you, and they both trust you. So no,

I'm not worried you're using or abusing me or my trust in you.

"I think you're crying out for a prissy, straight-laced, naïve woman, like me, to notice how smart and interesting and wonderful you are. I think you're looking for someone exactly like me to notice you. And now that I have, you're uncomfortable. And you don't trust it. Which I understand, given your history. Your upbringing versus mine. I was taught to trust myself and my gut before I trusted any others. You weren't given that luxury. You were betrayed. Hurt. So yes, I believe you aren't doing anything nefarious beyond what I already know about."

He paced more and muttered. Then he frowned and scowled at her. She could easily picture his personality landing him in jail. Being nervous, hyper, and angry, the negative energy was steaming off him. But she had to hold onto that and remember he still had a lot to work through and a few weeks couldn't undo all the years of molding he'd had to endure.

She got to her feet with a sigh and he stopped talking. She stepped out to pass him, reaching up to grab his arm and pull him to her mouth to kiss his cheek. "I'm going to get ready for work. You need to do that now too. But if you prefer, just stress over me loving you and stew on my trust for a while. I'm going now. See you tonight?" Her tone was so pleasant. It was annoying. She all but chirped as she smiled. And she knew its desired effect: calming him and bringing him back to the present moment. It was the easiest way for Rose to extricate Mateo from the loop of fear and distrust that constantly replayed in his brain. "Okay?" she pressed.

He nodded and let her go. She smiled softly before turning to leave.

One hard conversation down, maybe a hundred more to go?

CHAPTER 11

SOLVING MATEO'S DISTRUST PROBLEM and overcoming his doubts regarding her and himself would take more than a few good talks and lots of sex. She understood that. It required immediate action and even if she had no idea what to do next, she had to keep trying. She hoped by nurturing his trust and belief in her, he would hopefully learn to trust himself.

December brought the snow and cold, with roaring winds and constant precipitation. Snowdrifts over a foot high covered the land. The Love Shack had to constantly keep the heaters running. Rose insisted on helping to pay his utility bill as keeping the place warm was mainly her idea. And she managed to keep it snugly warm.

In the months since their "I love you" talk, Rose said it to Mateo almost daily. He never reciprocated. Although he didn't fully appreciate it, he quit pacing and snarling every time she said it. He apologized for the occasional times he burst out with a nasty comment about "fucking" in some version or another, which he only did to hurt her because he knew how much she disliked it.

He also used sex to show her the emotions he couldn't articulate to her. He wanted her to feel them from him. And in that context, she believed he did love her. On a daily basis. He loved to kiss and lick and caress her in the least touched places she most craved, even though she blushed whenever she thought about it later or heard him talk about it. But oh, God, he did it with such loving care that she knew she meant so much more to him than anything or anyone else in his life.

"You are the most responsive woman in the world when you're being eaten out," he muttered into her thigh one day after her body climaxed hard.

She finally landed, coming down from her spiraling high, swatting his face on her thigh and chiding, "Damn it. Don't call it that. It makes it sound so gross."

He laughed and lifted his face before kissing her thigh, her mound, her stomach and one nipple, then the other, her neck and finally, her lips. "You didn't consider it gross when you clamped my head between your thighs like a vise before screaming in ecstasy." His eyes gleamed with pride. Oh, how he seemed to love to make her come. And embarrass her about it.

"No… but can't you call it something that's not so gross sounding?"

"Face-planting you?"

"Worse."

"Cunnilingus?"

"No. That sounds like a scientific experiment."

"Okay… why don't we just use its actual name: oral sex?"

"No, that relegates it to being too clinical and there's nothing clinical about us. It's lovely and so intimate, the most intimate act of all… Doesn't it make you feel things?"

"Feel things? Sure. I feel you all wet and warm and smelling like—"

She kicked her legs and screamed. "Oh, my God. Stop."

He couldn't contain his laughter. She shrieked. "You did that on purpose."

"Every time. I love the outrage you exhibit when I say common sex words."

"Tell me… how do you feel about me? Do you consider that act a chore? Eating me out?" She shuddered, hating the phrase.

His smile faded. "No, it's definitely not a chore. It's more like…" He twisted his lips as he pondered. "Fuck. It's like a way to worship you. I can't believe you're here with me sometimes and I love putting my mouth on you anytime I want to and knowing you welcome it."

"Me too." She sighed happily. "That's how I feel when I do it to you; like I'm worshiping your body. Making you feel good makes me feel wonderful and…"

"I love worshiping you." He smiled as he stared into her eyes. Then he kissed her long and slow. "I can call it that but only if you never tell another soul. It makes me sound like a wuss."

She punched his arm playfully and bit her lip. Suddenly, a worried look appeared on her face and she asked, "You haven't told anyone about us? I mean, in those horrid, graphic details? I really couldn't handle any 'locker room talk' about me and our sex lives. That would humiliate and ultimately devastate me."

He gathered her in his arms. "You really take this stuff seriously, don't you? I've never known anyone who was so serious when it came to sex as you are."

"Yes, because it's that meaningful to me."

He nodded. "I would never tell a soul. You might hear me talking shit with Iris and the crew because that's how we bond. It has no meaning and she knows it. You know I'd never mock or discuss you or us with anyone. Besides no one knows anything about us."

Her shoulders dropped in relief. She pushed the silky strands back that sprang over his forehead. His hair remained short from Rose's frequent clips. "I would love to shout it from the highest mountain. But I also like having you all to myself."

He smiled and a boyishly bashful expression crossed his face. He liked having her attention. And teasing her for her prudishness about sex. He loved to see her near reverence in the way she treated him and their relationship. She believed he loved her already, but he didn't believe it yet.

When January came, Rose grabbed Mateo's hand and said, "Come on. I have a birthday surprise for you." She'd been looking for the perfect gift for a long time, and finally found it.

She dragged him behind her, driving to a small town thirty miles away and parking in front of an old grange that was routinely used by the local farmers and residents. Tonight? She came there for Mateo's surprise.

"What the hell is this?"

She grinned as she tugged him to follow her. They entered the building, which was cool and dark as the night. Snow swirled outside and Mateo complained, because he truly despised the snow. Rose wasn't bothered by snow. It was just another season for her to adjust to.

The group was comprised of six other people who looked like they were all seventy if they were a day. But that was fine. She turned to Mateo. "This group meets every other Tuesday to read and discuss Shakespeare. It's a Shakespeare Club." She beamed. Then she scowled as he turned and stomped out. She had to run after him to catch up.

He shook her hold off. "No." Harsh and mean, that was all he said.

She grabbed his arm harder so he couldn't shake her loose. He'd have to hurt her first. "Mateo, I'll stay here with you. I want to do it too. I enjoy Shakespeare, but babe, you *love* it. You've read every play and sonnet he's ever written more than once and you can recite most of the lines. So yes, this is definitely your crowd."

"You weren't supposed to tell anyone. And what were you thinking? Those old folks won't feel comfortable or glad to welcome a fucking Latino with a criminal record and a neck tattoo? You think they'll just scoot over and let me join their little gathering? Think. Think about it, Rose. I don't belong here in their eyes. And they're right."

Desperate to stop him from leaving, she grabbed him but he shook her off again. "Mateo. You're so wrong. Of course, they will want you. You know more about what they're reading than they do. You love it. And no one knows that. No one knows Shakespeare is your secret passion and they should. You could have been a theatrical, drama/band geek. But no one noticed your talent and skills. Except me. I noticed them and I want to do this with you. Fuck everyone else. They'll welcome you when they see what you know and how brilliant you are. Your tattoo and your record won't matter once they know you. And as to your being Latino? Well, if that is an issue to them, then fuck them. But that isn't going to be what happens. I mean it, Mateo, trust me. Let someone else see you as I see you. They will. I promise."

He didn't trust or believe her. He was angry and in a rage. Almost. However, her words wore down his resistance. He had a hard time opposing her. She took his hand and pulled him back inside. When they entered, they were greeted by the shuffling of seats, big, incredulous eyes, and fleeting glimpses that darted away as soon as they were observed. People even audibly gulped. It was the exact reaction Mateo predicted.

"May we help you?"

"Yes. This is the Shakespeare Club, isn't it? I saw your

189

advertisement for recruiting new members in *The Valley Gazette*. I called and talked to someone named Annette."

"Y—Yes, that is correct. You did." They tilted their heads. Rose wondered what they were thinking? Judging by their suspicious glances, they probably expected to be robbed by the newcomers.

"Good. We came to the right spot then." Rose smiled pleasantly and took a seat, pulling out the seat next her as she glanced at Mateo. He scowled at her as he observed the appalled faces around the room. Uncomfortable about himself, not to mention Rose and the collection of adherents to Shakespeare, he looked every bit as scary and intimidating as they all assumed. What they failed to see was how much they intimidated him. He flopped down on the chair, his obvious discomfort undeniable. Crossing his arms over his chest, he couldn't hide his glaring anger at Rose. His long legs stretched out before him, and he slouched as he scowled, appearing like the quintessential ex-con, someone who didn't care about anything or anyone.

She kicked his shin and he scowled harder at her, sinking further into the role.

Throats cleared and the seat shuffling continued. Rose glanced around at the pleasant, prissy and pristine people who were the opposite of him. Placing her book on the table and her paper tablet beside it, the perfect student as always, she said, "I believe you guys were reading 'Hamlet'? Is that right?"

Mateo pushed away the copy Rose gave him.

The group nodded in unison. One lady, a spry woman of the group, perhaps in her fifties, nodded. "Um, yes. We like to go around and take turns reading the lines of the play. Would either of you like to go first?"

"Sure." Rose smiled, although it was strained. She was more than aware of the stony effect Mateo's mean expression and scary appearance provided as he sat beside her. She read the part they indicated. Naturally it went to Mateo next, who didn't open the book. He just slouched and sprawled, giving Rose a death stare. She gulped hard as she realized she made a huge mistake and said, "Mateo? Y-Y-You're next."

He stared at her and his eyes sparked with hot fire. She remembered the dark depths and the bottomless ebony that made her think he had no soul. Now it made her skin prickle. Was it really such a terrible mistake? Mateo ignored the book. He didn't look around or seem to care about anything but kept staring right at Rose for a full minute. People began to cough and mumble until... He opened his mouth and started to recite his part. From memory. The next line was where he started from, voicing the words with clear, accurate perfection. He read from memory the same number of lines Rose read from the text. Starting with the long section as Hamlet, from Act 3, Scene 1:

To be, or not to be-that is the question:
Whether 'tis nobler in the mind to suffer
The slings and arrows of outrageous fortune
Or to take arms against a sea of troubles,
And by opposing them...

And on he read. It was far more than she could have ever memorized.

Big-eyed, Rose stared at him in shock. Of all the things he'd ever done to astound her, this was the most astounding. The rest of the group fell silent. They too were stunned and awed by Mateo. Submission to the moment and silence followed.

The first lady who spoke to them gulped. "You... you memorized the entire play?"

Mateo didn't blink, gulp or flinch but simply nodded. His scowl was still in place also.

Oh. Oh, my. Even Rose had underestimated him. The lady

nodded and said, "Well, that's very good. This will be easy for you." She glanced briefly at the startled, unsure, big-eyed man sitting beside Mateo. "You're up next, sir."

The man seemed stupefied by her address. "Oh? Oh, right. Yes. Umm… and where would that be?"

Mateo rolled his eyes, leaning forward and plopping his finger onto the man's book to show him where he left off. The old guy looked like an idiot for not following and Mateo simply ignored everybody else as though he were not so gifted or unexpected.

It was a stunning and satisfying moment. The most revealing moment Rose ever witnessed in all of her schooling and even her life. Mateo was simply… wow.

After that first recital, no one questioned Mateo. Everyone read the lines if they wanted to before they began an analysis. There were some interesting takes on it. Then, the woman who was named Deborah, asked Mateo, "Tell me… what do you think?"

Startled, Mateo lifted his eyes and his scowl finally departed now that the older, white woman sought his opinion. He blinked once, then twice. Mateo seemed to have the ability to look inside a person's soul and Rose was sure that was how poor Deborah felt. Rose could have kissed her for asking Mateo his opinion.

"Well, obviously Hamlet is one of the most tragically conflicted characters on the stage ever created…" Mateo not only could recite every word he read, but could also analyze and critique it.

Rose blinked her tears away. The moment was so touching to her. Her boyfriend was evolving… he was becoming all the things she loved, which she found endearing and amazing. Spending his entire life without anyone to notice, nurture or even care about his obvious gifts filled her heart and her eyes with tears. She buried her face into the text so Mateo didn't realize she was crying. She imagined the little boy that no one perceived or realized was a fucking genius. He never had a mentor or someone he loved to celebrate and cultivate his skills. No one ever asked Mateo, *what do you think?*

No one taught him to believe he was worthy, and his dreams to excel as the drama and band geek he should have been, were relegated to the back burner. He was groomed by his family to become a rebellious, scary, ex-con.

Although Rose revered her dad and Iris and found them smart and wonderful with mechanical things, Mateo's mind needed more. His goddamned brilliance needed to be promoted. He knew he was smarter than average people but he never shared it with anyone because he didn't know how to.

Yet, he exhibited his genius all his life by reading to escape his mental and physical confinement.

Rose fisted her hand as she realized she fell in love with the most brilliant, interesting, broken man she could ever imagine. And she loved him fiercely. He was all hers now. She vowed to take better care of him. She'd never underestimate him again and would find new ways to foster his flair for knowledge and expertise. Someday, the whole fucking world would know all about Mateo Alvarez. Her boyfriend. Her heart. Her love.

But for now, she could only blink her tears away. Caught in his gaze, which was much less contentious now that the group so fully embraced him, he gave her a small smile. Rose smiled back but hers was large, and brimming with unconditional love.

CHAPTER 12

*R*OSE TOOK HIM TO a freaking Shakespeare Club. Who did things like that? Who even knew about them? Who else ever cared enough to do any of the things she did? Just Rose. Who else would dare to subject the half dozen retirees, who were trying to enjoy their primary reason to keep busy and socialize, with him? The faces they had when they'd first beheld him. Appalled. Discreetly staring and looking away the moment his glance caught theirs. Skittering gazes, fisting hands, fluttering fingers and one woman even clenched her purse. The poor things. All of the bald, gray- or white-haired club members were initially terrified of him.

Rose did not fully appreciate how real their fear was. His simple presence put everyone on edge. Rose only saw Mateo's discomfort and knew he was feeling stupid. She didn't seem to notice theirs. And his attitude made him look meaner and tougher than he'd ever been. The indifferent attitude was one he often displayed to Rose when he felt out of his league and unsure with her. But now, Rose seemed to forget about it, or perhaps she didn't see it in him anymore?

194

He was puzzled and confused by Rose. Who else would drag him to a thing like that and expect everyone in attendance to accept him? Oh, yeah… Rose. Only Rose. She was the embodiment of everything and everyone Mateo lacked all of his life rolled up into one. She nurtured, cared, supported and fussed about him and his well-being, something his mother had neglected to do. Rose became his champion, supporter, fixer and encourager like a father might be, or maybe an older brother. She was his friend, confidant and the only person he finally felt comfortable with. She was his playmate too and she allowed him to frolic with her as much as he liked. Rose became truly everything and everyone to Mateo's sad, lonely, violent, and kind of miserable existence. When he came to River's End, it was no longer violent, sad and miserable, just lonely, quiet and isolated. As always, he was universally distrusted.

But not by Rose. Not anymore.

They left and she beamed at him as she gushed, "You do realize that you have a photographic memory? No one can memorize entire plays and recite them from exactly where another reader randomly ends. And then you counted how many lines I read and you read the exact same amount. Mateo. Oh, my God, you're…"

"Brilliant?" he supplied at all her oohing and ahhing. And his sarcastic tone and hurried annoyance were all a show. Goddamn if it didn't feel nice that someone *finally* knew. He didn't need any accolades or gold star awards for it, not even a decent GPA from school as proof. It felt nice that someone fully realized his talents and Rose witnessed them often. Yeah, he was pretty fucking exceptional.

"Brilliant. Amazing. Unbelievable. You are an unsung and complete genius."

He grabbed her when they were about to get into the car. They shivered as the snow fell around them. But still, he held her. She easily slid into his embrace, despite their jackets and hats and gloves. "Thank you," he said quietly, barely whispering into her ear. Not for the birthday gift but for every other damn thing she did for him. He blinked and his eyes prickled, almost like hot tears were filling them. But he blinked again harder to prevent such stupid sentiments from becoming visible.

Rose didn't. When he glanced down, tears streaked her face. He wiped them off. "Get in the car before you freeze to death." His tone was gruff, but his heart was melting.

Once inside her car, they both warmed up quickly. They always drove Rose's car because of its strong heater and general reliability. Mateo never minded driving his finicky vehicle since he knew how to fix it, anywhere and anytime. Rose didn't want to take any chances that evening in three-degree temperatures and a snow storm. Blizzards happened without warning around there. One thing Mateo wasn't used to were the cold winters here.

Tucked in beside the heater, she sniffed. "No one caught it, did they? The power of your beautiful brain?"

"Nope." He shrugged, staring hard at the road through the snow, ice and compacted drifts that obscured the streets.

"They're just oblivious. Anyone working with you should have noticed it."

"My family strove to do the opposite. No one gave a shit about my schooling or did anything to encourage it. I didn't do my school work, Rose. I just skated through. I didn't want to make myself a target for resentment."

"You still should have been noticed by an educator. So what if your family wasn't traditional? And your mom and dad weren't doting on you at home with their two point five kids and a picket fence? You should have been noticed. Your brilliance is rare, and I've never seen it before. You came from a poor family of color. I've had enough education to see the huge biases in our public education system. And unfortunately, you were completely ignored by it. People assumed you were one thing and that stopped them from ever considering that you could be special and rare."

"Rosie, I purposely bombed the state testing every time they were given out. I hated them. They insulted me. So I picked the wrong answers. That's how contrary I liked to be."

"You were just bored. Duh. Mateo, it wasn't even your fault. You were probably too exceptional for even their damn gifted or high-achieving programs. And your negative attitude shouldn't have been a disqualifier. Someone with a good educational background should have noticed what I witnessed and a long time ago."

She crossed her arms over her chest as if her last comment was final. He was silent for a few miles, then asked her, "Why the tears?"

"It breaks my heart that no one knew what a genius you are, and yet, even as a little kid you knew it, and still, no one noticed. You learned to hide and downplay it. You were just taken advantage of and cheated out of a life and that's what hurts my heart."

He smiled to himself. "So you're going to fix it?"

"Yes. I am. I love your heart. Your brain. You." She sighed. "I just don't know exactly how to go about it yet."

"I know of a few ways you could show it," he replied, resorting to his usual innuendo and the one subject he could respond to and communicate about: sex.

He squirmed in his seat and aimed a glance at the dark, snowy world. It seemed to symbolize how he felt as a kid. So smart that everything was easy for him to do, he was craving attention, dying for someone to notice his quick learning aptitude. Someone to foster it. To make something, anything, harder or more interesting for him. Having everything so easy bored him to death. He hated to be bored by anything.

But despite his brain power, he didn't have the emotional maturity to handle his genius. He knew how different he was, but didn't know what to do about it. He longed to find somewhere to fit in. Everything he was and felt and wanted were the polar opposite of what his family and gang affiliates wanted. He was expected to be like them, not as he was. Mateo felt blind and lost, groping in the dark for something familiar and being hit in the face by hard ice because no one cared or knew or noticed him.

Until Rose came along.

He glanced at her. She changed everything and became everything to him. What could she possibly receive of value from him?

"Would you go back to the Shakespeare Club?"

"Maybe. It was kind of fun reciting the lines to their old faces and watching their eyes bug out with shock and disbelief. Maybe I would just for the fun of it."

"Mateo. I don't believe you. You liked it; I know you did. You love Shakespeare. You liked discussing it and hearing the takes the others got from the material. I saw it. The flash in your eyes, the way you replied to the others who spoke. You even nodded your head a few times in agreement. Even if you didn't elaborate the first time, you will. After you feel more comfortable. So don't bullshit me."

He did love Shakespeare. He first read it in middle school and then began to devour every play and sonnet during high school. Alone, of course. He borrowed the books from the library. He also had one textbook he stole from an English class. Buying ebook versions when he was older and could afford them, he read the plays and sonnets again and again, just for pleasure.

"Mateo?"

"Fine. Yeah. I love Shakespeare."

"Tell me about it. How does Shakespeare speak to you? Why do you love him? Explain it."

He gritted his teeth and scowled but finally sighed and said, "The words are musical. And they speak to all people. His plays are ancient and use old English, yet they are still relevant and lyrical. His words and thoughts are parts of a song. It made me feel smug and shitty happy to be smarter than the rest of my classmates. Like it was a secret I shared with Shakespeare."

She nodded. "Thank you. That's what I guessed. But thank you for trusting me enough to tell me that. You must realize you're starting to trust me."

"I trust you."

"Sure you do. But I'm not talking about cheating on you. I mean, trusting your heart and soul to me. Your brain. Telling me your likes and dislikes, your thoughts and feelings. No, you haven't really trusted me with the real you, Mateo. It's so engrained in you to be suspicious and distrust everyone. I saw that from the start. But with enough time and effort, you'll get through it and there are no words I could say to prove it. Only actions. Consistently predictable and reliable actions. But you will grow to trust me."

"What do you mean? You sound like I'm a house plant that you're trying to keep alive."

"You kind of are. Yes. And the metaphors of water and plant food become my trust and love... but I know you get it." She grinned, knowing how cringe-worthy that was.

She was also right. About all of it. He chanced a look her way. "How do you know all those things are right?"

"Because your exceptional brain power doesn't extend to your heart. You're like a child that just discovered it's there... Your capacity to care for others and allow others to care for you. Right now, I have to read your emotions, since you can't tell me them, and I'm finding ways to help you realize them for yourself. And you will return to that club. You can't resist your love of Shakespeare even if all the old people assumed you were there to rob them at gunpoint."

"So you noticed that too?"

"Honey, you have a neck tattoo and a dark, forbidding look when you want to. Of course, I noticed it. I knew exactly how they felt because I felt the same way once. We'll work on your mean demeanor too. Someday. But for now, you need it for your self-protection. I get that now."

"And what? You're preparing to start fixing me?"

"No, more like, I'm allowing you to trust me and the world around you, so you don't have to guard yourself so much or so harshly."

He fell silent. He was annoyed. And unwilling to admit she was completely right.

WINTER WITH ROSE was unlike any other. It was filled with sex and lots of it. The night began at four PM and Mateo never once cared about it or got bored. The nights were spent talking and reading, things he never did with anyone. They also discussed at length what he read and devoured. He never had anyone to share his thoughts with, never mind, constantly. To the point of distraction. Every topic was important to Rose. She asked a lot of questions. She wanted to know what he knew. She couldn't read half as fast as Mateo or remember the minute details as well as he could, but she encouraged him to vent and explore what his brain soaked up like a dry sponge in a water-filled sink. Mateo absorbed the information just like a thirsty sponge. Without any work or effort, his brain assembled the information, and the metaphor of a sponge was the only way to describe how his brain registered the written word.

She was fascinated by the process. She would often just stare at him as he spoke or read.

One evening, he lifted his left hand and put his palm and splayed fingers right on her face like he was making a handprint. Then he gently pushed her face away without glancing up from his e-reader. "You're watching me like a science experiment again."

She giggled and distracted him from the late 18th Century France, an era that he was currently exploring. "I love watching a genius at work."

He set the tablet aside and scooted towards her as he pulled her to him. "Yeah? Then wait until you see my tongue at work; it goes way beyond brilliance to the realm of exquisite…"

Usually, their evenings were filled with new subjects to discuss. Mateo finally had someone who loved to listen to him. And he listened to her. She taught him about trust and emotions and feelings. She often demonstrated how his self-protection made him come off as uncaring to the world. He knew that, but not as fully as she explained it. She was the first person to encourage him to let his invisible wall down just a little.

He went to the Shakespeare Club, alone, without Rose. She guessed he'd open up more without her being there and he did. Rose didn't love Shakespeare, but the old, retired people did. They loved to quote and parse Shakespeare's true meaning. And Mateo looked forward to the Tuesdays when they met. Everyone, including Mateo, forgot he was forty years younger than them, and his many tattoos became invisible as they all participated in the conversations that usually exceeded the club's prescribed time frame. He was a valued member and became an integral part of their meetings.

In addition to the plays, they sometimes discussed other subjects besides Shakespeare. One man in the group was a favorite of Mateo's. His name was Roger and Mateo learned he served in Vietnam when he occasionally related a tale or two about it. Mateo started to glimpse the torture and guilt in Roger's eyes over the things he'd done and seen. Roger was tough. There was no doubt about that. One day, he asked Mateo to grab a coffee with him on a Saturday morning. After that, they kept doing it. The guy was not a wuss, and Mateo understood that very well, yet he too attended the Shakespeare Club. He admitted to Mateo that it was his wife's dream to attend it together. She'd nagged and pleaded and he'd refused… until she died… Now, he came for her. But after sitting there and listening, he realized how much he liked it. His regret that he never shared his wife's love of theater and Shakespeare haunted him and he often said if only he could go back…

Something about the old guy clicked with Mateo, even when it shouldn't have. Rose smiled when he told her. "Your experiences might be different, but the effects on your heart and mind can be similar."

She was usually right.

Mateo belonged to a club and found a new friend. Someone like the grandfather he never had. He also had a girlfriend who was beautiful, hot, kind and sweet, someone who changed his entire life. She was the only woman he wanted. So much happened from what he erroneously thought would simply be relegated to a singular experience of sex on the beach.

It was Annette from the club who first mentioned the community theater in Wenatchee was performing "Romeo and Juliet." Wenatchee was an hour and ten minutes from River's End. Mateo crumpled up the flier and shoved it into his pocket.

But Rose found it later. Why didn't he throw it into the trash at the coffee shop? Why did he drag it home? Rose was starting to undress him for some worshiping of her own, a wonderful blow job to put it in more adult terms, and she found the crumpled paper. She stopped undressing him and opened the wrinkled paper to read it. Glancing over at him, his hard-on deflated when her thoughts began clicking. The pleasure and delight her mouth had planned for him fell to the wayside. He sighed in disappointment as he flopped down beside her.

"No," he said before she could speak.

"But it's meant to be. It's your favorite Shakespearean play." Why did he tell her so damn much?

"Uh-uh, Rose."

"Rehearsals are conducted in the evenings and on the weekend. You could handle that."

"No. N. O."

"Little Mateo. Remember little twelve-year-old Mateo who wanted to take drama and band but had to lift cars for his selfish dad? Remember the boy you could have been? Do it for him. For your smart, articulate, brainiac Mateo. Do it for the child who never could pursue his wants and needs and likes. Do it because you *can* now."

"Oh sure, the neck-tat will really work well as the lead of a Shakespearean play."

She shrugged. "Wear a turtleneck then. Audition for it. They'll be so blown away by your performance, you'll have them in your pocket. You can reveal the tats later on."

"Rose…"

She smiled sweetly and addressed his pants again. "I'm just saying, think about it, honey." She was condescending to him. She already decided he'd do it even though she hadn't convinced him. She knew how to get what she wanted. Arguing with him wasn't the way. She humored him. He knew it. His body jerked towards her when she grabbed his hardening dick again with the softest, most loving smile.

Setting herself over his lap, she let her red hair spread over his legs like a beautiful auburn blanket. He soon forgot what she said, he was so lost to the consummate gift that her mouth became for him.

Goddamn if he didn't go to the stupid audition wearing a turtleneck. He was grumpy and surly about it all week. Not only to her, but also to Iris and Shane and Chan and Jeff. Iris flipped him off as she muttered, "You need to get laid, Alvarez, just so the rest of us can stand you."

He did. But that didn't improve his mood. He hated venturing into unknown spaces. He hated being exposed to new people, especially a crowd of them. Never mind they were comprised of small-town, theater wannabes. Ha. Why were all these people spending time doing some under-funded, under cared about and underrated, hack rendition, of one of the most famous plays in the world? Who were they to ruin such brilliance?

And why the fuck was he here? Adding to it? Or more like taking away from it? Why would he do this to himself?

But… he was.

Mateo was the only person of color at the audition. That exception made him downright nasty as he waited in the audience for his turn. Rose clutched his hand and he sunk down in the seat, his head nearly dipping below the back of the chair. He despised it. And he resented Rose right then as they waited for his turn. His leg jiggled, his stomach knotted and he feared he would be sick. He could not do it.

He'd already memorized the entire script, so that was nothing. But how did he say the lines? How did he perform the dialogue? He couldn't. He never tried. No way.

The crowd was mostly older people again. All were white and most seemed affluent. This was their something to do on Tuesday. People like him, on the other hand, were either working late or drinking or going to their second jobs to survive until the next day. He almost bolted out. He didn't belong there. He wasn't one of them. He was an ex-con with a neck-tat and a brother who was in a gang. He should have been in one too. His leg jiggled harder. Rose clutched his arm as if to anchor him there. He was about to get up and flee when Roger sat down. Out of nowhere, the old guy sat beside him. He nodded and smiled. "You gotta land a role in this play. No one wants to watch all these old farts butchering all the text and flavor of it."

Mateo slowly calmed down. He scowled hard at the old man and then at Rose, giving them both the kind of look to make people assume he was in a gang. But he stayed put. For Rose. And for Roger. Because Roger was right. They were butchering it to ribbons. Mateo could at least say the lines without having to think about remembering them.

He heard his name being called and stood to his full height. He was wearing clothes he'd never be caught dead in before: blue jeans and a white turtle-neck sweater. He thought he looked like a cheesy prick when he saw his reflection. But Rose assured him that her ex, the asshole, Benton Smith, would arrive in such an ensemble, so Mateo hoped it would appeal to this crowd.

But once Mateo stepped on the stage and the blinding lights allowed him to see the few sparsely filled seats, he forgot. Everything. He forgot Roger and Rose and all the people judging him and his words. He forgot he was a prison punk. And that he didn't look right for any of the roles. He forgot he was too tough and cool for something like this. Instead, he let the words speak for themselves and they leapt from his mouth and echoed down the hall. He ceased being Mateo Alvarez and became instantly transformed. He became someone new and different and better than he was. Losing himself in the words, Mateo realized how much fun it was. He felt wonderful and really wanted to do it again. He recalled himself watching a terrible amateur production of Macbeth at his high school. He remembered how badly he'd wanted to do it because he knew he was better than any of them and could never forget his lines.

A deafening silence followed his trance-like audition as soon as the words stopped flowing from his mouth. The hall was deathly quiet and he blinked several times as he tried to realize what had happened.

What had he done?

He was such a fool. He did the one thing he could not stand: he humiliated himself.

Suddenly, the room was loud with clapping. Lots of it. The audience was comprised of the crew, the producers and a few people who were trying out so it wasn't a large crowd, but they all clapped and whistled. Shit, one of the producers was standing up and clapping. A standing ovation for him.

Mateo quickly ducked off the stage, embarrassed he got so far into the role. He lost himself in it. Slumping beside Rose and Roger, he slunk down into his seat and didn't acknowledge them or say anything as he glared at his sneakers.

But when it was all over, they called his name. Mateo was selected to play the lead role, Romeo.

He stared at Rose, who smiled with wisdom and optimism. She never doubted him. She knew if he tried out for the part, it would be his.

A childhood desire finally manifested. And she was so right, it felt fucking amazing.

And important.

And it was very important to him.

Mateo's jitters were manageable because he'd practiced so long and hard. He was fully prepared. Three months of rehearsals had culminated to this special night. His time away from Rose was always encouraged by her and she was very gracious about it. Mateo learned from and talked to others. People he never ran into before. Almost everyone involved in the theater troupe was either retired or stay-at-home moms, peppered with a few middle-aged men who claimed to work from home. But all were avid theater lovers and wannabe actors. They took the project very seriously and their surprising intensity rubbed off on Mateo.

The day arrived when he finally had to quit wearing turtlenecks. Spring was coming and with it, warmer weather. Mateo dreaded the moment he walked in wearing a t-shirt with his tats showing.

There were a few double-takes. Then someone said, "Nice tattoo, I love dragonflies!" and all the tension vanished. Some of the others teased him and he was okay with that because he was part of them and he knew he belonged.

There were late-night dinners after rehearsing. And teasing and laughter over what happened at their rehearsals. They joked and laughed over the things they sucked at. And their meager budget made some of the props pretty cheesy, but no one cared. It was so much better than not doing it. He was in a group of people that were barely seen or acknowledged for a play most would never remember. But he did. And they did.

On opening night, Mateo was freaking epic. Rose gushed over him, and Roger and all the members of the Shakespeare Club surrounded him with hugs and high fives, which they really meant. They celebrated him as one of them and he was overwhelmed by their joy in his performance. He was blown away by everyone's support. His unconditional acceptance from both the old people in the club and those in the theater production shocked him. Both realms respected Mateo and were always inclusive towards him.

He was finally part of something. Two things, actually. And something changed in his hardened and stoic demeanor.

How could things he thought so stupid at the start, turn out to somehow change his entire viewpoint? Maybe even his entire perspective of the world? It was all Rose. In the crowd he caught her gaze and they stared long and hard at each other. Their gazes all but burning and throbbing. She was everything. She was all the hope and chances he could ever hope for. She was his conduit to a new and better life. She was his better. His moon and the stars. His true north and the only reason he even wanted one, was her.

CHAPTER 13

ROSE ENTERED THE LOVE Shack with a flourish, letting the door bang into the doorstop like she always did. She loved the small, cozy space. She'd added more candles and sprayed pretty scents in the air. It clung to the bedding and gave it more ambience. The winter cocooned it like a little nest and the coziness made her feel safe and loved. And oh. The things they did in there. The way he made her feel… She still blushed about them and never imagined she could feel or want them done to her so often.

She always hopped into the shack with eager exuberance. Glad for her day to end there. But this time, in early spring, for once, Mateo wasn't alone.

A man stood at the small back window. He was staring out and he swung around at her entrance. She gasped as she caught the man's profile.

Good God. It could have been Mateo's doppelgänger. Down to… yeah, even the same firefly tattoo on his neck.

Before she could begin to comprehend him, the small bathroom door slammed open. *Mateo*. She smiled in relief. Who was this other person? What was this about?

But the look Mateo gave her came straight from the pre-sex days. It was mean and hard and harsh. "I don't have the rent. I'll get it to you later."

Rent? Later? What the hell? And the look? She opened her mouth and her face scrunched up with puzzlement. "What?"

Instead of answering her, he turned to the twin. "She's my boss's daughter. She collects the money for the space I rent. Just give me a sec." He turned, grabbing her arm above her elbow and pulling on her. Not very gently either. Her feet nearly tangled as he tugged her around. She stumbled and scurried to right herself while wondering, *what?*

He shut the door behind them that fast and pulled her into his arms. He kissed the side of her face and whispered into her ear. "It's my brother. I don't want him to know what you mean to me. It never ends well. Go back home. I'll come and see you as soon as he's gone." He released her and his eyes sparked with regret as he added, "Sorry."

Turning away, he slammed the door. Rose was staring at the blank door… stunned.

Brother? Not to know what she was to him? It never went well? For whom? And why did he act like she was collecting the rent from him? What? And the fearful reaction as he came out of the bathroom and found her staring at his brother was another mystery. He was rough and harsh, but Mateo never spoke to her like that. Not anymore.

Reluctant to leave, but scared after what she witnessed, Rose finally left. She didn't think she had another choice. She wasn't about to start banging on the door and embarrassing herself with demands he obviously couldn't meet right now.

She went home, glad when she realized Iris was staying at Quinn's house. She paced and ate some noodles for dinner before sitting dejectedly on her sofa until freaking one in the morning. That was when footsteps sounded outside the front door and she heard a soft knock.

Her heart leapt and she stood up. Mateo came. Even so late. He came. She quickly opened the front door. He stood there, his hands in his jeans pockets, hanging his head, looking strange. Different. Confusing her.

She tugged him inside. "Iris isn't here tonight."

He sagged with relief and nodded, coming inside before she flung herself at him, wrapping her arms around his torso. He didn't hug her back which was unusual. But he did allow her to cling to him for warmth. "What the fuck was that all about?" For once, Rose decided to be crude.

Mateo disentangled himself from her and went to the sofa to flop down. He stared at his feet dejectedly. "That was my older brother. He's in a gang and he's not nice. I didn't want you anywhere near him. He showed up out of nowhere, about twenty minutes before you arrived. I should have texted you and warned you not to come. You got there sooner than I expected. I'm so sorry."

She flopped down beside him. "Do you fear him?"

He shot her a look. "Yeah. Yes, I do. And seeing you near him? It fucking terrifies me."

Puzzled, she shook her head. "But why? I don't even know him."

"He'll hate you no matter what. He hates everyone. He'll resent knowing I was with you. You'd hate the way he turned and talked about you. Or how I allowed it. But worse than that… anyone who gets near him, Rose, is in danger. He won't hesitate to hurt you. Rob you blind. I can't let him know how much I care about you."

She gripped his forearm. "Why did he come here?"

"He shot someone. The police are looking for him. He came to me to lay low for a while. He wants to stay with me until the heat passes. I waited until he fell asleep and then I snuck out."

"He's still in there?"

"Yeah." Rose bristled at the idea his brother was sleeping in their clean, neat, lovely space with so much goodness and love inside it. But that was between them. He already tainted it by making Mateo act so abruptly cold to her.

She licked her lips. Events and speculation had started percolating during the hours she'd waited and she'd contemplated his brother, trying to figure out what happened. Chunks of Mateo's history didn't always line up. Or they didn't until now, after she'd met his brother. Now she wondered how she'd failed to realize the truth long before now. "He looks exactly like you."

"Yeah. I know."

"You guys got your neck tattoos together."

"Obviously. It was his idea. Once we decided to get the neck-tattoos I came up with the fireflies idea since my dad talked about catching them as a little boy. My dad wasn't sentimental, ever. It was about the only time I can remember him sharing something personal with me. So I guess I memorialized that exchange with this. Manuel followed along."

"And he's dangerous?"

"Yeah. Always had a penchant for violence inside him. Had a stomach for it that allowed him to tolerate cruelty and barbaric acts that I could never handle."

She nodded and his entire life seemed to finally clear up for her. "Holy shit. Then he was the one who robbed the convenience store and shot the clerk. It wasn't any accident, was it? He did it on purpose and made you take the rap for it. Someone must have seen him. But you got caught because they saw that fucking tattoo. Right? You never did the crime. You just took the rap for it."

Mateo shot to his feet and started pacing. Staring up at him, she shook her head. "Why? Why would you do that, Mateo? Why would you take the blame? And never tell me?

After all these months, and all the intimacy we shared. How could you not tell me?" Her voice cracked. And her head shook. "Why in the name of heaven, would you not want me to know you were innocent?"

"Because I never said I was. And who would believe it? Everyone says they're innocent of the crimes that send them to jail. Duh. Everyone there is innocent if you ask them. No one would believe me."

"I would." She shot to her feet. "I always would have believed you. How could you not tell me?" The betrayal she felt ripped through her heart. It slashed a harsh trail straight through her. "Mateo, how could you not trust me?"

"Trust you?" The words spilled out like acid. "How could I? There was never anyone to trust before you. My own mother wanted me to confess to it. I was fucking sixteen years old."

There. Rose's body seemed to exhale. Not with relief but for finally reaching the truth. A reality that made much more sense than the one she'd perceived. Nothing she'd learned about Mateo and his kind heart would suggest he could commit the crime he was charged with. Yet he never said otherwise. He never even hinted at his innocence. She recalled the few times they discussed it and his word choices included phrases like "I was accused" or "they said" or "I was young when I went to jail" or "I'm a felon." He never really said he was guilty. He didn't claim to have done the crime. He didn't deny it, however, either.

"Made you confess to what?"

"Manuel had two other felony convictions and long sentences to match. He'd been busy, starting at age thirteen, when he began packing a gun, and robbing convenience stores for his personal allowance. Dad didn't let him get near the family business because he was sure Manuel would have gotten caught. He was too loud and unpredictable. His sharp, volatile temper goes from zero to ninety in seconds and he instantly resorts to violence. No one wanted him near the chop shop, so he was banned. That's why he joined a gang and became our contact to hook up deals. We provided all the orders and they supplied them. Sometimes, we'd get a half dozen of the same type of car or motorcycle; other times we specialized in high-end vehicles. But of course, I was sneaky, smart and excellent at stealing the cars. I never got caught. I never even had a close call. But I never packed a gun and I don't have a hair-trigger temper."

"Or his kind of temperament," she added softly.

Mateo's gaze was glued to the floor as he paced. He paused to throw her a sharp glare before he went back to pacing. He was scowling and his tone was angry toward her.

"He shot the clerk of the convenience store. There were witnesses, two of them and a grainy video tape. The fucking tattoo… he wasn't smart enough to cover it up. I always covered it. From the time we first got the tattoos, I put a bandanna over my neck so there were never any obvious marks for identification. Duh, right?"

She nodded. Duh, exactly right. There was no way Mateo would overlook the smallest detail, being as intelligent as he was. His innocence was always right there in the open for her to see. She was kicking herself, internally.

"But he didn't. The tattoo was evidence. A cop recognized it, of course, on review of the store security tape and soon they were knocking on our door. My brother was well known to most of them. Dad had a record too and often got questioned when local cars disappeared. But they could never prove anything. I did most of the scouting for inventory. I never did it close to home. When that happened, it was Dad or my brother, both being idiots. You don't shit where you eat, you know? They would find a local car or bike they just had to have, or an opportunity they couldn't resist, and I'd want to freaking kill them for taking the risk. That's how people end up getting caught. And we were known already to the law. So the tattoo was a big mistake."

"And your mother decided that you should take the fall?"

He stopped dead on his feet and stared out beyond her, looking at something she couldn't see. Was it his mother's face? Rose tried to imagine the moment she requested that of her son. He dropped into the chair across from her without looking at her.

"She did do that. Yes. You see, I was a minor still. So she quickly deduced if a minor confessed to the robbery and claimed it was an accidental, fear-driven shot, perhaps the sentence would be more lenient. And since my brother already had a long rap sheet and bad reputation, he would have gotten a decade or more in the slammer. He deserved it too. Because he shot the clerk on purpose. But luckily for me, the video camera didn't catch the shooting. The store display of Hostess Baked Goods covered my brother from the chest down. So all you see is his head and shoulders moving. You can't see how the shot got fired so Mom's story that it was an accident fits. As the truth would have also fit. My brother got antsy and pissed over how long the clerk was taking and he shot him, intending to kill him, but missed. He was always an impatient jerk, and he's damn lucky he only grazed the guy's shoulder. He is a fucking idiot as well as a mean son of a bitch."

She blinked back her tears. "Why did you go along with that, Mateo?"

He didn't glance her way as he replied, "I was sixteen. She was just as mean as my brother. She simply ordered me to confess to it. Threatened to kick me out so I'd never see any of them again. I had to do it for my brother. I owed him. Looking back, I still wonder why. All he did was show me how to be a thug and mark me for life as a criminal. The tat is what sent me to prison for three years. I rotted in the cell while my father got stabbed in the gut during a bar fight and I missed his funeral. When I came out, I was different. That was my penance, I suppose."

"Did you get a lighter sentence?"

"Yeah. I got a plea deal. I pled guilty and they reduced the charges. Being a minor and saying the gun went off accidentally because I didn't know what I was doing; and since the man wasn't fatally hurt, well, my mom was right, huh? It was a much lighter sentence at only three years."

"Three years at that young of an age is a lifetime. Oh, my God, you must have been so scared." She scooted closer to him, attempting to take his arm in hers and lean against his shoulder. She kissed his upper back. He kept his posture rigid and didn't lean into her.

"I was petrified. I was turning seventeen when I started my time. Tall, skinny and looking like the punk I never was, I didn't stand a chance in prison."

"What did you do to survive?"

"Joined the first gang that looked like me. I let them put these on me..." He pointed to some ragged, amateur tattoos on his arms and back. "I stayed under their protection and avoided being raped and tortured, but none of it came easy; there was always a cost."

"You had to join them."

"Yeah. It was petty shit. But I was mean to others. I saw things... God, Rose... I can't tell you about some of them. I survived, yes, but at the cost of my soul."

Rose shuddered as she struggled to imagine it. While she was joining clubs at the university and studying hard to pass her general requirements, Mateo was what? Obeying his prison gang in their enforcement and punishment of others? Trying to keep himself from being their next target? "It was either join up or become their next victim?" she asked quietly.

He nodded, keeping his eyes down. "I never raped anyone. I beat up a few guys. I stole and intimidated and made sure everyone believed I'd do much worse if they didn't comply. Inside, I made it seem like this was the best thing that could have happened to me. I looked mean and connected, so I could pretend to be that way. I played the part and... yeah, it was great stuff. When I was released, I got the street cred I lacked during my youth. Everyone expected me to hook up with the gang that kept me safe inside. I owed them, after all... But I only foresaw more prison or a cruel death by them. And my own mother would have freaking applauded it. Dad was already dead, and another gang took over his shop. My inept brother, for all his blustering bravado, couldn't keep the shop running without Dad. He has no brains and no courage or bravery. He instantly capitulated our once small legacy without even trying."

"So you..." Rose started to say before she stopped herself and shook her head. "Your mother didn't contact my dad, did she? She would have never encouraged you to leave her or your brother. She fully expected you to follow in his footsteps. She knew you were the brains and could make money for them. You pretended to be her when you contacted my dad."

The smallest smile crossed his face. "Yes. I wrote the letter to him as my mom. I remembered your dad from when I worked there. He was always nice to me. He had that great laugh and he and my dad shared a strange vibe. They had a true friendship. I hoped I could use that to get the fuck out of Texas. And your dad made it happen. He invited me up here, after my mother's sad request to help her son leave a dangerous town before falling into drug addiction or having to join the same gang as her other son. Blah... blah... blah.

"I had to do it, Rose. I had to get out. I came here and it felt like I could breathe for the first time in a decade. Maybe my whole life. I loved it. I can't describe it to you. I could work without fear of being arrested or shot by rival gangs or thieves. We weren't the only chop shop in town, and we had to jump through hoops sometimes under threat of being shot for making the wrong move. I was always good with mechanics because I learned from my dad. Like yours, he invested his knowledge in me. Then, the same crew who once couldn't get past my initially shocking looks, treated me like anyone else. Your dad gave me respect. He knew my fucking history and he still set out to show me the business. His trade. He even trusted me. He gave me access to his office and the safe and even more telling, his damn daughter."

"Iris?"

"Yeah. He never once told her to be cautious or careful of me. He also never interceded in our feud-turned-friendship. I assumed he would, which was why I was so hard on her. I was so ready to have her daddy fire me. The first few months, I expected it all to go to shit at any second. Any second. It always ended like that for me. You know? But Shane just laughed and smiled at our antics. Iris grew more comfortable and she invited me out to drink and eat and hang with her. She was fun and nice and funny and she made me feel like her brother. Not a scary thug or criminal."

"Oh, my God, and I was jealous. Thank God for Iris. She never judges anyone. Like my dad. Unlike me. Yeah." Tears filled her eyes out of a sudden, burgeoning love for what her sister's kindness and sense of fairness and fun did for the lost boy that Mateo was when he first came to River's End.

"And then I was judging you as everyone else was. As you predicted. And after all you went through…"

He finally turned his head and made eye contact with her.

His dark eyes were serious and too full of images she could not begin to comprehend. No matter how much he told her. The rejection of his mother. The betrayal by his mother and brother. The fear he had to endure at such a young age just to survive. And then to be evaluated and tossed away by a so-called polite society.

The most intelligent, kind, loyal, trusting boy lay beneath the outward ink and brooding eyes. He didn't smile or engage, because he hated to be rejected. Rose made the same mistake. She was as bad as all of them, like all the self-right-eous assholes rolled into one.

He turned, lifted his hand and touched her cheek with it. The soft, gentle touch was something she'd grown used to. She cherished, adored and luxuriated under his caress. "Then there was you."

"Judging. Bitchy. Awful me."

His lips twitched. "You were so beautiful, you hurt my eyes. You made my heart leap with, for the first time, hope. I wondered what it was like to be with a woman who was good and decent. Until you, it wasn't that way. The women I associated with were as tough and criminal as I was. But not you… I wanted something to happen with you from the first time you were too scared to hold my gaze. I believed it was impossible, but you gave me a glimpse of what could be. You were the first woman I dreamed and hoped for. Despite being judgmental and bitchy, what you consider awful behavior, you were more than amusing to me. Like a little gnat biting me. Compared to my own mother? Ha. Until the impossible happened and you looked at me differently."

She crawled onto his lap and tears streamed down her face as he spoke about her. The day when she'd entered his tragic, heartbreaking story. She wrapped her arms around him and cradled her head against his chest. She cried for him. For the boy he was. The boy that was lost and hurt and sent to prison where men could hurt and change and taint him.

"That you could manage to see past all of those things. And be attracted to the likes of me… you have to believe that I never foresaw that. You have to know what you mean to me…" His voice was low and sad as he drifted off.

She nodded her head. His hand stroked her hair as she clung to him. She cried for him. He was stoic and rigid, but he let her. Bending down, he kissed her forehead, her hair, and her ear. He rubbed her back. He comforted her as she wept for him. Finally, she shook her head against his chest and placed her ear above his thumping heart. "Why didn't you just tell me?"

"I didn't think you would believe me. No one has ever really seen the true me, Rose. Let alone, believe me innocent of something so obvious."

She lifted her tear-streaked face. "I do. I would have. All these months, I've loved you, adored you, and trusted you despite thinking that you shot a man. How could you imagine that the breaking point for me would be the truth? When it's just the opposite?"

He shrugged his shoulders and his gaze darted every-where. "I just never thought anyone would."

"You feared I wouldn't believe you."

"Yeah."

"But I do. I believe you."

He hugged her to him and breathed harshly into her hair. "Now you have to see why I can't let my brother know about you. He'd find a way to hurt you. He'd steal from you. Or do something evil. Or he'll try to convince me… oh… just please stay away from him. You're the most… no, you're the *only* real thing in my life that I give a damn about. You're the only thing that matters to me, so please promise me."

"I promise. But how did he get here? And why the fuck

did you let him into your place? Our place? And why do you send money to the woman who all but sold you down the river?" Anger started to percolate as the reality of his story fully started to materialize in her mind's eye. A story of betrayal and a mother forsaking her son for another. Another thug that didn't deserve it.

"He knew Shane. He knew the name of the shop. I didn't try to hide it. I just said Shane reached out and offered me a gig here and I took it. Then I never went back. My mom was destitute and my brother was in and out of jail and…"

"And you send her the money you need to rebuild your own life, the one that she destroyed and never allowed you to get started? You give your money to that woman? You still insist on supporting her criminally guilty son? The one who came here… Why would you do that again, Mateo?"

"He shot a rival gang member. He has to disappear or they'll kill him for it."

Anger exploded in her veins. "Look at this more closely. Look at what you're going to do. You say I'm the only meaning to your life. You love working for my dad's legitimate shop and being respected by Iris and Chan and Jeff and all the customers of the valley, right? Or is all that bullshit?"

"Yeah… Yes, I do."

"Then why would you allow a gang member into your life who's hiding from a rival? Listen to that question, Mateo? How do you think that story will end? And anyone close to it? Well? No sane person would allow your brother to come near them or their residence or their loved ones. Fuck him. That's what you do. You tell him to fuck off for all the times he let you down as a minor, a little kid, and for selling you down the river for *his crimes*. Oh yeah, what a man. What a brother. How old was he when that happened?"

"Twenty."

"He was a man and you were a boy? See that clearly for

once. See it crystal clear for Christ's sake, Mateo. He was *a man.* But he was never a real man and he still isn't. Running to you again to fix his mistakes. Never mind the lethal consequences? Well, as far as I'm concerned, he already landed you in lethal consequences. Right? You're a felon for life. According to everyone else, correct? I mean, the chances of having it legally changed are pretty small."

He flinched. "Right. And can you live with that?"

"Well, I already planned to. I'm the one who proclaimed my love for you, remember? Not the other way around. And then you doubt I can live with that? Yes. I can. I will hate it more now since it's not even true. But I should have realized that on my own. The longer I knew you, the less it made sense. I thought you had childhood influences I could not understand and that's how it happened. But this? Your brother. Tell him to get the fuck lost. And never come back."

"What? Just give him some money and send him on his way?"

She screeched and jerked off his lap before she started pacing. "No. No. You absolutely will not give him your honest, hard-earned money. Your hard-won place of respect here. People appreciate what you do and how you do it. No. You tell him to get the fuck away from you and never come back here. You cut him off. You tell your selfish mother to get her money from the son she didn't sell down the river and forsake. You stop it here and now."

"Rose… goddamn. They are still my family. She's my mother…" He ran his hands with obvious distress through his hair. His voice rose as he stood.

Frustration almost made her screech again. "Yes. Don't you see it? They know you're intelligent and they know who can make more money. They don't care what it costs you or how badly they treat you. Did they ever apologize? Huh? Even once?"

He scowled. "No."

"There. You see? No. Be done with them. Cut the cord. They already cost you three years and a permanent record as a felon. They destroyed you and now they want to prevent you from building a new life? You live in a shack... why? For them? So you could send all your money home?" She paced as she flung her words until she saw the confusion in his eyes. She was agitating and hurting him when she simply wanted to protect, cherish and help him. She had to make him see he was so much better than them, and he deserved so much more too.

She rushed to him and flung her arms around him. "You are worth a thousand of them. They will never see it. They'll simply use and abuse you. Don't you realize that? They are the very definition of toxic and you don't owe them anything. You never did. You gave them years... *years* of your hard work, Mateo. You gave them more than they ever gave back. Okay? But you deserve the money you honestly make. You had to start far behind the starting line of life with a prison record they arranged by the felony they foisted on you. Now? You lose the job here? You can't easily find another. How many Shane Rydells are there who would hire you? See? They trapped you with a record. That felonious crime will follow you. You gave them all but your blood. Now they are coming for that. Realize that, please. You deserve to start building your life here... for us. We deserve it. Not them. Don't you see? You deserve a real life, Mateo. One you worked for and earned and dreamed about. And I want to stand beside you."

His eyebrows rose and lowered. Puzzlement shone from his eyes. He never gave himself the permission to stop taking care of them. As hateful and detested as they were to him, he felt bound to them by invisible chains. "Just don't send her any money? Kick him out of the shack?"

"Yes!" she nearly screamed.

"I'm not sure how to go about…"

"Let me do it."

His head whipped up. "No. I told you…"

"If you can't trust your brother to see me and know who I am, why would you let him near you? Listen to yourself. You warn me of the danger and the fear you have about him listen to your own words."

He flopped down again and she knelt on the floor in front of him, on her knees. She clasped his hands in hers and kissed his knuckles. He stared at her movements, her face, her lips and then her gaze. "I love you. I know you love me. I do. I know you can't say the words to me. But you told me from the start, remember? You make love to me to show me what you can't say to me? What you feel? Right?"

His dark eyes held hers and nothing twitched on him. He was as serious as the moment he first looked at her. "Yes."

She knew he loved her. It was as close to an admission as he could confirm for her. But she knew it was enough. She felt it. All the time. "I want a life with you. Always. So I can't have some gangster brother popping up when he's on the run from the cops or other gang members. I would move your mother in with us, with me, if she were loving and kind and even remotely maternal and needed your money and your help. But that isn't the case, is it?"

He shook his head.

She sighed and kissed his hands again. "I see what they've done to you. They've literally marked you on the outside, and scarred you on the inside. I love you, Mateo. With all those marks and scars. Everything about you and inside you, I LOVE. Do you understand me? And how much I love you?"

His gaze grew bigger but it was weary and hopeful. So much hope shone in her eyes. Her heart shattered at seeing the youthful boy who clung to her gaze while glimpsing the distrust that loomed behind it. A war he waged inside himself that she couldn't really love the tatted up, boy-gangster and felon, Mateo Alvarez.

"I want to marry you and build our life together. I want kids and the Love Shack to be our getaway, a place that no one but us knows about, where you can always show me what your words can't say, so that my heart knows. I know how much you love me. It's not a secret. I'm not needy or unsure of myself. I know what you feel about me. But letting your family leech off you and hurt you is potentially bringing danger to us. Our future. No. I won't do it. You don't want to do it and you don't have to. I just don't think anyone's ever told you that."

He stared at her. Then at their clasped fingers. Her head was bowed before him. He suddenly grabbed her shoulders and smashed his mouth on hers. His powerful feelings and sensations were almost violent as he all but inhaled her before he devoured her. When he allowed barely a sliver of space between them, she smiled and touched his cheek. "See? You show me what you feel. The words I say to you? This was your response, wasn't it?"

He swallowed hard and the firefly on his throat bobbed. Then with caution and deliberation, he dropped his head in a half-nod. One time. One short, expressive nod that said everything. *I love you. I adore you. I want to marry you. I want to have kids with you. I want to be with you. I want you with me always.* But most of all, it said, *I trust you. Please don't hurt me.*

She smiled softly and said, "Please send your brother away. And cut your mother off. And you know I would never advise that if it weren't the best thing to do." She held his face in both of her hands. "Understand this: they will never want what's best for you. They only want what's best for them. They are selfish and harmful in your life. The only way to get what you want and deserve, is by claiming it. You have to separate yourself from them for your own well-being… and now, for me."

He didn't answer her but simply leaned forward and his lips landed on hers. The kiss was slow and soft this time. So many different expressions were revealed by his kisses and touches. Rose learned to read them. Decipher them. Cherish them. She gained confidence and trusted that Mateo was hers, even if he could never say so.

She stood on her feet, took his hand and dragged him into her bedroom. So rarely did they stay at her apartment or go to her bedroom for fear of Iris seeing them. Now that she fully understood what her dad's shop and his job meant to Mateo, Rose would be more careful to preserve it. She could never allow her presence in his life to snatch something so important from him. His confidence and self-image were tied up in them. So their secret relationship status was something she guarded fiercely for him.

But that night he made love to her with such tenderness and later whispered into her hair, "Okay."

Okay? So he'd forsake his brother and his mother? And start keeping his money? And continue to love her? And start building a life with her? All that was tied up in one word. And odder still, for her that was enough.

CHAPTER 14

"WELL?" ROSE ASKED AS she sashayed to the left and then to the right. She was showing off the burgundy dress that flared over her breasts and the white lace that offered peek-a-boo glimpses of the skin on her smooth back. It clung to her hips and reached the floor. It was by far the most expensive and exquisite dress she'd ever put on her body.

"I... Wow. Damn, Rosie. You look perfect."

She was attending a charity event in Seattle with her sister and parents. Quinn Larkin was sponsoring it. Rose still wondered about her sister's billionaire and his true intentions towards her sister. But he kept Iris so busy during the time Rose was holed up with Mateo at their Love Shack, that Iris didn't notice how often she was absent from their apartment. Being so busy with her new relationship, she was totally oblivious to Rose's.

Iris bought the dress and spent an obscene amount on it, in Rose's opinion. But of course, her sugar-daddy-with-the-big-bucks, Quinn, purchased it. Iris freaked out and suddenly realized she could only go to the event in a man's suit, since she adamantly refused to wear a dress. She gave the dress to Rose, who now modeled it for Mateo.

He ran his hand over her silk-clad waist and over her plump butt. "God, Rose…"

She tugged on his hand and pulled the dress up until it was bunched around her waist. Then she climbed on Mateo's lap, straddling him. She pressed down and he gasped when he realized she was completely naked underneath. She moved and gyrated over him. He was instantly hard as only his nylon basketball shorts separated them. Rose's dress spilled around them like huge petals of a red flower. She reached under, pulling him free of his shorts before slipping above him and finally taking him inside her. Her eyes fluttered and moans and sighs escaped her. "I belong with you. I like the pretty dress. But I'm only going there for Iris. So don't start with the 'I deserve better than you,' shit. I deserve you." She lifted her hips and slid down on his hardness with each sentence as if to emphasize her words. His mouth opened in ecstasy at each thrust from her. Now, Rose was on birth control so they no longer had to use condoms. She was sore and stung at first when they went wild with the raw, unprotected sex.

Sighing into his mouth, she clung to him and rode him. His hands circled her waist and the expensive material bunched together with his grasp. As he lifted her up and down on his shaft, she suddenly leaned over his shoulder, breathing hard, like a piston as she swallowed the length of him with her wet pussy. She rode him harder, panting as he held her still when he finally pushed as hard and far inside her warm wetness as he could. She squealed and called his name, kissing the side of his face as he held onto her, just as eager as he. The chaste feel of her lips on his cheek made him smile. It was so innocent. She always did it, but especially when she saw Mateo feeling insecure. "I'm yours. Just so you don't forget it."

She also knew the fancy dress and the event she was attending were foreign to him, so they brought out every insecurity he harbored, which were many.

Not being good enough for her was probably the biggest phobia. The most obvious. The thing that turned him the surliest.

But Rose fucked him in her pretty dress. She let his hands crumple the material as his body slid in and out of hers. Yeah, Rose knew how to banish Mateo's doubts and fears and she could take him from raging to benign. He smiled as he kissed her sweaty brow. "Right back at you, baby girl."

She lifted her face and giggled. He could feel her body wiggling as she laughed because he was still inside her. Now limp, he could easily get hard again if he stayed there much longer. He loved her damn giggle, which was innocent and sweet. Rose disapproved of crude or rude remarks, but she didn't mind so much anymore with him.

"Yeah, I noticed. Hard to forget this…" She smiled greedily and the lust sparkled in her eyes as he easily flipped her over and buried himself inside her again.

"I'm always hard for you, baby girl." He grinned and they were lost again. To each other. In their own world. In the quaint Love Shack she'd named, which they'd christened so many times… Mateo was even growing fond of the goddamned shit-hole. But he detested it from the moment Rose left it until she returned. Only with her inside could he tolerate it.

He loved having her inside it with him.

Rose attended her weekend with the rich and famous. Wearing that dress. At least, she remembered having it all curled and bunched around her waist when he showed her what her dress did to him, and not once but twice. Mateo got even grumpier and surlier the weekend she spent with her family. Chan and Jeff noticed his miserable mood and ignored him. He worked longer and harder on the weekend, and when he ran into a few clients, he had to restrain himself, lest he totally drive them away.

On Sunday night, Rose got home. Mateo sighed in relief when she came directly to him. She was gushing about Quinn. When her sister dressed in a tuxedo, Quinn not only called her up on stage with him, but they also danced to Iris's favorite song and plenty of photographs and videos were taken. They were later shown on gossip sites and tabloids. Rose was more than impressed by Quinn Larkin's public displays of acceptance in his love for her sister.

Mateo wished he could give Rose something besides a fucking shack.

Rose noticed he was quiet so she slipped onto his lap. She kissed his chin. Once, twice, until finally, he couldn't resist her and dipped his mouth down to her lips. She stared up at him with big, blue, lake-tranquil eyes. "I liked seeing that someone loves my sister exactly as she is. She's totally herself. The thing is: I'm the kind of woman that Quinn *should* be chasing. Wearing that gorgeously appropriate dress and my hair swept into an updo, I looked so good. I really did. You know I don't brag about myself often. But I was the perfect date that Quinn should have been with. He looked hot, every inch the CEO and billionaire. And Quinn should have been the guy I wanted to be with. Looking at us, anyone would have thought we were the 'it' couple."

Her explanation wasn't helping. Mateo stiffened his back and dropped his hands from her waist. She kissed his neck. He found it hard to resist her lips softly brushing over his tattoo and she often followed that up by licking it. She did that quite often as if to establish he was hers and his tattoo was also hers. It was part of them now, just like her soft hair.

"But I couldn't wait to get back to the Love Shack. With you. Quinn needed my tomboy sister as much as I needed my tough-assed you. You are the only man who fulfills me. And calls to me. And challenges me. It was fun to dress up, and see what too much money and wealth can afford, but I wouldn't trade any of it for what we have. Not even this Love Shack for all his damn money. Why? Because I wouldn't have you."

How the hell did one reply to that? How could he maintain the wall around him after hearing her sweet words and heart-felt declarations after months of sharing the shack with him? After she declared her love for him and the space that they monopolized? How could he doubt her? After all she did, like the Shakespeare Club and the play and her unflagging support throughout their time together. And finding people who appreciated what he had to offer when it came from his brain and heart. How could he not trust her?

But still the words were lodged in his throat. He leaned his forehead onto hers and closed his eyes as he whispered, "Rose, I…"

She kissed his closed eyes, leaning her head on his. "I know, Mateo. I've known for a long time."

He let her kiss him to know that she was his only truth. She had become his entire world. His whole life. It was too much responsibility to put on another, but he couldn't help himself.

He didn't know how to stop. He didn't want to anymore.

He swiftly cut his mother off and never sent her another penny. Only a short note stating he no longer had a job or any money to send. That was it. He ignored her unending calls and texts that got nastier the longer he didn't answer them. He threw his big brother out that night without a penny and told him to lose his address forever. He surprised himself and Rose by doing exactly what Rose said. He also thought of himself for once. It made him hurt and ache but he did it anyway. He tried to be as selfish as his mother and brother were.

And Rose? Rose managed to change his whole life. He rewrote his entire forecast for the future. She improved what he thought about his past, his actions, and his mistakes. She validated his passion for reading and the endless variety of subjects that constantly captured his ceaseless curiosity. Rose normalized what he considered being a freak. She spotted and nurtured all the unusual and interesting aspects of his personality and yeah, she was kind of special for seeing it like that. Rose made Mateo feel special too, and no one else ever did. Not even the teacher that commented on his quick mind and uncanny retention of details and facts, but never encouraged him or pursued it beyond a few questions. Nor the friend that he helped out with math problems that he did in his head. Nor the mother and father who used his natural talent to make him steal cars. And cook the books on their illegal enterprises until they finally betrayed him—"sold him out" as Rose put it—in favor of the criminal brother.

Mateo earned money now. His paycheck belonged only to him. Not just to afford more ebooks and fancy kicks, but to start a savings account and to have more dinners out and to buy gifts for his girlfriend.

Life was idyllic. Something he never imagined it could be. Never. He even started to trust the world. He still attended the Shakespeare Club, which was now full of his supporters. Who knew old retirees would listen or care about what he had to say? They were awed by him, not fearful.

He joined in with the theater troupe when they started planning what play would be performed next spring. It was huge and new to be part of a group like this. He never knew he'd fit in or want to with people who were so different than him. But he did. All of it.

But of course, that was a mistake. Believing he could actually forge a new life with Rose and somehow escape his past, his destiny, his crimes and the history that tainted his future was a mistake.

He entered Shane's shop one morning and knew in his gut that the idyllic time with Rose was over, and he was truly the cursed sham he always believed himself to be.

THE SHOP WAS DESTROYED. Vandalized. Mateo looked around it, blinking in shock. The vehicles that were parked there were all smashed up. Windshields shattered, the bodies and hoods dented irreparably. Tools and small parts and screws were thrown everywhere. It would take forever just to clean up. He stared at the disaster with dismay. Appalled. Disgusted. The place was completely trashed but there was no sign of forced entry. The door was even unlocked. He winced when he caught sight of the van in Iris's bay. Dear God. The violent destruction was devoid of any human thought or mercy. That kind of anarchy was something he'd witnessed only from his brother.

Fear rippled through him. *His brother.* Fuck. Damn. Shit. His brother knew where he worked and that he'd disowned him and his mother in favor of this place. For the chance to build a good reputation and an honest name. His brother had deliberately destroyed Mateo's only decent chance to make something meaningful of himself?

Fuck. Although he didn't do it, he'd brought the vandalism and violence to the Rydells. He sucked in a breath of air as if someone punched him in the gut. He'd brought this violence to Rose. And her dad. And her sister. What if Iris had been in here working late? She so often did. What if his brother had entered then?

Fuck. Mateo was responsible for this even if he didn't know it at the time.

He backed up a step, then another and shut the door on the sickening chaos and destruction. He could barely stand it. Realizing all the damage he'd indirectly brought to the only family he'd ever really felt close to was tormenting him. The same people who gave him a second chance. The woman who gave him a new life and love and feelings and a future.

He knew he'd ruin it along with everything else he touched. It was the reason why he'd resisted Rose for so long and denied the feelings he felt. His life always went to shit. Something always went wrong, and usually not because of his fault or from his actions. He never deserved her or the confidence she invested in him.

Look at the results of that. Look at the devastation he'd brought to her and her family.

He turned away, feeling heartsick as he ducked back into his truckbefore pulling a U-turn. He had to find Rose and explain or… what? What should he do? He didn't know. But discovering it without any warning? That would be a mistake. He wanted to call Rose and tell her. But the words failed him. The humiliation of his lousy family and the trail of destruction that followed him was too much to explain. Everything she said his family would do to him had been done.

Finally, at the usual starting time, Mateo pulled back into the shop parking lot. Someone else was there. A sheriff's car was parked beside Jeff's old Mustang. Mateo entered the open door, flinching once again at the scene of destruction. His stomach knotted and churned. He was so ashamed that his presence there brought utter ruin to the one man who gave him a second chance. Shane was like a father to him… and he repaid him by what? First, he seduced his daughter and now this? He sabotaged his place of business?

"Shane?" Mateo said as he glanced around, his gut tightening. "What...what happened?"

Shane and Sheriff Lazaro turned towards him. "Someone broke in obviously... but then, you knew that."

"I didn't do this." Mateo stepped back automatically, shocked at Shane's accusing tone. Sure, his record and felony conviction made him the cops' first choice of suspect, he knew that, which was why he ran at first. But Shane? So quick to make that assumption? Mateo was hurt. It stabbed him in the heart when he realized how much he cared about Shane's opinion of him only to realize how easily Shane pointed the finger at him.

Shane's jaw tightened. His hair was pulled back in a ponytail. His eyes with laugh wrinkles surrounding their usually warm depths flashed with regret as he said, "I saw your truck earlier."

Mateo nodded. His shoulders collapsed and his heart sank. He was stupid to panic and run. "I got here early and saw the shop and freaked out... you know... considering my past..."

"Yeah, I considered it..." Sheriff Lazaro said. "Mind if we step out and have a chat?"

Mateo nodded and his heart sank. Oh fuck, yeah. He minded. How dare they both make the obvious assumption. How easily they threw him under the bus. The trust he thought he'd found here? Poof. Gone. One false accusation and it evaporated. He knew it was flimsy shit and always believed it was until Rose changed his mind. Even though he knew better. He would always be a felon. Always. His tats confirmed that. This would be the last they saw of him.

He pulled his phone out and shot a fast text to Rose. God, he was so weak now. When he was arrested as a youth, he called no one. He never sought comfort or solace from another human being. No one contacted or visited him during the three years in prison. No biggie. He dealt with it. But now? A burgeoning sense of panic filled him. Rose. Rose had to know what happened. Why? Because he needed one person, Rose, the only person who might believe him.

Shop was vandalized. Police questioning me. I'm sorry. I didn't do it. I think my brother did.

Her response was instantaneous. *I'll be right there.*

And she was. In the moments it took for him to step outside so the sheriff could ask him to come down to the station for further questioning, he saw Rose. She was there that fast. Her car slammed to a halt and she jumped out in a pair of sweats and a t-shirt. Her hair was still messed and snarled from his hands last night, and she hadn't brushed it but pulled it into a ponytail. She stormed towards them.

Rose screamed at her dad and the sheriff. For Mateo. She stood up for him and never once questioned him. Somehow, she knew for sure he didn't do this.

Mateo's heart hurt from seeing Shane's doubt, but Rose's? He steeled himself for her. She was his champion and advocate and warrior and she truly believed him. "Tell them, goddamn it. You tell them Mateo would never do this, right now, Dad! You know he didn't."

A lot of denials. Blah, blah, blah... Questioning him was routine and all that, but Mateo knew it wasn't. They thought he was guilty and he'd most likely take the rap for it. There went his job again, and his gaze hardened as he stared at Shane. He didn't want it anymore now. Not if Shane were so easily persuaded of his guilt, after almost four years of loyal service without a single misdeed or act of poor conduct. Mateo had full access to the cash drawer and none was ever missing. And oh, the ironies. None was missing now.

Off in the distance, Mateo spotted Iris standing there. Watching him get cuffed. His friend. His best friend. His first real friend. But she didn't charge forward like Rose. After a few words of protest, Iris started to back away as if it pained her too much to even look at Mateo. Like she couldn't face the situation. What? Was he now out of sight, out of mind? She'd worked with and trusted him before anyone else and still, she didn't rush to his defense. She stood back, oddly quiet with a dazed, strange expression. The denouncement by Iris and Shane almost slammed him to his knees. If not for Rose, he might have surrendered to their preconceived suspicions and simply taken the blame if only so they could maintain their erroneous beliefs. His neck-tat, that seemed like so small an item, was the very thing that made him appear guilty to so many.

Except Rose.

He shook his head at her. She was making too much of it. Her dad was watching her with wonder and something sparked in his gaze. He met Mateo's eyes and oh, hell, yeah. He knew. He knew Mateo slept with his daughter, and no doubt, he also, believed that's all it was. That's all Mateo was good for. Mateo's sadness and disappointment with his mentor, the man he'd pinned all his hopes on, burnt up and turned to ash.

Then Iris turned away from him and left.

But not Rose. No, Rose fumed and swore on his behalf, darting ugly glares at her dad and the sheriff. Rose had no fear of anyone. Must be nice. Unfortunately, that would never be his reality.

Rose followed him to the police station, pacing the small foyer where he could see her. Like a caged animal. Fiercely rabid. She was furiously vocal and when she was ordered to calm down or leave, she told them to arrest her.

Only the privileged Rose Rydell, one of the famous Rydells, could get away with threatening the sheriff. Mateo knew he would incur added charges for that. He was detained and had to spend the night until the judge appeared for an arraignment. His bail was steep, due to his criminal record and background in Texas where his family had known gang affiliations. His heart plummeted to his feet. God. Jail. Again. He felt queasy and sick to imagine it.

Rose posted his bond. Dazed and shocked to be released so quickly, he looked up and there she was.

Stopping dead at the doorway of the courthouse after being released, Mateo was so glad to see her. Her hair was freshly washed and swinging free; she'd styled it so it framed her shiny face. Her eyes showed lack of sleep. She opened her arms wide when he stepped out. She never doubted him. Rushing forward, she nearly launched herself at him. Crying with relief. And anger. And desperation. Mateo sucked in a breath of fresh air and buried his nose in her citrus-smelling air.

"I will kill my fucking father for doing this. Come on!" she said when she finally released him and held her hand tightly in his. "I love you and this won't stand. You know that."

Ha. As if. First of all, Shane knew about them now. That alone would have gotten Mateo fired. But the trashed shop? Who else but Mateo would Shane consider a suspect?

"Your dad wasn't rushing to my defense. Maybe he was unsure, but he definitely wasn't against me being questioned and then arrested."

"Well, I am and he will regret this."

Mateo stopped short and tugged her hand. "Don't you see, Rose? I'll always be the guilty suspect. The first target if anything goes wrong. Being an ex-con and felon, I belong to the least sympathetic group of people. Even you must see that. You can't will it away. This is my reality. I look the part and I have the record. I doubt this will be the last time you post my bail if you decide to stay with me." Bitterness singed his words.

She flipped around and took his chin in her hands. "If? *If* I decide to stay with you? For fuck's sake, Mateo, we're together always. I'm with you, now and forever. So what if I have to pay your fucking bail again? And we have to fight and fight and fight? I will never give up on you. And I know you're innocent of any wrongdoing. So there it is. You're a victim and if I have to, then I'll be one too just because you are. But I would never exchange you for a million other guys. All the Benton Smiths and his ilk; white rich boys who look honest, forthright and moral, but they aren't. You, Mateo, you fucking are. So shut up about all the *ifs*. Or trying to convince me to stay away from you. Fuck that. Got it?"

Weariness plagued him. "Rose, it's not fun or sexy to align yourself with a felon. It might seem like it's us against the world and all that at first, but a decade from now? With a kid or two that depend on you? Fuck. How fun do you think it will it be then?"

She simply screeched. "I don't consider it fun. And it will always be you and me against anyone who does you wrong. Or me. So there. That's it. Now come home."

"Then what? I just go to work? As if nothing happened?"

She twisted her mouth back and forth and then nodded. "Yes. I think you do. Until my dad confronts you or tells you differently. Fuck him. Make him come to you."

"Rose?"

"What?" she snapped and her tone turned grumpy. Her hands were on her hips and her eyes were flashing blue fire at him. "What, Mateo? Are you going to warn me to keep away from you some more? Protect lil' ol' me from your hideous reality? What?"

"I love you."

She snapped her mouth shut and her eyes grew to huge saucers. "I'm sorry this happened. I'm sorry you have to be with a felon and fight for me, but when you came charging up against your dad and the cops, so fearlessly and most of all, so sure, so damn sure, I finally realized that I trust you. I do."

Her smile was soft and sweet as she grabbed him and hugged him. "Of course, you do. And I love you too. Forever. No matter what. Right?"

He shut his eyes and clung to the red-haired girl. They were standing in the parking lot of the courthouse where he just spent the night in jail. He smiled. "Yeah. No matter what."

$\mathcal{H}$E SHOWED BACK UP at work and Shane nodded at him. It was a cool look. He'd obviously been notified of Mateo's release. Did Shane know it was his own daughter that paid his bail? No thanks to Shane or Iris. If not for Rose he'd be rotting in a jail cell still.

Fuck them. If he didn't need the damn job and money, he'd walk away right then and there.

If not for Rose. He needed Rose. So he tolerated them.

The shop was cleaned up. Chan and Jeff had helped Shane. They told him all about it on his first lunch hour back. They back-slapped him and told him they were sorry the sheriff had assumed he was guilty... because they didn't think he was. Mateo had stilled at their automatic faith in his innocence. He hadn't expected it. Not from them. He nodded his appreciation.

"The fuck that sheriff think you'd do that to Shane. No way."

"Shane knows that too. He's just upset. He'll come around," Jeff added with a lazy nod.

Maybe there was more in River's End for him than even he realized.

Iris? Who the hell knew?

She didn't even fucking show up. And never asked what was going on or if he was okay.

Mateo was miffed. He'd expected a declaration that she indeed knew he wasn't guilty and would stick up for him and help him beat the rap; but instead, all he got was avoidance. She was sick and gone for a few weeks. And when she came back, she was in a foul, black mood. Grumpy, surly and unwilling to speak to him or anyone else.

She left at lunch and barely came back for the afternoon shift and rarely stayed until the usual closing time. She never stayed late anymore. She didn't finish the car Mateo was supposed to paint, which was their shared side gig. He was so pissed he had no words for her. He didn't trust himself to speak to her.

All in all, it was a terrible few weeks. Surly and rude, the co-workers barely spoke. There was no kidding around. No bad jokes. No off-flavor jokes even. There was serious work. Talking only within the capacity of their work and nothing else.

It was the worst he'd felt since finding Rydell Rides, River's End, Shane and Iris.

Thank God, he had Rose. She was all that was left for him.

Then, there was a knock at the Love Shack's door. They were together, of course, and they glanced at each other, puzzled. Who in the hell could it be?

Mateo opened it to find Iris standing there with Quinn towering behind her. "I need to talk to you," Iris said, her mouth in a tight line.

"No thanks, Iris. I've had enough of your family for a

while. I didn't wreck the shop. I don't need to deny it again to you, of all people."

He wasn't in the mood to see her. To be honest, he wasn't so grateful to Shane and his family anymore. He no longer felt like he had to suck up his feelings and take any treatment they gave him. He was angry that they'd doubted him. Completely pissed that he had to prove his innocence to Shane and even though Iris didn't ask him, she also didn't come to his defense in any way.

Rose turned out to be his ride-or-die friend. Realizing that, he squeezed her hand tighter as he glared at Iris.

Rose nearly slammed the door in her face.

He shouldn't have loved that. But he did. Rose's fierce loyalty towards him was new and amazing. She was pretty unreasonable about it. Despite being rude or confrontational, she went ballistic when it came to protecting Mateo, and damn! Did he love it! The feelings she aroused in him were deep and he felt a big rush when he realized for the first time in his life, one person felt that way about him. One more than he ever imagined could.

Iris wedged her foot in the door Rose tried to slam and her next words changed everything. "I know you didn't." She rushed her sentence, adding, "I know you didn't because I did."

That did the trick. Everyone was glancing at each other in total shock as Rose let the door go slack and Iris and Quinn came inside. And then she told them an alarming story that changed everything. She was terse and to the point.

She was raped.

It happened in the shop, late one night after work, about three weeks ago. She subsequently returned to the shop at night to make her peace with it. But something went wrong and it triggered a rage in her that ended by destroying her dad's shop. She was the vandal. Iris did it.

Mateo's ears buzzed and his stomach pitted out. He instantly forgot his hurt feelings and betrayals, which were so small compared to what Iris was going through. All alone. She hadn't told Quinn or her dad or Mateo. He was her best friend and she still couldn't come to him.

Rose was strangely silent. She watched their exchange as Mateo rose to his feet and asked Iris if he could hug her. All the former concerns regarding his arrest disappeared. As far as he was concerned, the entire thing was relegated to history and all was forgiven. He tried to imagine the horror his little Iris had to navigate through all alone. Until then. She was so small, strong, and fragile that it broke his heart to imagine any man forcing himself on her against her will. Her strong will was an undeniable asset and Mateo worried this could break or ruin it. Her self-image was tough and she was always able to take care of herself.

It even put Mateo's own tragedies into perspective. He and Rose could only stare at each other when an exhausted Iris finally left. They were both starkly affected. Rose's blue eyes were huge and terrified and Mateo waited for her words, but she had none. He opened his arms and she got up and rushed to him, nearly knocking him to the ground. Then she burst into gasping, hiccupping tears. This was the bleeding-heart sister, the loyal Rose that he recognized. Not the stoic, quiet, cold attitude she'd just shown Iris.

"Why didn't you react more to her? Were you really still mad about the arrest? God, Rose, she didn't mean—"

Rose shook her head vehemently against his chest. More hiccups and sobbing. "No... I couldn't speak. I don't care about the arrest now. She didn't mean to get you arrested. Of course not... she was raped. Iris. And I was so mad at her when all this time, she couldn't tell me..." More sobs. Crying.

Mateo let the first round of emotions play out. Then he

set her back and said gently, "You need to go to her. Be there for her. No matter what."

She nodded. "I know. I'm so scared. What do I say? It's Iris. Things like that can't happen to Iris. Not Iris, of all people. She's the strongest woman I know…"

"Not anymore." He kissed her forehead. "Now you're the strong one and you need to give her your strength."

She clutched him tighter. "I can't. I can't do it. I'll fail her…"

"No. You won't. You'll get more strength from me, as I do from you. Right?"

Rose sucked in a breath of air and her sobs started to lessen. She finally nodded and replied, "Yes. You're right. I need to see her. But first we need to see my parents."

Rose slipped into her parents' house. Her dad and mom were seated at the table. Together. Their hands clasped. Eyes downcast. Tear tracks still stained both their cheeks. Her heart lurched.

Her dad turned at her unexpected entrance and his eyebrows shot up when Mateo followed her inside. Reluctantly. He preferred not to come with her. She'd insisted upon it and tugged him behind her.

There was nothing more clarifying than the news she'd just got about her sister.

They eyed her, then Mateo who stood just to the side behind her.

"Iris…" Rose's voice cracked as she sniffed and had to press against her eyes.

Her mom let out strangled cry. Her dad answered his tone as tortured as her own. "Yes. Your sister was raped and she's the one who vandalized the shop. That was a huge mistake. I see that now."

Their gazes were stoic as Rose pursed her mouth and her eyes flashed. She set down her purse with a cool, anger-laced undertone as she said, "You should have known that. You should have stood up for him. You should have bailed him out. How could you have him arrested?"

Shane's gaze felt burdensome on her. She found it hard to glare back at him. She often defied her dad, but in subtle, undetected ways that only she could manage. But this was entirely new for her. She never attacked him with what she thought and felt. And needed him to hear. Iris spoke to him in her quiet way, but never Rose.

"Seems you could have told us a thing or two." Shane's flashing eyes sparked as they met hers and they held a long staring contest. She refused to look away. So did he. He crossed his massive arms over his chest. "Explain to me, Rose, how you came to be there that morning?"

She crossed her arms too, mimicking him and his disdainful look. "First, you give me a good reason that you believe Mateo could have done that. He would never betray you. You, of all people. The person who gave him a chance right out of prison. The person he loyally served for nearly four years now. You know you can trust him. You know he isn't a criminal and he never was. You were the closest thing he had to a mentor and father-figure. And you damn well knew that, Dad. You squandered his trust in you. I just don't know how you could do that. You're not the man I thought you were."

Shane blinked with obvious surprise. Her words lost their anger-laced tone and instead, she was cool and disappointed. She remembered how he used to talk to her and Iris when they did something wrong without a good reason.

"He trusted you and you broke that trust," she finished.

"He… I… I just didn't get a chance to… to think it all out. A lot happened in a short amount of time. I was confused and surprised. Iris was acting strange, you were yelling about Mateo, and the sheriff kept asking questions, and Mateo lied about being there. He came there earlier and he left. Then he came back. That was and is suspicious."

"Rose. He's right. I was acting weird." Mateo's soft, hollow tone came from behind her. She glanced back. He stared down at his feet. Unwilling to engage.

"At the time, he thought his brother broke in and wrecked the shop."

"His brother?"

"Yes. The one who looks just like him with the same neck tattoo? I recently insisted to Mateo he disown him. Mateo did. Of course, his brother wasn't happy about it. He thought maybe Manuel came back to his place of business, and took out some revenge on him. Given his history and that it might have been his brother… yeah, maybe he wasn't acting perfect. But still… you should have known." She glared and crossed her arms again. "Did you actually think he did it?"

Shane tapped his foot and fidgeted. Rose held her breath, knowing this was a make-or-break moment for her, although she doubted her parents understood. She loved Mateo and she chose to give him her undying, one hundred percent support, right there and then. And if she lost her parents because of that, she'd still do it. She believed in Mateo—and them—that much.

"I—I… No. I don't think he'd trash my—our—shop out of the blue. Everything was confusing at that moment and he remained silent and wouldn't answer… so I got temporarily miffed. But no, you're right, I think I always knew Mateo wouldn't do that to me."

Her shoulders relaxed as her breath whooshed out of her lungs. Shane passed a test, and Rose wasn't sure he understood the consequences if he'd chosen the wrong answer. It also proved to Mateo that someone besides her believed him. And would stand up for him. Two people still saw the best in him and he needed to hear and believe that now so much.

She glanced at Mateo. He was stricken while staring at her dad. She grabbed his hand and shook him out of his trance. "See? He's not a total asshole." She smiled softly, trying to lighten the moment and the gravity of her dad's initial doubts about Mateo… At least they didn't betray him like his own damn family did.

Mateo didn't smile. He swallowed and stared harder at Shane as his hand clung to hers. Her parents' eyes followed their linked arms and hands. "So what is this?"

"This is us together."

"I can see that," her dad grumbled. "Why don't I know anything about it?"

"Because you're an old-fashioned idiot who scared Mateo away from dating his daughters. And since he's an ex-con and felon, he's extra indebted to you for giving him a job and he didn't want to do anything that might ruin it. Or shatter your trust in him. And we fell in love in spite of all that and we hid it."

Both her parents' eyes bulged. "In love?" her mom gasped.

"Deeply. Crazily and forever." Rose smiled easily. This was the fun part for her and she had no fears or doubts or regrets.

"When did this happen?" her mom asked as her dad continued glaring and tapping a finger on his elbow. His arms were still crossed and he looked menacing.

"Oh… last June."

Her dad emitted a strange noise. "Last June? Holy shit. What else don't I know about my children? Iris and her stupid billionaire boyfriend and violated… And you Rose, the one I rely on to be sensible and do the responsible thing no matter what the others might do or say. Why wouldn't you just tell us?!"

"Uh… because of the threats to Mateo about dating your daughters."

Mateo was frozen. Scared. Unsure. He never sassed her dad. He might talk and laugh and shoot the shit, but he never was confrontational. He couldn't even speak now.

"I asked him not to date Iris simply because you two work together and it could have become awkward for all. And your prison record factored into your job with me. And I didn't want a lover's spat to go wrong... And, she's my daughter. I've never been quiet or shy about where my loyalty lies and she'd win it every time. I'd have to fire you if something went wrong. I never said daughters, as in the plural. And I certainly never mentioned Rose because that dynamic, and this... crap. I never foresaw it coming down the lane."

"Oh," Rose said as her response was aborted after hearing her dad's reasonable request. It was about Mateo's job, not his daughter's virtue.

"Yeah, oh, Rose. You should have told us. Me."

"You could have been more receptive so I could." She glared back. Her arms re-crossed. "Did you ever consider that Mateo is young, handsome, loyal and smart? Why wouldn't I be attracted or interested or friendly to him?"

Shane drew up to his full height and replied, "Because, Rose, you were so afraid of him. You were the one who said a damn prison record meant he must be scary and dangerous. You never said it out loud but I knew the damn neck tattoo was why. So don't stand there sniffing your nose in disdain at me, after it took you years to see who and what Mateo is. I knew who he was three years before that. So cut it with your attitude." He turned and his gaze softened at he met Mateo's weary eyes.

"And I am sorry if you thought I'd worry about you dating my daughters. Or being part of their lives. No, it wouldn't worry me. I know you. And the type of man you are. It was simply owing to the smallness of our shop that I warned you about Iris. Not a comment on your character or my balking at you dating my daughter."

"Oh." Mateo's mouth popped open and he was obviously as stunned as Rose was. He had no initial response. All of Rose's righteous anger died.

"Yeah, oh. You two were judging me perhaps too harshly. What I will take responsibility for is being there that morning in front of the vandalized shop. I did hesitate. I paused and that was enough for the sheriff to take my hesitation somewhere I never meant for it to go. I was just so appalled by the destruction... I... God." He ran a hand over his scalp. "I'm sorry, Mateo. I can't undo my hesitation, but I will give you my sincere apology and hope I haven't lost you. I can't imagine how I'd ever replace you. Yeah, you're a stellar mechanic, but you are far more valuable to me because I can trust you. How precious and rare to have an employee like you. And hell, you must know you're like a son to me, if I failed to make that clear to you. But you are."

Rose lost all her anger and disdain before she simply flung herself at her dad. Surprised, he stepped back but caught her and patted her with his paw-like hand. She gripped his shoulders in a hard hug and whispered, "Thank you, Dad. He needed to hear that." She appreciated what he just said to Mateo. And for not being archaic after learning Mateo was sleeping with his daughter.

He whispered back in her ear. "So did you. For some reason, you inflate what Iris means to me compared to you. I love you, Rosie, and if Mateo makes you feel as fierce and sure as you just were to me when you spoke on his behalf, then of course, I'm happy for you. I support you."

She'd been so wrong. She harshly judged her dad when he was working on behalf of Mateo too.

"I guess I overreacted before hearing the truth."

He patted her shoulder. "Rose, you always do that. It's

what makes you, you. You're passionate and strong; and when you think something isn't fair, hell hath no fury... I love that. I knew it would serve you well in life. And look at you. Look at what you bring to your job. This is what makes you such a formidable advocate for getting dyslexia training to teachers and remediation courses in schools. You're a fighter and you do just that. For me. For this place. For Iris, Violet and Daisy. For Mateo. For the kids. It's why I'm so damn proud of you. So don't apologize for it."

She leaned back, meeting his warm gaze and feeling sheepish now for underestimating him. He tugged on a strand of her hair with affection, just like when she was a little girl. "And don't sneak around with me. Just be upfront about your life. I'd rather know about it and deal with it than not know. Even if I get mad, I always come around, right?"

"Yes." She smiled. "Yes, Dad, you do. I'm sorry for under-estimating you."

They shared a smile before he let her go and she turned to her mom who gave her the same hugging and soothing. Shane walked right up to Mateo, all six-foot-four of muscle and bulk before he simply swept Mateo up in a huge hug. Not a man-hug where they both patted each other's backs, but a real hug. Mateo, being so tall and skinny, was no match for Shane's strength. The look on his face was comical as her dad embraced him. Mateo's body straight as a bamboo reed, and her dad still hugging him until he finally relaxed. Mateo didn't hug her dad back, but he also didn't resist it. Mateo knew Shane was sorry and he meant everything he said.

That's what Rose loved about her dad but temporarily forgot for a few months. But it was exactly what Mateo needed. More than all the words in the world. Her dad's hug assured Mateo that he was one of them. He was accepted, cared about, and not just another employee. He was good enough to be a part of all of them. And nothing else would have expressed that to Mateo. So the tears filling Rose's eyes were happy tears after observing the beauty of her dad's generous personality and his acceptance and forgiveness for all.

Her mom squeezed her against her mom's side, staring at the hugging men with a small smile on her face. "I can't believe I forgot what he's like."

"His heart is as big as the world. And he's never been afraid to share it. I knew you were hiding something. I couldn't figure out what it was. Just remember: you really don't have to hide anything with us. We'd rather deal with the truth than have you guys hide or be ashamed about anything with us. Okay?"

Rose nodded and hugged her mom. She was so lucky to have enlightened parents, who were more understanding than most and she vowed to never forget that again.

As much as she needed her parents, Mateo needed them more.

CHAPTER 16

ROSE WALKED INTO THEIR apartment and found it silent. Deathly quiet. Even Quinn wasn't there. But his body guard was, something she'd discovered when it was texted to her with an explanation. She nodded as she passed the man in question. Then she simply slipped into bed with Iris. Hugging her tightly and letting Iris speak… or not, Rose simply stayed with her.

Later, she and Quinn shared a drink and tried to process what happened. His eyes were red-rimmed and he'd obviously been using his hands to comb his hair until it was sticking up haphazardly. Her heart twisted for him, for her, for her parents and for Mateo… but mostly for Iris. This? This went beyond anything she'd ever experienced. She stated that to Quinn and he appeared surprisingly vulnerable and honest about how lost he was, just as much as she.

Together, they made a pact to support Iris together as well as separately in all the ways Iris needed over the coming months, even if it went on for years. Her rape wasn't something that could be ignored or accepted. It would take time, therapy, unconditional support and lots of tears. From everyone.

After comforting her sister, Rose went to Mateo and he held her as she responded to him. They relied on each other for support.

Then one day, Mateo came home and everything about him looked different. His face was haggard, his stance poised and tense. And he was very dirty and covered in bits of white dust. "What's all over you?"

He shook his head and his eyes seemed wild. "Drywall dust."

"What? Why?"

He flopped down on the small two-person table, staring down at the flat, blank surface. His head was shaking as he ran his fingers restlessly through his hair. "They're tearing it down. The whole fucking thing. And I was helping out. It's…"

She sat beside him, taking his hand. "Mateo, what happened today?"

"I found her…" Mateo's voice shuddered. Rose knew instantly that *her*, was her sister. It could only be Iris. Everything revolved around Iris for them. In heartbreaking ways. They compared stories of what happened with her. Rose often slept beside her, only abandoning her post when Quinn arrived or Iris stayed with their parents. Tonight, Iris was at their parents' house.

"She was just sitting beside the spot. The spot on the floor I've walked past a hundred times… she kept staring at it. Her tears fell on the cement. Iris crying? I've never seen her cry before. Remember two years ago when she dropped that heavy drill on her big toe and broke it? She never even shed a single tear. She cursed and yelled and planted her fist into anything she could find, including my arm but she never cried. But this time. She cried. And she remained there, silent, as if she were lost in a terrible world that we can't even imagine."

Mateo got so choked up, he buried his face against Rose's neck. He let the tears slip from his eyes while Rose stroked his head and she cried.

He shook his head as he withdrew from her. "Your dad was there. After I found her, I helped her up. Iris. I lifted her like she was a little old lady with bad knees and a bad hip and couldn't walk properly anymore. God, Rose, she was so dazed. It was…"

She nodded. "I've witnessed her silent cry of streaming tears; it hurts worse than her sobs. It cuts you in half. You want so much to help her, save her, crawl inside her head and banish whatever she's remembering. *I know.*"

Their gazes met as tears blurred their eye colors. She touched his face. "I know this is hard. But I'm so glad you're just as affected as I am. That you care as much as I do. That you get it. I would have a much harder time if you didn't."

He gripped her hand. Nodding. Eyes stricken with grief that mirrored her own.

She closed her eyes. "I never really believed there could be an *us*. Not here. Not like this. Or that something like this could happen." They paused to observe a silent moment of their individual and combined grief.

He leaned back and said, "Anyway, your dad saw Iris in that moment… and he went fucking ballistic. After I led her to the bench by the river, she asked for a few moments alone. So I left her and when I got back up to the shop…" His entire body shuddered. "Jesus, Rose, Shane was pouring cans of gasoline all over the front shop doors. He wasn't screaming or yelling or moving fast. He was moving slowly, with deliberate precision. It wasn't a fit of rage; he knew exactly what he was doing."

"What was he doing?"

"When I ran up behind him and demanded to know that, he said, so quietly that it sounded lethal, he said he was burning the motherfucking building down."

Rose gasped and flipped back, looking more startled. "What?"

"Yeah. Burning it down. Iris got hurt in there and she could never get past it if she had to work around the same spot where she was violated. How could I argue with him? And why should Iris leave her job because of what happened? He was moments from igniting it when Jack came jogging up, followed by Ian and Joey. They came to convince him not to burn it down. But oh, goddamn, their faces were stunned. They had no idea about what happened to Iris. They know now. It's a punch in the gut every time. Anyway, Jack convinced Shane a fire could endanger the entire valley, duh! But fuckin' A, Rose, they're still going to tear down—"

"Tear down what?"

"The shop! All of it. They're tearing the whole thing down. Instead of burning it to the ground, they're paying a demolition crew to take it apart piece by piece. It was Jack's idea. Shane calmed down and agreed to do it. Then Quinn showed up. I was pulling the free screws to remove the metal siding on the outside, and inside, I was smashing the drywall. It's happening right now."

She sat back on her heels, totally flummoxed. "Holy crap."

"I know."

Questions flooded Rose's brain. "Yes. Then what about your job? And all of their jobs? And crap. And Iris?"

"What about Iris?"

"She walked up as Shane and Jack argued and tried to make them see reason, but it boiled down to this: how could she ever work there again? It happened right there. She'd have flashbacks every time she went there. I agreed there was no way around that. Your dad claimed he had all the money he needed and since it was his business… Then he said fuck the business and if he wanted to destroy it, he would. His daughter got hurt there. It no longer had any right to exist."

Her mouth was still open. "Wow, just wow."

"He's right, you know. She could never recover and work in there. But shit, Iris's life revolves around that shop. Working with your dad. She lives for it. She loves it. I can't imagine Iris, not…"

"Iris." Rose smiled softly. "I know. I never had a calling like Iris did. She simply was a mechanic from the toddler years on."

Mateo leaned forward. "The thing is, if it were me and it happened to you, I might have torn down Shane's shop with or without his permission. I can't fault him for that. So I'm helping."

She grasped his hand. "Good. Yes. I've never heard of anyone doing something like that for a raped woman. It's awesome. And of course, it's my dad." She shook her head. "And I'm glad you're all in and you all get it."

"He's going to pay the crew still so…"

There was nothing to celebrate. They simply fell into silence and went to bed.

"I wish you could have told me about your feelings for Mateo." It was finally a normal Monday and Rose was back to work at the office with her mom. A place that felt sane and normal and familiar after the latest shocking tragedy of Mateo's arrest and Iris's revelation of rape.

"I know. But it was for him. The trust issues, and the deep-seated belief that no one would want him, let alone, allow him to be with me. It's a miracle I got past it."

"And he's what you want?" Her mom's tone was curious.

"Yes. Forever. It's done, Mom. And yes, he has a neck-tat and a prison record but if Dad had been a bachelor longer, he might have ended up with both too. So you can't cast any stones at me."

Allison smiled slightly. Then she gave a small head nod as she said, "Touché. Okay, I guess I passed along some of my genes to you. My looks, my career interest and choice of education, my dyslexia tutoring, and finding your other half in a package that's the antithesis of you."

"You did. And so you know, he's an ex-con and he always will be, I know that. But he didn't do it. His older brother, who looks more like a twin, has an identical tattoo and a long rap sheet. He did it. His mother made Mateo take the fall because he was still a minor. And that's the truth."

"If you believe it, then I'm sure it is."

"It is."

"I had something else to discuss with you. About him."

Rose tensed, realizing why Mateo was so guarded. She was exactly that way about him nowadays. "What?"

"I contacted a colleague in the education department at the University of Washington. I told her about Mateo, his above average intelligence and how he slipped through school without any acknowledgement or special courses. Her passion is studying the differences in various learning styles and why some children with high potentials are addressed while others are ignored in public school settings. Anyway, she'd like to interview Mateo as part of her course work."

"Oh. Okay. I'm not sure he'd like that. But I can ask him."

"Well, in exchange she offered to give him an IQ test. It is included in her study and thesis at no additional cost. It would prove to Mateo what you already know. It might open more doors too, beyond the shop. And it sounds like it should be done."

That jolted Rose's attention. "Do you mean it?"

"Yes. And I really think you should persuade him to do it."

She nodded, already formulating her plan to convince him.

∼

"WELL, Mr. Alvarez, I can't tell you what to do with it, but you need to do something."

He eyed the lady doctor with unmasked suspicion, still incredulous that he was there. Her name was Dr. Marsha Von Hauser and she had so many degrees and initials after her name he couldn't begin to untangle them. Somehow, Rose convinced him to travel to the other side of Washington State where it was stupid crowded and the weather cooler and grayer. After sitting through interviews and several tests, he was itching to get back to River's End. To his normal life and familiarity. To Iris and the new shop they were currently designing. She'd asked him, Mateo, of all people, to be her partner. Fifty-fifty. Shane was retiring and Rydell Rides would soon be hers and she simply wanted to give Mateo half of it.

He finished all the tests and interviews. So many of them. Questions about his childhood and every grade of school. Finding the exact place where his gifted intelligence should have been noticed and nurtured. All the tests that failed to show it because he'd deliberately failed them. How many teachers simply overlooked him? How did they allow their biases to feed the picture they already had of him, putting him into a box and making him stay there? He resented the trip down memory lane, but he did it for Rose. And she stayed right beside him then and now as they waited for the results.

Grumpy and tired, he sighed. "What does that mean?"

The lady with deeply set, dark eyes, and a soft, kind

mouth smiled. "It means you have the second highest IQ of anyone I've ever tested. That's a lot to say. And your brain is a rare and beautiful gift to the world. You can't waste it. You have been gifted with it and you need to find a healthy way to explore and challenge it. Not a professional opinion, mind you, just my personal take. I have several doctors who would like to discuss some other options with you—"

She kept talking like he was a newly discovered alien entity. He didn't even have a high school diploma. He was just a mechanic who lived in a shack. It didn't fit. Overwhelmed, he suddenly bolted upright. The chair he sat in smashed into the wall as he left it. "Excuse me," he mumbled when their eyes followed him, wide with shock and surprise.

Breathing hard, his hands sweating, he ran. He went down the hallway of the university corridor he was in. Him. Mateo Alvarez! What the fuck was he doing here? So what if he had a gift? Fuck. When did his life or his superior brain ever work right? It was annoying. Wanting so many things he couldn't give to it. Never satisfied. Never content. Never fitting in.

Not until he met Rose.

He strode far and fast. Out of breath, he finally stopped when he found a bench that had a view of Mount Rainier. It was a cool, but sunny day. Pleasant. The water glowed against the city-scape and mountains.

Then he felt her cool, soft hands on his shoulders and smooth lips touched the top of his head. It was Rose, of course. She found him. Came to him. She sat down beside him, holding his hand. Her leg pressed against his, and she leaned her head on his arm. She let him be quiet to think and breathe.

"I was going to be a partner in Iris's new shop. I was going to be an equal owner. That was further and higher than I ever dared to reach in my life. It was a known success, Rose. It was more than enough for me. It was everything."

Her head shook and she said, "I know. Based on what you used to know and were told. Those were the chances and choices you had until now. But Mateo, you are truly gifted, which is so rare and unique. You read all the books and subjects you can't get enough of. What if you could learn about things that I can't understand? What if you finally got all the attention your clever brain and you deserve?"

"I can't... I didn't go to high school."

"That is a laughable problem to them. You take a test, one they say you'll ace no problem and then, you can enroll in a merit-based BA program that you can pass as fast as you can do the work. They expect two years for you to complete it. Then, you can pick any field you like and become a leading expert who can improve and change it. You can decide how to formulate it. You can save parts of it or change it to your own liking. Baby..." She tilted her head up. "You're that smart! Which is why you're so curious about everything and your thirst for knowledge is about to be quenched. I watch the way you hunger for knowledge. It wasn't cool so you joked about it, but it's cool now and it's very real. I would tell you to go home and be a partner to Iris, if I believed that would make you feel complete and happy. You don't owe anyone anything. Not a soul. The education system failed you. The court system failed and the prison system wants to keep you shackled to it. I think this would be the best path for you. It will open up your potential and you'll learn about all the things you always wanted to know... You'll receive endless information."

"What? They're going to enroll a tatted up ex-con? Get real. I can't even speak properly."

"Yes. They will enroll you. They don't care about your tats. And they already know you're an ex-con. You speak just fine. If anyone doubts you, just start quoting Shake-speare. Have them pick a play and start reciting. And as for the tats? Everyone has them now. And being an ex-con? Youthful mistake for not being noticed, like a challenged genius."

"Rosie?"

She gripped his hand. "I know it scares you. All these expectations. Believing in things you never knew before. Especially because it's academics. But oddly enough, Mateo, it's exactly where you belong. I can't begin to satisfy your brain when it longs to know and do so much. I can however, love you through it. I can support you and care and be your friend. As you are mine."

"I can't do it."

"You can. If you want to. I'll be right there beside you. Every step, wherever you want to go."

"Iris and I are building the business of our dreams. We planned for years to do this. It's happening now. I'd be a business owner. Me! And you want me to give it up for something unknown… like this?"

"I want you to have everything you truly deserve."

"Owning a business in a field I rock at is far beyond what I thought I'd ever have."

"But, Mateo, you can't deny your endless curiosity. Your capacity for all kinds of information… Taking a new path to explore what you've never had the chance to see before will tell you if you are indeed happy being a business owner and a mechanic with Iris… There could be something else you don't even know about yet. You're still young and we have plenty of time. Why not take a day or two to figure it out? You can always go back to Iris. You know that. But this chance? Seems worth exploring."

"I don't know…"

"I do. I'll support you and be right there with you, either

in River's End, or to the ends of the earth. I'm in, no matter what you decide."

He gripped her hand so tightly, she flinched. He gave her a small, strained smile of apologyand released the pressure a little. Only a little. She was his lifeline. His hope. His heart. He might have a huge brain capacity but not for daily life and people. She was his conduit to the rest of the world. His source of bravery. Love. Acceptance. "You'd do that for me?"

She smiled up at him. "You silly genius. I'd do anything for you. Whether or not the IQ test proved how smart you are. You knew that, already. Right? Ride-or-die? Well, I'll ride anywhere with you. And the thing is: we don't have to include the dying part. We're going to live a long, productive, successful life together. We're going to challenge your brain to its fullest capacity and pursue all the doctorates you choose. We'll get married and have four kids and live in a pretty house with a little bit of land. Here or there. Or in River's End... but somewhere you will finally have a home. And always, no matter how distinguished you get, we'll sneak off to our Love Shack and remember how we started this long, wonderful, prosperous life that now lies ahead of us."

He shut his eyes. Her belief in that was almost vivid enough to paint a picture for him. A picture no one ever painted before. Dreams no one expected of him or for him. But Rose. She did. Then and now.

"Four kids?" He finally prompted when all the rest seemed too much to conceive. Too deep to ponder. His anxiety would stir if he started thinking about it for too long.

"Yes. I want four kids. And you'll finally have the love that was denied you. Me, my family and our kids. You'll find respect in whatever career you choose. But love? Acceptance? Friendship? Joy? That will come from us. Your family."

Family. The one thing he never knew, or how deeply, he

needed it. "Can't we start with one and see what happens? I don't know about four…"

Rose laughed and rested her head back on his arm. She sighed. "Okay. We'll talk about having one for now."

He sighed. "But we'll plan for four."

She giggled. His heart swelled when she didn't answer and he knew she was planning their future, and hell, if that wouldn't be what happened. Rose always got what she aimed for.

Including him.

And when Mateo received offers for positions under various renowned professors over the next few years, Rose went with him. She followed Mateo to three different states. He received his high school equivalency certificate. Then he got a bachelor's degree in science from the University of Washington and went on to medical school at Brown University. His end goal was to pursue medical research in the field of brain cancer. And through it all, Rose watched, congratulated and supported him. She pouted when he worked too hard and reined him in when he got too busy and narrowly focused. She did the tutoring with her mom, all of it online remotely, and when his degrees were completed, he knew what he wanted to do next.

He asked Rose Rydell to marry him.

And Rose said yes to Mateo Alvarez. Not the doctor. Not the Mateo who was well on his way to greater things, but the ex-con, the neck-tatted mechanic who loved and worshiped her, the man who would end up having four kids with her, the man who said she was the sole reason his life changed and he finally found something real and valuable. It wasn't his brain. Or his abilities. It was Rose finding his heart, and showing it to him until he finally knew what true love meant and he chose to give it to her.

ABOUT THE AUTHOR

Leanne Davis has earned a business degree from Western Washington University. She worked for several years in the construction management field before turning full time to writing. She lives in the Seattle area with her husband and two children. When she isn't writing, she and her family enjoy camping trips to destinations all across Washington State, many of which become the settings for her novels.

Made in the USA
Columbia, SC
05 August 2020